THE
UNUSUAL
ALLIANCE

Anthony DeLeon

The Unusual Alliance

© 2021 Anthony DeLeon

Paperback ISBN: 978-1-66780-043-1

WELCOME TO THE FUTURE OF A UNIVERSE THAT YOU MIGHT be familiar with. The year is seven years after the fall of the Sol solar system, Earth has been abandoned and humanity stands near extinction. With the help of several new intelligent allied species, humanity survives and forms the Galactic Alliance Military. Also knowing humanity didn't know shit about dick, the allied species agreed to form a council of government to help guide humanity's interstellar journey. However, things take a turn for the worse, when a cryptic message is sent referencing strange beings called "World Eaters", and the finding of an unusual vessel with a crystal that has immense power, echoes through out the galaxy. This crystal is one of twelve, each with a unique ability and will bring unwanted attention from every kingdom, alliance or militia. A human scientist is working on what might be the last hope to stop an evil that will consume every planet in the galaxy.

THE LIEUTENANT

IN A FAR CORNER OF THE MILKY WAY GALAXY, ON THE SMALL planet Helix Prime, there is a secret facility that is heavily protected in the middle of the desolate part of the planet. Inside there is a large laboratory with white tiles on the walls and the ceiling, the room is crowded with big machines and computer consoles. The screens on the computers are interactive holograms and the other machines act as stabilizers with anaconda size hoses attached to a glass cylinder in the center of the room. Hovering inside the cylinder is a semi large crystal. The crystal is chaotic in shape with several colors and triangles. It is slightly opaque with extra pieces floating around it with tiny singularities at the center of them. Two scientists are working on one of the hologram computers.

"That's it! Look here! This spectrum shows that it can do much more than we anticipated." one scientist says to the other who is sitting in front of the console screen.

"But Dr. Teyach, this also might mean it's too much to handle, we have to take another scan."

"Olson, we don't have time, we must begin testing!" Dr. Teyach walks away from the console, his coat stained with coffee and some sort of green substance. The bit of stubble on his face goes perfectly with his no sleep and hasn't showered in a week look. He makes his way to the cylinder with a slight limp and stares at the strange large quartz.

"Sir, with all do respect, we still need a sample of the virus, or at least a suitable replacement that is similar to the Phazaren strain." Olson pleads to the hell bent doctor. David Olson is your typical young teacher's pet, brown-nosing kiss ass. He was born with money, that's probably how he afforded eye surgery to get his eyes replaced with R.A.I.S eyes - "Because they have a better percentage rate," he always says. It's an odd look, a human with big bright orange mechanical looking eyes. It's just not right.

"Sir I just think…"

A loud alarm goes off, followed by an explosion in the distance. The doctors' turn to the door with a frightened look. Dr. Teyach turns around and accesses a console to close up the cylinder container with a metal shield. His hands glide over the holograms quickly.

"Olson, close the blast doors!" Dr. Teyach yells back at him.

Olson runs over to the console by the doors and just as he begins working, the two big doors blow open. The initial explosion tosses Olson into the corner of a near desk, cracking his skull. Dr. Teyach is blown forward into the cylinder, smacking his forehead into the glass cracking it, leaving a blood trail as he falls down to his right. Dazed, he tries to slowly get up. He looks through the smoke and fire while coughing and sees a dark, skinny and hooded figure walking toward him carrying a purple crystal energy blade, curved like a sickle. It drags across the metal floor burning a long lava-like mark into it. Dr. Teyach manages to put his back to the cylinder, as the attacker advances. The Doctor looks to the left, and sees an exit, the sickle blade flies past him stabbing the cylinder and slightly burning his ear off. He screams in pain, grabs his ear with both hands and looks up. The tall female with long black hair wearing a maroon colored armor and purple glowing eyes that match the blade, looks down at him with a sharp metallic-like smile.

"Hello doctor." She says. Teyach faints.

In another part of the galaxy, the Guillotine, a large cobalt and silver military vessel with a massive cannon just underneath the bridge of the ship is flying to one of the eighty-seven docking stations on Terra-127; a huge space station that resembles a jellyfish or a wilted flower some say. The Guillotine is known as the Galactic Alliance Military's fastest ship with enough firepower to destroy a small planet. The size of the vessel can hold up to ten thousand occupants, somewhat comfortably. As for Terra-127, the massive space station is a gift from the second intelligent alien race humans came in contact with called the R.A.I.S [Radioactive Artificial Intelligent Synthetic]. These robots are humanoids that share their minds with all the others of their kind and they have three organs similar to humans, the heart, the lungs and the stomach. Their muscles, bones and skin are nothing but wiring and highly dense crystallite armor with minor levels of radiation. Terra-127 shares the same type of crystallite armor on its giant crystal blue dome and shield strips that drape from the top giving it that jellyfish look minus the radiation. Terra-127 is the base of operations for the Galactic Alliance Military and Humanity's government. There are 4 levels on the Stem of the station and every level has three smaller levels called Tiers. Each Tier has a small city on it and each Tier is about one hundred stories from the one below it. The presidents of humanity, along with other high-ranking officials live at the top of Level 1. Civilians or military families live on Level 2 and 3, level 4 is for military warehouse and storage.

The Guillotine, slowly makes it's way to the docking link bridge, with bright red lights every ten miles on either side, allowing ships to be registered and scanned as they dock with the station. On board, Colonel Commander Stephanie Ashley Williams is walking down a bright white metal corridor. Two Alliance R.A.I.S soldiers dressed in a basic black armor and weapons magnetically attached to their backs accompany her to the bridge. Stephanie's long shinny dark red hair hangs down in a tight ponytail past her shoulder blades. Her hair, takes on a life of it's own as the ends curl upward with every step she takes. Her uniform is armor mostly and underneath a black skin-tight suit with shield tech built into a small blue lining sewn down the left and right side of the suit. The suit is covered in only some places with black and cobalt armor plates. The back piece of armor drapes two red cloths down to just above her ankle. The cloths have the Galactic Alliance insignia in blue printed on them. The left breastplate has all sorts of badges and metals some have crazy color combinations and others just gold, they go hand in hand with her strict, but fair attitude.

As they arrive at the doors of the bridge, two thin scanner rods on either side of the hallway turn red and scan as she and the others walk through. The two rods, once halfway to the door, break into four rods, two on the bottom half and two on the top half; they scan the rest of the way to the doors then retreat into the walls and slide back to the beginning. The doors open quickly despite their heaviness; Stephanie and the two soldiers walk on through to the bridge. Its spacious open cabin allows for four computer cockpit areas, two of them smaller "D" shaped pits, and the other ones are big triangle- shaped. In the center stands an elevated platform with a ring shaped like a balcony. Behind it is a throne with console holograms above the side arms. Stephanie makes her way up the small flight of steps to the throne and sits throwing her legs over the left arm side and hits the right side console. A contact list pops up on a holographic screen, bright and clear as day.

"We are about to dock with Terra in two minutes, Sir," says one of the pilots. "Thank you cadet, let the rest of the ship know" Stephanie says as she scrolls through her contact list. She picks a name by touching the holographic screen then begins writing a message, taps the screen again to send it out.

On the receiving side of the message, there is a hologram clock alarm in a dark apartment that projects the time and year of what it would be on Earth from a small black pad. The time is a little after eight. The image then changes to an unopened letter indicating a new message. The main room of the apartment is filled with only a small round table with two chairs, many posters of different bands and movies, small figurines of different alien races and one small couch. In the bedroom, there is a full size bed underneath a small window and a mirror that takes up the whole wall across from the bed. The alarm goes off for two minutes and then stops. A holographic virtual interface that can be programed with any personality appears over the black pad

"Get up Ms. Williams! Wake up; you're going to be late! You also have new message!" says the two-foot pink and white Sieren holocharacter wearing a black and pink plaid schoolgirl outfit. A Sieren (Sear en) looks humanoid. Their irises and pupil are galaxies, stars and all. Each Sierens eyes differ from each other along with the color of their fox like tails, and fox like ears on top of their head. They are the most powerful alien race in the known universe with the power to read/control minds and whole lot of other shit.

The woman lying in the bed turns over and looks at the hologram with her deep dark blue eyes.

"Forward it to my com," she says as she throws the sheet off of her in a bit of a fit. Getting up slowly she rubs her head.

She has a slight migraine and a bit of Déjà vu from a very strange dream. She has been having the same dream every night for weeks. One where she is surrounded by fire and faces that can't be seen, but the their aura feels familiar. She shakes it off then grabs and moves her legs off the bed. She reaches for her spandex-like black pants on a nightstand near by. A scented candle and a Planet Side clock telling the time on three planets Phazel, Typhas and Ohyron sits on the nightstand. As she puts her pants on a dark blue light goes from the ankle up to the hip on both sides of her legs, then she reaches for her boots and slides them over in front of the bed.

The boots are made of Carik crystallites, a type of crystal used for shield technology and armor for ships. They also have Dra'Konein metal plates the strongest known metal in the universe. It's from a practically extinct alien race of seven foot tall, walking on two feet, dragons. This is what gives the boots a dark navy blue tint. She slides one leg into the high combat metal boot with an opening that looks like a flower with teeth on the inside of the petals due to the three inch needles on the inside lining of the boot.

Casey's condition is called Molecule Dysplasia and she is the first and only case. The molecules of a certain affected area become unstable. The molecules and atoms will vibrate to the point that the bones become jelly or even nonexistent. The needles inject a small amount of a molecular solution that keeps the bones of her legs working, about every two hours forty needles (twenty each leg) release the solution into her legs allowing her to walk. Its not painful, well the injection part is not; just annoying to see that humanity hasn't found a better way. She secures both legs inside the boots then holds the buttons with two fingers on the ankle of each boot simultaneously. The red linings of the boots close over then it clamps down to her legs. She lets out a painful gasp.

"Motherfucker!"

"Oh are you alright? Should I call the medical staff?"

"No I'm fine Sarah that's not necessary" She looks down at her legs, stands up slowly then walks over to the mirrored wall. She's wearing a medium size grey T-shirt with the words "To Defend, To Protect, Galactic Alliance Military" on the front. She places her hand on the right side of the mirror and it becomes invisible. The view of a closet appears half -filled with different uniforms and the other half has weapons. A bubbly sound comes from Sarah's console,

"Casey you have another message! Wow, you are popular today!"

"Thanks Sarah, you always know just what to say," Casey says sarcastically while taking her shirt off.

"Just forward it like the last one," she says after putting on the Aero armor shirt outfitted with the same blue energy as her leggings.

She begins grabbing her weapons and holsters them one by one. All military personal is required to have at least three firearms with them while on duty, but today is the day Casey might finally leave the Terra space station.

So, what better way is there to feel prepared than with a count of three different sets of pistols, two sub-material machine guns, two light energy daggers, one Anti-matter shotgun, one Aloverse (Creates mini black holes) rocket launcher tube and her custom made Assault rifle, with many different settings. Now, it sounds like a lot but most of it is actually small or lightweight. Two pistols are strapped to her thighs; two strapped at the hip and the final two are placed on each side of her chest. The daggers go on her back on the right and left of her hip and the sub machine guns go in the middle of the two daggers.

Once she has most of her equipment on, aside from the shotgun, rifle and rocket, she pulls a short black leathery jacket out and puts it on. She pulls the two sides together and puts her right hand over base of the two sides then slides her hand up with out touching it. A dark blue light zips the two sides together. After that, she grabs a ruler-long metal plate and slaps it on the back of her jacket. She grabs her shotgun, which looks and feels very light. She throws it on her back. The metal plate opens three slots and magnetically locks the shotgun in place. She does the same with a small six-inch tube. She grabs her rifle, her somewhat bulky wrist communicator and walks through her small apartment to get to the door. "Have a great day Ms. Williams!" Sarah says to her as she transfers herself to the light fixture above her bedroom, illuminating the rest of her apartment and the door. Casey stands at the door, turns around and puts her soft jet-black long hair up in a tight ponytail that ends up between her shoulders. She puts the rifle on her back in the center between the other two weapons just barely missing her hair.

"Thank you Sarah, make sure you lock up while I'm gone."

"You got it Ms. Williams!" Sarah says excitedly. The grey door slides open to the left and Casey leaves. As soon as she exits the door she walks down a small flight of steps and continues through a light blue painted hall to an elevator at the end of the hall. The elevator arrives with an open view of the colony's large and brightly colored city and a rail in the middle of the window. Casey walks on and hits the "floor" button. She lifts up her wrist communicator and brings up a screen with small apps; she picks the one that looks like a letter flying through the air. When the app opens up, the word "messages" crosses over the top. She checks the first message,

"Hey, Lazy Ass! I'm docking as we speak, meet at Zalzoes?" Casey smiles and replies, "Okay, but you're buying!" She then checks the second message,

"Lieutenant Williams, Report to the Adris Building, 84th floor, Suite 808 immediately!"

She looks out over the city and sees the ominous looking twisted black and maroon hotel building. A sense of uneasiness falls upon her as the elevator slowly descends into darkness as it passes through the building to the floor level.

On the ground floor, she walks out to an open lobby with two desks across from each other with R.A.I.S clerks at each one. There are some plants and chairs by the entrance to make the lobby seem more welcoming. She continues through the lobby to the exit, but stops and looks up at the hologram screen above the two desks and sees the time. Her heart sinks into her stomach,

"Oh shit," she says to herself before running out the exit doors. She exits to the building. (Now before this continues let us take a minute for those who might get confused or are old, there are FOUR levels on the space station, and THREE mini levels on each level called Tiers! This is very important!) The apartment building sits more elevated above the city on Tier 1, Level 2. She runs down a small flight of stairs into a small-over-crowded sidewalk. She continues running in between people and the sidewalk eventually turns into a wide bridge walkway that moves like an escalator, held together only with light of two color schemes, lime green and red, red for going, lime green for coming, divided with a fence made of two blue colored beams that come from a post on either side. Casey shoves people left and right trying to get across, eventually she ends up jet jumping over the median with her boots. The boots letting out little bursts of focused energy from the bottom, allowing her to fly for only a short period of time. She lands hard on the other side, gets up and begins running on the opposite walk way. After shoving a few people and running for what felt like hours to her, she makes it across the bridge and comes up to a big open two way gondola, again one way for going and one way for coming, the only way to get from Tier 1 to Tier 2. Casey looks at the one for coming in on the left and then at the one for going down on the right. She sees a way to get on top of the way for going down. She runs straight hopping up on a set of three medical supply crates, setting her up for the perfect jump to get on top. She makes it up on the third crate, only to be lifted by a construction robot that causes Casey to bounce up too high and over shoot the gondola. Angled face first and falling all the way down to Tier 2, a quick "Shit" is all she could get out as she flails around trying to fall in a more elegant way. She uses her boots to try and control her falling with the flight setting, but only one boot lights up, causing her to spin around in circles and fall between two semi large slum apartment buildings that hovered above the Tier 2 city. She reaches for her wrist communicator hits two buttons, accesses her boot's commands and shuts them down. "Got it," Casey says to herself proud of what she has done. Just then she realizes, she is still falling, but before she can react she slams down on the top of one of the buildings in Tier 2 on her right side, with her energy shield lighting up before she hits. Her impact causes the small part of the roof she is on to collapse and the balcony that is beneath it goes too. Casey, hair flying loose, is now falling with hazardous debris following her all the way down. She thinks fast using her wrist com to activate the boots and launch herself further up the alley and away from the debris, but hits the ground, lighting up her crystal energy shield once again and launching her to the edge of the alley into a puddle of artificial rain water right before the metal silver side-walk. She pushes herself up and out of the puddle with her hands, as she lifts her dripping hair up. The bad thing about light shields is, they protect you from shear force, but not from water or any liquid thrown in your face. She looks at the time on her wrist. Casey jumps up and exits the alleyway. She pulls outs a small four inch cylinder from her jacket pocket, twists the top and throws it on the ground, smoke comes out and rises up fast. She steps into it; jumps around in it and her clothes and hair become dry when she steps out of the smoke. She kicks the can back into the alley while tying up her hair and runs down the sidewalk. She is about five minutes from the Galactic Alliance Training Facility. The compound is massive, taking up a half of the city on level 2 Tier 2 of Terra-127, with a four-story high wall, armed turrets lined up around the perimeter and two gates, one on the north side and other on the south. Casey is on her way to the north side entrance that has heavy artillery auto turrets at the top of the steps on either side of the two scanning doorways to enter. Inside the doorways are a metal fence and a half glass ticket booth. Military personal place their left hand on the glass and scan the ID tattoo three semi thick horizontal black bars on the left wrist. The scanning either allows you access or will deny you. Casey runs to a left gate with no waiting, most likely because everyone else was on time. She places her tattooed hand on the glass; the scanner reads her wrist. The booth lights up green, and then turns red and the words "Three consecutive times of tardiness, need approval" run across the glass above her hand.

"Ah fuck me!" Casey says banging on the glass. The booth opens with a slightly overweight red-haired, freckled man.

"Well, if it isn't Ms. Williams. Looks like you're the first one here again." He says sarcastically.

"Come on Roy! Please let me in!" Casey begs with both hands on the booth.

"I don't know. What are you going to do for me?" Roy says

"Uh how about I don't put you on latrine duty!" she says. Roy laughs,

"Ms. Williams this is the second week you have been late three times in a row. I'm going to have more authority than you when the general finds out."

"Roy, just open the fucking gate!"

"Fine, only because I love it when you get mad," he laughs. The giant gates open, and Casey runs through to a building directly across from the main north gates, but an electrical surge comes from the two circles on either side of the pathway and electrocutes her to the knees. She lets out a scream of pain as she crumbles to the ground; the electrical current slows down just enough to hold her in place. Three men appear.

"Ms. Williams, how nice of you to fit us into your busy schedule." The tall Commander made of forest green armor plates with streaks of black says stopping in front of her.

"Well you know me, I always have time for you, sir." Casey says clenching her teeth while trying to breath. The Commander turns off the restraint with his wrist comm. Casey falls over then gets up slowly and salutes the Commander. General Commander Heathrow is the only R.A.I.S. Commander in the Galactic Alliance. He stares at her with his black headlight - like eyes then signals his men with his head to walk away.

"Casey what's going on with you? You can't keep doing this. You're leaving me with no choice." Casey cuts him off

"No, please Commander Heathrow, just one more chance please!"

"You need to get your shit straight Casey, I don't care if your sister is one of the highest ranking officers, you don't do your part."

"You have no part," Casey says simultaneously with him.

"I understand Sir"

"Obviously you don't!" says the Commander,

"As punishment I'm taking you off weapons training with the new recruits, I'm bumping you to ammunition until I can figure out what to do with you." She looks at him with slightly teary angry eyes, then stands at attention and salutes him.

"That will be all Ms. Williams." Heathrow and his lieutenants start walking away and as they do one of the lieutenants throws a crumpled up piece of paper at Casey's face, while she is still at attention. She waits until they are gone to let out one little tear; she picks up the paper and unravels it. She reads "Fai Kiet" a Nexus word that meant "crippled whore" or something close to that. Pissed off, she crumples up the paper and walks toward a large opening with an arc over it. Three symbols hang on the arc, an orange triangle, a yellow square and a green circle. She walks up to the entrance and throws the paper in a slightly tall black trash receptor on the way into the Recreational Plaza. This plaza is made up of different restaurants and other recreational centers in the center of the base. She reaches the center of the plaza where Zalzoes, the most popular restaurant, is located on the corner across from the entrance walkway. Casey walks halfway across the street, then stops and waits for higher-ranking officers riding in a smaller black jeep-like vehicle to passes by then continues and heads into Zalzoes. She passes by the bar on her left and a crowd of people filling up the five tables on her right. She heads to a booth next to a window where a woman with long red hair is siting and scanning her wrist comm. She gets up to the table and stands at attention real quick then sits down across from the woman.

"Why do you always do that? You know how many people salute me every day? I don't need my sister doing it too," Stephanie says, as she looks through her wrist comm. "You and I both know you love it when people salute you and especially love it when people say 'Sir yes sir' to you," Casey says jokingly while releasing another salute.

"Wow and here I thought you wouldn't have a sense of humor after Heathrow was done giving you 'the talk.'" Stephanie retorts.

Casey glares at her.

"Hey this is your fault, don't look at me like I'm the bad guy." Stephanie says chutting off her comm. A green haired Nexus waitress comes up to the booth.

"Hey guys!" she says very cheerful.

"Hey Selina" both sisters say simultaneously.

"Now, I know you guys are busy, so what can I get you?" Selina says with the same happy ass attitude. Casey looks at Stephanie,

"The usual." Stephanie says with a smile.

"Two spicy chickens" Selina says writing it down. "Alright I will get that for you guys!" Selina runs off to the next table.

"I really don't like her." Casey says shaking her head.

"What's wrong?" Stephanie asks.

"You can't tell me you like her happy ass attitude." Casey says.

"No you idiot, I'm talking about work, you've been late and now demoted from weapons training? You're the best shot we have!"

"I know!" Casey says.

"You know your going to have to see the psychologist? And they keep records."

"I know I know!" Casey says with her hands on her head looking down at the table.

The sound of high heel shoes clicking comes closer to the booth, Casey looks up to, see a woman with long dirty blonde hair tied up in a bun, wearing glasses and dark green suit with a skirt standing at attention.

"Colonel Commander Williams, Lieutenant Williams." The woman stands at attention.

"At ease." Stephanie says to the woman.

"I am Corporal Lieutenant Kristin Conway, I am also the psychologist stationed here." she says while looking at Casey.

"Aren't you a little young to be a psychologist?" Casey asks.

"Aren't you young to be a Lieutenant?" Kristin retorts back to Casey,

"Regardless, Ms. Williams please stop by my office when you have finished your duties today." Casey looks at her with a smile.

"Tell you what, I'll think it about." She says.

Stephanie smiles and looks away.

Kristin puts on a content smile, pauses calmly, fixes her glasses then says,

"Well, you two have a good lunch! And as for my office, it's not a request." She smiles and leaves.

Casey crosses her arms weighing them on the table while looking out the window. "Talk to me Casey."

"I just don't know what it is I'm doing or going to do. I haven't been anywhere besides Carsecs since the accident happened and I thought if I joined the Galactic Alliance that I could go to see the galaxy and go to different planets like Typhas or Phazel, but instead I can't even leave Terra!"

"Casey, these things take time. Instead of jumping around like some vigilante super hero you should give your self time to heal." Stephanie suggests.

"It's been two years since the accident and the fact that I am jumping around proves I'm ready. All I want to know is how long? And why am I the only Lieutenant who isn't allowed to leave Terra?"

"Casey, that's ridiculous. "

"It's true!"

A semi loud ring comes from Casey's wrist COM notifying of a new message. She raises it to her face and opens the message, "Lieutenant Williams, Report to The Adris Building, 84th floor, Suite 808 immediately!" Casey suddenly gets a nervous sinking feeling and quickly closes the message. Stephanie tries to glance at the message but is only able to see the numbers 808.

"What's up? Is that Stacey?"

"Uh yeah, I gotta go." Casey responds nervously getting up out of the booth.

"Wait what about your food?" Stephanie yells.

"See ya!" Casey yells as she runs out of the restaurant.

Outside, Casey runs to an alley and turns her wrist COM on to accesses her contacts. "Hey Sarah can you trace the messages you keep forwarding to me?" she says into her wrist comm. Sarah pops up on a hologram screen,

"It's already done, Ms. Williams, I took the liberty of tracing them the moment we received the third message," Sarah says.

"And?"

"They seem to be originating from the Adris hotel, on the 84th floor," Sarah responds while showing Casey a hologram of the building and a red blinking spot to show the 84th floor.

"Alright thanks Sarah, keep forwarding the messages to me."

"Of course, Ms. Williams." Casey closes the hologram, and looks up to Tier 1 between the somewhat visible light roads and sees the Adris hotel. She looks at the time on her wrist and walks out of the plaza heading to a large building in the back of the complex.

The building is the most secure of all others and has a symbol above the door, a small sun with smaller triangles on three sides. The door itself is large and impenetrable. This is the ammunition building; used mainly to store only the big kind, Akrian artillery shells and Machinok anti-matter battery charges. Casey places her hand on the right side panel of the door; it scans then shows her credentials and the words "approved" underneath her picture. The door slides to the right, Casey walks in and sees two window service counters and a large heavy door with no handle, one of the service counters is dark and empty, the other one has someone in it. Casey walks up to the counter,

"Hey, so I was told to report here, did you want me to go in the other booth or," Casey pauses waiting for a reply, but the man behind the glass is a senior officer and by that it means his wrinkles have wrinkles. Casey thinks the only reason why he wasn't saying anything was either his hearing aide went out or he is literally too old to respond quickly. The old man doesn't acknowledge her; instead he just lifts his hand and hits the button on the panel in front of him. A loud unlocking sound comes from the large heavy door and it slowly opens. Casey looks down the short hallway then walks down through the door and into the large open warehouse with a pile of ammunition. She steps down to a flat level with a laser gate and a small table to the left of the gate controls, on the table is two pairs of magnetic gloves. Casey walks up to the table and disarms her upper half. She grabs a pair of the gloves and opens the laser gate to the rows of ammunition.

The warehouse is set up with five rows and six racks each row with pockets of empty slots, the racks are five feet wide and seven feet high. Casey walks over to the pile of ammunition, mostly heavy artillery shells. She puts on the gloves, turns them on and holds them palm down over the hexagon shaped long box. It magnetically flies up to her hands, stopping it right before it hits her palm. The gloves have a circle on the palm that magnetically locks with the two corresponding spots on the shells. They allow the user to lift heavy objects without having to worry about the weight of the object. Casey walks the shell over to one of the slots on the rack and rests the front of the shell on the edge, then disengages one glove then the other from the shell and pushes it forward into the slot. She continues to do the same thing for about twenty-five more, on the twenty-seventh one she pushes it in then puts her back to it and slides down. She sits with her knees up, crosses her arms over and puts her head down. The large deadbolt safe door opens with a loud

"Oh, Ms. Williams!" coming from the opening. Casey raises her head quickly and flips her hair away from her face. A beautiful bubbly blonde woman comes skipping toward Casey.

Stacey Maze; is a Lieutenant for the Galactic Alliance and Casey's oldest and really only friend.

Her hair is long with a wavy curly style. Clearly she is done for the day and is about to go out. She has green eye shadow and a small amount of blush. Her ears are pierced in two spots and the only tattoo she ever got is a small diamond with a dragon laying over it right behind her ear. She stops three feet in front of her; Casey gets up and brushes her self off.

"What's wrong?" Stacey asks.

"Nothing." Casey quickly responds,

"Casey, what is it?"

"I'm fine Stacey, really." Stacey stares at her with her forest green eyes for a long serious gaze, and then pulls out a silver pouch with green across the top and smiles. "Well I brought lunch!" she says.

"Good because I'm starving." Casey smiles.

Stacey walks up to the laser gate platform and places the silver pouch on the table. The pouch puffs up and opens at the top, then decompresses around the two somewhat small burgundy metal boxes and two twenty ounce blue thermoses. Stacey grabs both of them and places them next to one another; she then places her thumbprint on the tops of both of the boxes. The boxes split in the middle the top half breaks down into small squares and folds back until the top half is gone showing the hot meal contained within. The two of them grab their meals, sit on the platform and begin eating.

"So your sister is worried about you," Stacey says.

"Yeah I know, things just have been difficult lately," Casey replies.

"Is it Shane? I will fuck that guy up if he's bothering you!" Stacey says. Casey smiles "No I can handle him." She looks down at her food.

"I just feel like I should be doing more, you know?"

"I don't follow" Stacey says before taking a bite.

"I just want to go to different planets, and see new cities, really see the galaxy and everything it has to offer."

"Casey you do get to do that, the Galactic Alliance…"

"The Galactic Alliance never goes planet side unless it absolutely has too, they have a ton of rules and restrictions." Casey finishes Stacey's sentence for her.

"Case, they have to, it's what keeps us organized and what keeps us alive." Stacey replies,

"I know, I know" Casey replies.

"What's gotten into you lately?" Stacey asks.

"Nothing, Probably just stress, I guess." Casey says then looks down at her food again. Stacey puts away her food and pulls a small disk from her belt, she presses the center, a series of small hologram rectangles pop up. Casey looks over at it; Stacey skims through the many rectangles and selects one. The rectangle becomes larger and a video begins to play.

The video starts with a drunken Stacey talking about her and Casey going to see a movie with some friends. As she is complimenting Casey, a man comes up and shoves Stacey out of the way. She curses at him, punches him and then the video ends. They both laugh,

"I can't believe you still have that!" Casey says still laughing.

"Oh yeah, I have most of our fuck ups on holocam."

"You mean your fuck ups, I'm just the innocent by stander." Right when Casey finishes her sentence three beeping sounds come from her wrist comm. She stops laughing and looks at her wrist. She checks it; there are three new messages all from the same ID number. She closes it quickly and her mind begins to race with thoughts and questions, how the hell did they get her COM ID number? Or is it a trap? Could it be a promotion? Or maybe just another sick joke by Shane. Either way, there is only one way to find out.

Stacey nudges shoulders with her, "Hey, you alright?" She asks while taking another bite out of food. Casey snaps out of thought,

"Yeah, No, I'm fine."

"Was that your sister?"

"What?"

"The three messages you got," Stacey says while pointing at her wrist.

"Oh, yeah, She wants me to help her with some new recruits that are terrible with simple Rx7 rifles." Casey says while taking a drink, Stacey stares at her hard,

"You're lying." Stacey says.

"What?" Casey asks while trying not to smile.

"Oh my Cortex, it's a guy! Isn't?" Stacey teases.

"No, no." Casey says but quickly thinks about the situation and changes her answer. "I mean, yes!" Stacey's face lights up.

"I knew it!" Taking a bite out of her sandwich.

"You caught me! But, right now I have to leave and go meet him, so can you do me a solid and cover the rest of my shift here? I only have an hour left." Casey pleads with her hands clasp together. Stacey puts down her sandwich, grabs her friend's hands and says

"For you, anything Space Case." Casey smiles,

"Thank you, I owe you one." Casey says.

She picks up her stuff and heads out the building. She runs off to the left and climbs up on top of a building. Once on top she backs up, runs and jet jumps up to the wall of the whole base. She climbs up on the wall then runs along the wall up to the corner that is directly above the gondolas pathway. Casey jumps and lands on top of the gondola that is going up to Tier 1.

THE ADRIS HOTEL

CASEY JUMPS OFF THE GONDOLA ON TO THE LOADING PLAT-
form in the middle of a small crowd. One of the gentlemen in the crowd
leans forward and yells,

"Hey what the hell is your problem?" Casey taps a pistol on her hip.
The man backs up,

"What I meant to say." He nervously says, "Was that you should have
a great day."

She puts her pistol away and begins walking down a flight of stairs.

She exits out to the park that is adjacent to the vehicle parking for the
gondolas. The park has a field of artificial grass and shrubbery with a small
river going through a kid's playground on the left end of the field. Casey
runs the walkway across the river to the end of the park and comes up to
a corner of light roads. A light road is made up of different types of crystal
energy, a visible electrified barrier that corresponds with vehicle tires that
also have streaked crystal energy running down the middle of the tire.

When a light road is green, vehicles can move, but when they are red,
vehicles will stop and cannot move until it turns back. She looks down at
the road and then up at the hotel that is in the center of the city. She knows
that light roads don't hold you up unless you're in a vehicle. She looks to
the left and sees a moving truck coming down the green light road. She

runs back a few feet then charges at the road timing it just perfectly to put her hands on top of the truck. She hangs on the side for a few seconds then pulls herself up.

Once on top of the truck she sits down with her legs crossed over each other, facing toward the front of the truck. She brings up a map on her wrist COM. The holographic map shows the road she's on and the buildings on either side. She scrolls down on the hologram, and stops over a bridge, just up the road. It is above the light road that leads straight to the Adris Hotel. She taps her palm with her fingers and the map shuts off. She looks up further down the road and sees the bridge coming quick.

She gets up slowly, once the truck makes it to the middle of the bridge, Casey dives off the left side of the truck and lands feet first on a smaller hovering cobalt taxicab. The taxicab bounces down from the weight of landing on it.

The taxicab hits the light road, but only for a second then comes back up to normal hovering height. The driver looks up out his windshield to see what hit him and looks around to see if anyone else has the same problem. Casey kneels down on top, keeping one foot ready. She looks forward and sees the plaza that is in front of the Adris Hotel. The plaza is large, separated into three quadrants and has one large statue of a R.A.I.S Soldier.

Casey jumps off the taxi and gracefully rolls when she lands on the ground. She stands up, brushes her self off. Ahead, there is a hooded figure standing across from her near by the entrance. The hooded figure stares at Casey with bright red eyes. She puts her left hand on one of her pistols as a large group of business representatives engulf her on every side. Casey looks for the hooded man in the sea of people but doesn't see any trace of him. She shoves past everyone and gets to the statue in the middle of the plaza. It has maroon and black shrubs all around it.

Casey looks all around the statue and checks the plaza, still no sign. She backs up cautiously toward the entrance then heads inside the building.

The main lobby of the hotel is massive. Two giant chandeliers made of red and black diamonds hang above. There are two matching service desks, one on both sides of the room. There are two waiting lounge areas with coffee tables, large rugs and couches in the middle of the lobby. She slowly takes a few steps into the lobby while checking behind her for the hooded figure. The lobby is empty aside from the one receptionist and a security guard. There is a red haired, dark blue skin toned Nexus woman behind the service desk.

"Oh great! You're finally here!" she says to Casey.

"Were you the one who sent the messages?" She asks.

"If I can just have you wait over there while I let them know you are here." the receptionist says while completely disregarding her question.

Casey takes a deep breath, to keep calm and not slap this bitch's face off. She puts on a smile, walks over to the waiting area and sits down on the couch adjacent to the center wall.

Casey waits impatiently before getting up and walking over to the receptionist. She is talking to someone in her language with an earpiece. The Nexus woman holds up her index finger and continues talking. Casey rolls her eyes, turns around and sees the restroom sign hanging above a hallway. She heads to the restroom, does her business then walks out. When she gets back to the lobby, it's empty, no receptionist and no security guard. No one is coming in and no one did in the time she waited either. Casey scans the entire room, but no one, she steps out a little bit and turns around. The couch she was sitting on has been moved and the wall it was against suddenly shifts and a door opens revealing an elevator. Casey takes a quick look around the lobby again and looks back at the elevator. She breathes deep and walks into it. She looks around inside, there are no buttons and the ceiling is one solid piece of black diamond. Casey immediately regrets her decision, but the doors close the moment she tries to leave.

The elevator starts moving, there are no lights or any way of tell how high or low she is going. It makes no sound she only feels the slight uneasy feeling of it moving. The elevator stops, the doors open slowly, Casey steps off quick and into a long maroon and black hallway with no exits or stairwells just rooms. She begins down the hallway; there are a total of eight doors on both sides of the hallway and one pair of double doors at the end. Casey checks the door numbers as she goes. She already has a feeling that the double doors have to be the right ones considering the four doors she's past don't have anything on them, not even access panels. She pulls out her right leg pistol and continues down the hallway and stops right before the solid black double doors. Curious, they have door handles, not access panels.

The numbers 808 are on both doors in red diamonds, Casey clicks the safety off and opens one of the two doors, checks behind the other door, takes a few steps forward while checking the left hallway as she passes by it and heads into the kitchen of the suite. She sees a man in a suit standing facing out of an eight-foot window across from the kitchen. Casey ducks down behind the sink.

"Ms. Williams when you're done wasting your time, I would really like it if we could get down to business." The man by the window says with a bit of a slur. Casey recognizes the voice; she stands up slowly and stares at the man. He turns around and faces Casey. His tie is loose and one hand is holding a glass of scotch.

"What took you so long?" Says the old dark skinned tone man as he takes a drink.

"Mr. Sullivan?" Casey says as she walks out of the kitchen.

"Oh shit I mean, President Sullivan!" Casey quickly salutes.

"Really? Put your fucking hand down." Sullivan says while shaking his head and slightly loosing his balance.

"Sorry Sir." Casey says relaxing.

"You know Casey it doesn't take a detective to know this is an off the books meeting." Sullivan says.

"I got that when I saw how drunk you were Sir." Casey says walking over to the living room space of the suite.

"Duly noted, but down to business, please have a seat." He waves his hand to the two couches in the center of the room with a table between them. Casey walks over to the couch across from him and sits down while Sullivan fixes another scotch on the rocks.

"So how are things? How's your sister?" Sullivan says while finishing up and turning around with two glasses.

"I'm okay, and Stephanie loves the Guillotine or maybe just being in charge." Sullivan sits on the couch across from her and places the two glasses down and a small dark blue pyramid on the table.

"I do miss being in the service." Sullivan sighs while looking up out the window.

"What's that?" Casey says quickly keeping her eyes glued to the small pyramid.

"The Service?" Sullivan becomes confused,

"No you imbe…" Casey stops herself from insulting the president of humanity and calmly takes a deep breath and says slowly

"No Carter, I'm talking about the piece of shit you put on the table."

"Well Casey, I was getting to that, but I figured we had time to go down memory lane, like the time I showed you how to play poker." Sullivan says with a smile.

"With all do respect Sir, you lost every time, so if anything I was the one teaching you." Casey responds.

"Now I can see why everyone likes your sister more." Sullivan says taking a large swig from his glass. Casey turns her head slightly with a smirk on her face; She wants to answer with a smart remark on how perfect her sister is however she knew not to be sucked in by the subject.

"Why am I here Sully?" She leans back and crosses her arms. Carter drinks and leans back. Casey stares at him; she can see the stress and lack of sleep in his eyes. His face is worn and even though he is wearing a suit she can tell he hasn't been eating. This is concerning, he is like a second father to Casey since her father went MIA and she knows it isn't the job that is making him drink this much or look this way. He takes one more sip, exhales and leans forward.

"We've lost all contact with Sol, now either the virus wiped them all out, or the new threat near Tiabanus has finally made its move."

"What's near Tiabanus?" Casey asks.

"Don't know much, except that they are very powerful whatever they are." Sullivan stops to take a drink.

"Why am I here then?" Casey asks.

"About a week ago, an unofficial building in an unofficial place was attacked and Dr. Carl Teyach was kidnapped along with a very powerful crystal, that could save not only humanity but every living thing in the galaxy from something far worse than the Phazaren virus." Carter takes a sip, sets the glass down then picks up the small blue pyramid,

"Basically you are here because I was given a set of instructions with this device to give to you." Carter says.

"By who? I thought you're the top of the food chain." Casey says.

"By whom," He corrects her.

"Casey this serious, this isn't a joke. When you take that key and leave this room you will be on your own you will not be a part of Galactic Alliance. Instead, you will have your own ship and crew, but you don't get to choose." He says then takes another sip.

"Now, as for the key, it's been coded to your DNA and it contains the location of your ship, mission details and your pass to get in. There, you will meet the first three members of your crew. You'll find profiles of allies on this device and it is imperative that you convince everyone on the list to join you. Now, hold out your hand." Sullivan finishes with a hiccup.

Casey zones back in from staring down the blue pyramid,

"Wait what?" Casey asks.

"Let me see your hand." Sullivan says.

"Hold on, go back what are we talking about here? I feel like we skipped something. Why is it coded to my DNA? Why do I need to get everyone on the list? And what list?" Casey frantically asks.

"The one on this key drive, Keep up Williams! Honestly, if you can't convince them, then your chances of survival are minuscule; but that seems to be all the time I have, so if you could just possibly hold out your fucking hand we might actually be able to get on with our lives." Carter says coldly while holding the object from its point. Casey can see he is dead serious.

She looks at the pyramid then slowly lays her hand flat over his free hand. Carter places the base of the pyramid over the center of her palm. The base opens with six pin legs that latch into her skin and lock themselves underneath the skin of her palm, she screams.

Carter grabs his drink while she walks around holding her hand crying.

"Now you must make sure no one sees you on the way there, or out of here. This meeting never happened."

Casey continues pacing back in fourth holding the wrist of the hand that hurts.

"Maybe I should have gotten the other sister." Casey abruptly stops stands up straight and clears her throat.

"Oh I'm fine." Casey says still holding her hands out at both sides.

"Well In that case good luck!" Without warning, two big security guards come from both sides of the room, grab Casey under both arms, lift and throw her into an elevator that has opened up in the suite.

"Hold on! Wait!" Casey tries to escape but the doors close and the elevator begins to descend. She looks around frantically but once again no buttons. She backs up and knocks her hand against her leg causing a stabbing pain where the pyramid is attached. She lets one tear out. She touches the pyramid and it lights up with an address, 639 Building H Level 4 Tier 3. It's in the warehouse district.

Casey remembers the place after being stationed there for 2 months, She and Shane broke up and she wasn't able to work around him, not because it hurt every time she saw him kind of thing but because Casey would literally try to beat the shit out of him and one time had succeeded. In return Commander Heathrow forced her to be moved to the shit end of Terra. This time is different.

The elevator stops and the doors open to a solid grey hallway with one door at the end with a hologram of the word "Exit" across the top half. Casey makes her way to the door, she pulls a small black disc from her wrist com and puts it on the handle of her assault rifle on her back cloaking all the weapons on her back. She places two fingers on the back of her jacket's collar and brings them over her head causing a hood to materialize. The door doesn't have an access panel but has an old fashion push to open exit. She pulls the hood down low and pushes the door open to an alleyway that leads to the main street. She keeps her head down, her hands her pockets and walks to the nearest tram.

She heads down a flight a stairs that leads on to a subway-like train and it's packed, barely any room to stand. As soon as Casey finds a spot, the doors close and the train begins to move.

Unfortunately the only way to get to different levels on Terra is the Tram system, four trains go from the top of level 1 all the way to level 4 in about two hours because of all the stops on the way, Three of the trains are used for military transport of materials, while the last one is crammed with civilians. It's a shitty thing for a government to keep their people in the dark on just how many of them are left due to the virus and then make the last bit of them cram in to do their daily commute.

This causes tension between the Galactic Alliance and the civilians. Casey always made sure to leave her GA badge at home. It's hard enough walking around armed to the teeth and people not ask you if you're with them or a bounty hunter. She preferred bounty hunter, mainly for the freedom of it. People tend to look the other way when you're a bounty hunter. She looks up to see the train's progress, just two more stops she thinks. The train stops, Casey looks towards the end of the cabin.

A hooded figure with red R.A.I.S eyes is staring back at her. She feels the weight of evil from the eyes. The train begins to move and passes through darkness for two seconds; once the light hits the train the figure has disappeared. Casey looks around the train, but there is no sign of the hood. She didn't understand why this thing is following her and how no one else seems to have seen it. She begins to wonder if this all just in her imagination

The train makes its final stop; Casey gets off quickly and heads for Tier 3 the warehouse district.

An elevator door opens to an empty hallway, Stephanie walks out with her assistant, "They have just finished sweeping the room for DNA, it should be about 5 minutes before they have any results." said the intelligent brunette. Her name is Gussie and her hair always looks like she spends her time reading and working. Yet she is always organized with a different pair of glasses for everyday of the week and her uniform is always steam pressed. She doesn't really care to do her hair or makeup, to her life is about learning.

They continue down the hallway to the last room 808. Stephanie walks in, past the cleaning crew who are moving two security guard bodies into bags in the living room. President Sullivan is sitting on the couch with a bullet crater in the back of his skull and the top half of his face is gone. The assistant instantly runs to the side and throws up. One of the members of the clean up crew walks up to Stephanie.

"We got a hit on one more DNA in the room." He hands her a holographic pad, she looks at it then turns it off.

"Let's keep this between us for now, understood?"

"I would Commander except they have already been sent to Commander Heathrow. Sorry Sir." The man says then walks away. Stephanie walks fast out the room, and her assistant runs after her.

"Gussie, I need you to send a message to my sister." Stephanie says.

"What do you want me to tell her?" Gussie asks.

"Tell her to run." Stephanie says. The assistant works on her pad as they both walk on to the elevator.

"Commander, what's going on?" Gussie asks.

"Not sure yet." The doors close.

Casey runs across the street to Building 639 after walking around the warehouse district long enough for the artificial rain to kick that only happens when the sun is blocked out for the night. She walks up to the entrance. The door only has one panel with a square keyhole. Casey lifts her hand to the hole the pyramid releases its grip and flies into the square keyhole. The door opens and the pyramid drops, Casey catches it before it hits the ground with one hand while the other holds her pistol. She attaches it to her belt and makes her way in. She checks both sides of the door as she walks in.

All the lights are out except one at the end of a hallway. She makes her way toward the light, hearing music and the sound of a blowtorch searing metal. Casey changes from her pistol to her rifle. She changes the shot to incinerate. She hugs the wall, as she gets closer to the end. She peeks around the corner to see, another hallway leading away. The wall on the right side has a couple of wire fences covering a blown out area. Casey takes a couple steps out and looks through the wire fence down to the lower level. There are two R.A.I.S women and what looks like a vessel under a brown tarp. She tries to get a better look, but the sound of a Ragnarok x79 shotgun heating up stops her.

"Drop the rifle meat sack." Says the voice behind the shotgun, Casey hands over the rifle and puts her hands up.

A R.A.I.S woman with an aluminum short haircut and green eyes зпу з

"Let's go," while keeping the gun on her.

Casey walks to the end of the hall and down the stairs to the lower level. The other two R.A.I.S women stop what they are doing and look over at Casey. One of the models is tall and slim with a gold and silver coating on her metallic body. Her eyes are a florescent yellow and her aluminum hair is a tied up, the same as Casey's. The other model is small and child-like. Not too many R.A.I.S children models are left, no one takes them seriously. Her metallic body is white with red coating. Her eyes are florescent blue and her aluminum hair is in pigtails.

"Tiny, I found this one sniffing around, should I incinerate her?"

Casey's eyes go wide,

"Jo, put the gun down she is with us." Tiny says.

"She is?" Jo asks.

"I am?" Casey asks.

"Obviously, how else would she have gotten through the front door?" Tiny asks.

"She could've hacked in!" Jo yells.

"Just put the damn gun away!" Tiny yells.

Jo struggles, but finally lowers her weapon and hands Casey back her rifle. The small R.A.I.S walks up to Casey.

"Hello there, don't mind her, she's a little hostile towards humans, well everyone actually, I'm Tiny Tiffany. You can just call me Tiny and that beautiful specimen working on the spare power converter is Trea Treasurella." Tiny says as she shakes Casey's hand and nodding in Trea's direction.

"You must be Casey Williams." Tiny says.

"Yeah, how do you know my name?" Casey asks.

"Sullivan told me you would be coming. Do you have the key you used to get in?" Tiny asks. Casey pulls it from her side belt and before she could give it to her, Tiny snatches it from her hand.

"Uh." Casey utters confused.

"Follow me Ms. Williams," Tiny says making her way up the on ramp of the ship underneath the tarp.

Casey follows her into the ship, they walk down a curved hallway, and the height of the ceiling is much higher than most privateer ships. The atmosphere on board feels more relaxed than any other Casey has ever been on.

"It took us quite some time to restore this baby but she's well worth it. This ship is more advanced than anything else in the galaxy right now." Tiny says while leading Casey into the main room area of the ship, with boxes of food, ammunition and medical supplies. There is also a couch off to the left and a hologram projector in the middle of the room.

"Is that a couch?" Casey asks confused

"You are very observant for a human, Ms. Williams." Tiny says as she walks up to the projector and plugs the pyramid into it.

The whole ship lights up, blue lights travel in between the floor panels and red lights travel between the ceiling panels. The ship lifts up off the ground slightly; Jo gets worried and starts loading boxes faster. The projector turns on and the first hologram is the words "Welcome back Casey".

"What does that mean? Welcome back?" Casey asks as she slowly walks up to the projector; Tiny puts her hand on her chin

"Time travel?" she whispers to herself. Casey gives her a confused look,

"Hold on, are you saying I have been on this ship before?"

"No, but time travel, would explain why this ship is here, I believe you sent this to your self from the future."

A video pops up with a blonde woman with short hair dressed as a General. "Casey If you are watching this, then that means I failed. I failed you and all of humanity," the woman says.

"Who's the human?" Tiny asks.

"My mother." Casey says quietly.

"Don't let Dr. Teyach get the…" Casey's mother says right before the video ends.

"What happened? Play it back!" Casey yells teary eyed.

"I can't, it deleted right after it played, but the message was sent to the ship years ago." Tiny says working on the pad.

"What?" Casey says when a semi loud sound comes from her wrist COM, new message from Gussie appears with one word "RUN". Casey becomes nervous and confused. Tiny messes with the projector moving files and passes by a live feed of news from Terra. She immediately brings it back.

The words "President of Humanity Murdered" are at the top of holo-gram-like screen. Tiny makes it larger.

"That's not good." Tiny says Casey looks up from her wrist and sees the news feed. "What the fuck?" Casey says. She gets closer to the projector.

"It can't be, I just left there." She says out of breath, as though the wind just got knocked out of her.

Tiny turns up the volume, the news anchor is speaking loudly.

"We are getting confirmed reports that former Lieutenant Casey Williams is the suspected shooter and is now hiding somewhere in the warehouse district as seen on this video of her exiting the Tram, If anyone has seen her please notify the proper authorities."

"Really? A hood? That was your disguise of choice?" Tiny asks incredulously.

"I didn't think I was being accused of killing anyone!" Casey says.

"Well, why did you kill him?" Tiny asks freaking out

"I didn't!" Casey says frantically.

"Oh, well they think you did." Tiny says more calm while looking at the screen and seeing the live feed of a raid in progress of the very same warehouse they are in.

"Well that's not a good sign, Jo you better hurry up out there!" Tiny yells out to her.

"Some help would be appreciative you know!" Jo yells back while setting two boxes down at the top of the ramp.

"Go help her, I will get the ship working." Tiny says.

"Wait we're just going to run?" Casey asks.

"Casey you have just been marked as the murderer of the president of humanity, do you really think they will let you live?" Casey stares blankly at Tiny.

"Fuck" she says then quickly runs back to the ramp.

Trea passes her as she heads to the cockpit. Jo walks up to the ramp with two more boxes and hands them to Casey. Two shots hit the side of the ship, causing Jo to dive for cover. Casey drags the two boxes inside then takes a peak and sees a squad of Galactic Alliance soldiers tearing down the wire fence covering the hole in the wall. Jo runs over to the other side of the room and grabs the last two boxes. Casey pulls a pistol out, hits a switch that changes the shot type; the word "Bubblegum" comes up on the side. She aims and fires four shots each one hitting each soldier trapping them in a bright pink bubble.

"Jo, let's go!" Casey yells, Jo runs over to the ramp and throws the boxes into the ship. Another squad runs up to the fence shooting at Jo and Casey.

"Trea, we need to get this bird in the air!" Tiny yells while working with the projector. "Working on it!" Trea yells back while flipping switches and pushing buttons. Casey helps Jo into the ship and closes the hatch.

Two soldiers pull out RPGs and ready them.

"Trea!" Tiny yells.

The ship begins making a charging humming sound and a hologram of the ship appears above the projector. The words "Flight mode" are above the hologram. The tarp above the ship falls off revealing a brightly orange, red and blue colored ship.

Outside the warehouse, more Alliance soldiers and vehicles surround the building. Stephanie steps off a transport ship that arrives on the roof of the building across the street. The warehouse begins shaking, and then explodes. A strange rocket shape ship bursts out. This medium size vessel begins shedding layers that form into four large vibrant blue wings making it resemble a bird. The blue energy lines make the wings to look like feathers. The tail of the ship is also feather like, with strands of the same energy, while others begin to turn red and orange. This ship is more than just an advanced bird ship.

To the Alliance soldiers watching it rise is a sign from the Nexus Religion; that states, "End of days is to follow after the revival of a Phoenix". The ship flaps its wings launching it upward quickly. The wind generated from its wings knocks soldiers and vehicles back. Stephanie is baffled at the sight of the beautiful ship as it makes its way out of the Terra's shielding atmosphere.

THE MERCENARY

THE BRIGHTLY COLORED SHIP FLOATS ABOVE OMICRON, THE large green and blue planet that Terra orbits. Casey walks up to the projector. Tiny opens a file that shows a list of eight names. Casey taps on the first one and the screen shows the name "Hyda Toocaro" at the top.

"What is this?" Casey asks.

"This is, your help, which if I may express my opinion, is not of help, they are more of a bunch of powerful losers, if anything." Tiny says.

"I don't know about this. I mean I just got accused of killing the president, this will make things worse."

"Ms. Williams, no offense but you need to stop acting like a little bitch; we have a job to do and if we don't do it, there won't be anything left in the galaxy. So, instead of wasting time like every pathetic character in every hero story, just take it in stride for now. Do us all a favor, quit second guessing yourself and pick a god damn name." Tiny ends her rant with a smile. Casey remains speechless then looks back at the projector and picks the first name on the list.

"Great. Last known location was Farses, Trea fly around a bit to throw them off, then takes us down to the far side of Omicron."

"You got it!" Trea replies over the intercom. Tiny walks away to check the ship's cargo.

Casey begins reading the profile on Hyda Toocaro. He is a mercenary, half Nexus and half Human. He has strange energy force ability and
doesn't use guns, only energy swords. In one case, he used a steel relic blade
to execute an ex alliance military soldier, slowly and painfully. His slightly
long hair is dark silver almost grey; he looks mostly human aside from the
bright green Nexus eyes and Nexus-like ears.

"If I were you I would hire him on some lie, because people like him
don't really like being the "save the world" type, not unless you make it
worth their while." Tiny advises as she checks the integrated hologram on
the back wall of the main room.

"Don't worry I got an idea." Casey says.

Tiny walks up behind her with the pad still in her arm.

"Ms. Williams, I will find some more information on the ship, and
relay any information I have. This ship is registered to you and it would be
wise to know how to use it." Tiny says.

"It's under my name?" Casey asks.

"Yes but if you happen to die a horrible death, I will be taking it from
you." Tiny says calmly.

Casey gives her a fake smile, and grabs the pad from her.

"Also you will be needing one of these to stay in contact with us."
Tiny says. She extends her cold metal-like hand that holds a small earring.
Casey grabs the earring and places it near her lob. The earing makes an
incision then secures itself to Casey, no blood and no muss, no fuss.

"We we're off to a rough start, but now is when things start getting
interesting Ms. Williams." Tiny says as Casey continues to go over the
content on the pad. Phoenix functions run across the top of the screen,
"Cloaking, Deflection," "Wingspan," "Weaponry" and "Cortex travel."
Casey begins to research the functions.

At the top level of Terra-127 there is a meeting being held by the
military leaders and the new president in charge is Jacob T. Hogon.

"We must find her at all cost, allowing her to live will have people thinking we can not keep them safe." Commander Heathrow demands while seated at the long levitating metal table. All the other generals and commanders are on both sides while the president sits at the end.

"With all do respect, Commander Heathrow, I think its best, I bring her back and she stands trial." Stephanie says walking into the room.

"Whose to say you won't betray us as well!" Heathrow exclaims.

"Oh shut the hell up Heathrow! I told you sending your men in there would just cause them to run, Mr. President let me bring her in." Stephanie says.

Hogon sighs,

"Very well, we will give Commander Williams ninety two hours to bring her in, if she fails to do so, then Heathrow it will be your turn. This meeting is adjourned." The president stands up and exits the room. All the Commanders and Generals pass by Stephanie on the way out. Heathrow stops next to her

"You better hope you find her before I do." Stephanie gives him a cold smile as he walks out of the room.

Casey's ship, known as the Phoenix, makes it way down over a large blinding white city that is surrounded by forest. Not much to this city other than refugees trying to make a living, dirt roads and corner markets. There is no real rich and poor, it's just poor.

The Phoenix quickly cloaks itself above the somewhat tall apartment building in the slums of the city. Casey jumps out and slows her way down onto the roof with her boots.

"Alright I looked up our little friend and he is currently working on a bounty, a Solarian named Jai Krait, wanted for murder. I would suggest finding him first." Tiny says through the COM link piece in Casey's ear. She walks to the edge of the roof and looks down at the droves of aliens and humans filling the dirt street.

"I don't suppose you know where he is?" Casey asks.

"Good luck Ms. Williams!" Tiny replies.

She sees a bar a couple blocks down and thinks it looks like a good place to start. Casey jumps over to the next couple roofs, using her boots that allow her to drop down to the street and walk into the bar.

It smells of alcohol and gasoline inside. The building has three entrances, the main doorway where Casey came through and two more on the left and the right of the building. The bar is full of drunken aliens and the booths on both sides of the room are filled. Casey walks up to the bar. She notices a table off to the side with one Solarian in a hood sitting and smoking. She walks over to the table and sits down across from the alien. He puts the cigar out in the ashtray on the table, and raises his head to look at Casey. His face looks like a preying mantis, with large orange eyes. He has a total of three pincers on both sides of his mouth and his skin is a pale green color.

"You are one ugly motherfucker." Casey tells him.

"What do you want, human?" the Solarian says.

"Oh good, you speak English, I'm here looking for a person who is looking for you and seeing as how I got lucky and found you first, you will be coming with me." Casey smiles while readying her pistol under the table. Jai readies his two extra hands as he puts them under the table.

"So, how about we take nice leisurely walk out of here?"

"I don't think so." Jai says right before he flips the table toward Casey. She falls back in her chair and fires a couple shots at him. No one in the bar reacts as Jai dodges and heads out the left doorway. One unlucky person at the bar gets one of Casey's shot in his arm. They scream in pain.

"Shit." Casey says while getting up.

"What happened?" Tiny asks over the COM.

"The motherfucker ran! I'm sorry!" Casey yells back at the man on the floor holding his arm as she runs out of the bar after him.

Jai runs down the main street shoving people out of the way. Casey chases him through alleyways and small shops until they come to an open plaza with a very large and very old well in the center. Jai stops next to the pound and grabs two civilians, using them as a shield as Casey points her pistol at him. Not able to get a clear shot, Casey switches her shot to Net and fires it in the air above Jai, only to have it thrown back at her by a hooded cloaked man wielding a blue energy light sword. Casey jumps sideways to dodge it and the cloaked man lands at the edge of the well. He attempts to stab Jai but Jai blocks it with his other two hands holding small green energy daggers. Jai lets the civilians go to grab two energy swords on his belt and tries to use them against the cloaked man, but he summersaults over Jai and pulls out another sword. Jai's arms bend back to strike him; the man blocks them with his blades. Jai continues to strike but the man blocks each one. Casey gets up, puts her pistol away and rushes over to the fight. Once she gets close enough, the man kicks Jai to the side. He points his flat palm at Casey. A blue wind like force pushes Casey out over the water well. She stops herself from falling in with her boots, levitating over the center.

The man stands up straight with his hood still covering half his face. He smirks and nods his head down at the pound. Casey looks down and sees a shadow make its way to the surface. A large Pylon Worm, (a nasty cross between a whale shark and a python) snaps its mouth trying to swallow Casey. She lands on its nose quickly pulling a grenade from her belt and throws it into its mouth and she shoots it with her pistols. The explosion kills the worm sending guts and Casey flying lighting up her shield.

Jai recovers and runs away into the city. The hooded man pursues him, eventually catching up to him. Jai grabs him with one of his four arms and throws the man eight feet out in front of him. He activates two swords as he walks closer to the man on the ground. Casey sprints to catch up to them and readies an energy whip from her wrist COM device. Jai raises his blades up to strike the hooded man but Casey lassos the two arms holding the blades together and pulls him back hard. She then jet-jumps over Jai and punches the cloaked man in the face keeping him down, then quickly pulls out a pistol and shoots a high powered spin and shot into Jai's face, killing him instantly. Jai's body crumbles to the ground and the man recovers now with no hood covering his head. He tries to reach for his energy blade to attack. Casey steps on it and puts a pistol right in his face.

"I wouldn't if I were you." Casey says confident in her aim.

"What the hell do you want?" He replies.

"You are Hyda Toocaro are you not?" Casey asks but the man remains silent. "Its ok, I figured you were when you pushed me into the Pylon." She continues.

"My name is Casey Williams and I want to hire you." Hyda looks over at Jai furiously, then looks back at Casey, but still remains silent.

"Don't worry you can still have the bounty for him and I will also be paying you." Casey says while putting away her pistol and lending a hand to help him up. He grabs her hand, gets up and brushes off his missed matched uniform, parts of it from a galactic alliance officer, and the other is custom made Nexus robes. He isn't very tall, maybe about 5'6.

"I needed information from him and you killed him before he could tell me anything!" Hyda yells.

"Bummer. But any information he had couldn't have been accurate." Casey says looking back at the body and putting away the energy whip.

"What makes you so sure?" Hyda says still angry

"Because Mr. Hyda, the next person on my list to hire is a private detective who knows practically every piece of scum in the galaxy and you are going to help me convince him to join. In return, I'm sure he will have some information for you." Hyda takes a deep breath.

"So how much are you going pay me?"

Casey smirks and hands him a three-inch flat rectangle then walks away. Hyda slides his thumb across it and a hologram pops up with a long number it's triple the amount what he was getting for the bounty of Jai.

He looks up and sees her standing further down the street looking back at him, waiting, as though she knows she has him. Hyda laughs a little, picks up Jai's body, and follows her.

After they drop off the body and collect the bounty from a local bookie, Casey takes Hyda to the ship. It's parked above the same roof where she was dropped off. Once on board the ship, takes off to orbit. Hyda follows Casey into the main cabin, where Tiny is working on an open compartment in the floor near the projector. He continues to look around the cabin, he notices the an inscription above the projector on an archway it reads; "The Phoenix exist where Time does not." Hyda then looks at the holograms from the projector, three in particular, one of a Groutarian, the next one is a Katharac and the last one is a Sieren (Sear-en).

"So what exactly do you need my help with?" Hyda asks.

"Don't worry, those three will be on our side, well hopefully anyway. The one in the hole there is Tiny, and the two piloting the ship are Trea and Jo, you will meet them eventually." Casey says to Hyda as he looks back in the compartment,

"Yeah hi." Tiny says while closing a fuse box like object.

"Hello." Hyda says.

"Have you never met a R.A.I.S before Mr. Hyda?" Tiny asks without looking at him. "Yes I have, just never had the pleasure of working with one." Hyda says.

"Well you're in luck, she is a bit of a know it all R.A.I.S." Casey says working with the holograms.

"I love it when you point out the obvious, Ms. Williams." Tiny responds,

"I hate you, Tiny." Casey says.

"So why am I here?" Hyda asks.

"I need your help saving a scientist, but before we get into that we need to gather a team including a Groutarian. The only way to get him is to get some gem and the only way to get the gem is to get a thief and the only way to get the thief is to hire this man." She pulls up the dossier on a human private detective named Demi Castalo. Hyda reads the information on him, "Fired from Galactic Alliance Military for sexual harassment and making a fool of his superior officers when it came to intelligence and hand to hand combat." Hyda backs up from the screen.

"Sounds like a handful." Tiny says appearing right next to Hyda, causing him to jump. "Wouldn't you agree Mr. Hyda?" she says this time while staring at him.

"In my experience, Humans are always a handful." Hyda says.

"Oh, I like him!" Tiny says excited while grabbing Casey's arm and looking in his direction.

"So, what's the plan, Ms. Williams?" Hyda asks Casey looks back at the hologram.

"I was thinking we ask him in an aggressively, nice way. I used to be a detective for a brief time on Carsecs, before I joined the Galactic Alliance, so I have a way of getting information out of people."

She walks away from the projector and to a wall COM and presses a button.

"Trea take us to Carsecs." Casey says.

"Take us to Carsecs, what?" Casey bites her bottom lip with an exasperated look and clears her throat.

"Take us to Carsecs, *please*." Casey says emphasizing, "please."

"There you go! Remember manners are what separate us from the primates, Ms. Williams!" Trea says over the COM.

"Listen here, you bitch!"

"Oh sorry the COM has to be shut off during a warp jump." Trea says cutting Casey off before she can blow up on her.

"Trea! Trea!" Casey screams while hitting the COM button then taking a deep breath. The ship begins humming before it warps out into the void of space.

The Guillotine makes it's way above Omicron,

"Sir, something just warped out of Omicron space without using a wormhole." Gussie says standing next to Stephanie's chair.

"How is that possible?" Stephanie says to her assistant.

"Not exactly sure, but something definitely ripped through space." She says.

"Can you find out where it went?" Stephanie asks.

"It left a small trace signature, it will take me some time to piece where it went." Gussie explains.

"Understood, Gussie." Stephanie says then nods to the pilot. Stephanie brings up her contact list and tries messaging Casey. The message reads, "Where the fuck are you?"

The Phoenix comes out of warp above the large grey planet of Carsecs. Carsecs is a planet is for mining, but it's a medium size moon, Catarac or also known as Merchant Moon is the one of the largest economy hubs in the galaxy. These two places are responsible for most transactions between "Allied Species".

The ship makes its way toward the brightly lit moon.

"We are making our way to the Catarac landing port." Trea says over the com. "Thank you my love, come to the main room when you can." Tiny says to her while readying a rifle. Casey checks her own weapon.

"Alright the plan is simple, let me do the talking and if I need you then jump in, got it?" Casey says.

"Understood." Hyda replies while fixing his cloak. The ship shakes slightly as they land. Trea walks in the room.

"Ah good! You will be accompanying Ms. Williams on this one." Tiny says.

"What? Why?" Casey asks.

"Because I need her to do something for me." Tiny says then hands Trea the rifle. Trea grabs it and puts it over her shoulder.

Casey, Hyda and Trea exit the ship and docking area and into a long glass tunnel with a one-way escalator-like floor that leads to the inner city.

"Ms. Williams, what do you have against R.A.I.S?" Trea asks.

"I don't have a problem." Casey says.

"Really? Because, I get the feeling you don't trust me or Tiny for that matter." Trea says. Casey turns around and looks at her.

"R.A.I.S have given humanity a second chance, for which I am grateful for, and yet they never asked for anything in return. Now even the Nexus have asked us not to involve them in our little fuck up with the virus, but R.A.I.S said.

'Here you go take this wonderful huge space station, but we will not tell you its true purpose or reason'. So if I had to guess its because every last one of you has a hidden agenda, seeing as you all share parts of your mind right?" Casey finishes her explanation.

"You know Ms. Williams, some would call that paranoia." Trea says with a smile. "Maybe, I call it not showing your full hand until two or more players fold." Casey says then turns back around.

"Am I going to have to separate you two?" Hyda says from the sideline. There is silence from both of them as the moving floor takes them to the end.

They get off and walk to the main doors that are opened by two large ugly Solarians. They walk into a sea of all sorts of aliens walking in both directions. They struggle and squeeze past to head down the intersecting main street. Casey is fascinated by some of the races she didn't even know existed. Catarac is a place of import and export seventy percent of all trafficking businesses in the galaxy travel through this city. They continue down the street passing by many civilians and many local shops, Trea stops, touches her ear, looks ahead then breaks off from the other two. Casey looks back to see Trea taking off into the crowd, but continues forward. Once they reach a clearing in all of the foot traffic, Casey contacts Tiny on COM.

"So how about you tell me where to find Demi, seeing as how you can tell your friend to ditch me." Casey says.

"You know Ms. Williams, you are eventually going to have to trust me, and to answer your question, I did the liberty of running a voice recognition over the whole city. He is currently in a nightclub called Vixen. It's to your right." Tiny says.

"How do you know where we are?" Casey asks.

"Do try to keep up, Ms. Williams." Tiny says while working with holograms on the ship. Casey looks around and spots a camera on the roof of the building across from her. She walks off to the left as Hyda follows her a few steps behind.

Inside the lively club, there are many Nexus and R.A.I.S dancing and enjoying drinks at the bar, one green skinned Nexus is enjoying a drink with a well-groomed, black haired human.

"So, tell me why is beautiful creature like you in a place like this all by herself?" the human asks with a crisp British accent. He straightens his purple and black tie inside the blue vest of his suit.

"Who says I'm by myself?" the Nexus woman replies while taking a drink.

"Well its quite obvious with the clothes your wearing and the very nice perfume emanating from you that you are here to be picked up. Or perhaps, you're not seeking company. However, the drink you ordered shows me that you currently separated from someone and need to feel wanted. Furthermore, this place truly indicates that you are looking for a dashing human such as myself to sweep you off your feet." He finishes while getting closer to her.

"Well as impressive as your deduction skills might be, I have never been with a human male before," the Nexus replies sipping her drink and getting slightly closer to him.

"Well I find that to be serendipitous, because neither have I," he says as he brings his arm around her. A hand grabs his arm and pulls him back.

"Wow! That was terrible, but I don't think this woman is that stupid." Casey says while putting a pistol in his back.

"I wouldn't be too sure of that." Hyda says from behind the Nexus woman startling her.

"How about we have a nice little chat in the alley, Mr. Castalo." Casey says while pulling him away and walking him out slowly.

Casey slams Demi into the brick wall of the club.

"Well aren't you a beautiful sight for very weary eyes." Demi says right before Casey hits him in the stomach and then pushes him against the wall again.

"Hey, take it easy this is a very expensive suit." Demi says while trying to catch his breath.

"Well, if you don't want it stained with plasma burns I suggest you start talking." Casey says as she points her gun at his chest.

"Okay hold on, what is it that you want to know, besides my COM number." Demi says with a smile before Hyda pushes Casey out of the way and knees him in the stomach.

"Now, that was not necessary." Demi says falling to his knees.

"Tell me what you know about Corbus!" Hyda yells down at him,

"Oh, is that what you want? Sounds like somebody is looking to die." Demi says laughing.

Hyda goes to strike him again, but Casey stops him.

Casey picks up Demi, straightens his coat then lets Hyda hit him in the stomach again knocking him down to the floor again.

"Look Demi, the truth is we need your help with a very important mission, for which we will pay you, and not kill you." Casey says while kneeling down to him. Demi looks up at her, then at Hyda.

"You know all you two had to do was get to the point of your bloody visit." Demi says. "We're sorry, but we needed to know that you weren't a threat." Casey says while helping him up.

"Well you are definitely going about it the wrong way." Demi says getting up slowly. "I don't know exactly where Corbus is, all I do know is that he is traveling with Tartoroc. I do apologize, I can see you are seeking revenge."

"The Rebel Militia." Hyda says under his breath.

"And as far as your mission Lieutenant, I'm not sure I will be much help." Demi says. "Actually Demi, you will be more help than you think." Casey says while straightening his coat.

THE THIEF

CASEY, HYDA AND DEMI GET BACK TO THE PHOENIX; TREA IS already on board and is handing a small grey metal box to Tiny when the others walk in. Casey walks past them to the holograms. She begins going through the files until she reaches one named Rayza. She passes the hologram around to Demi.

"So, let's see how great of a detective you really are." Casey says while he opens the file and goes through the content. Hyda goes straight for the couch and lies down. Casey sits on the couch, but Tiny interrupts her break.

"I need you to put your hand on this scanner." Casey gives her a confused look,

"Why?" she asks.

"Ms. Williams, do you always have to question everything?" Tiny says.

"Only with you Tiny." Casey replies as she places her hand on the clear glass slab.

It scans her hand twice, and then Tiny pulls it away right when Demi shouts,

"Brilliant! Oh Ms. Williams she is a crafty Cat, but I'm smarter."

"Did he find her already?" Hyda says while lying down on the couch.

Casey walks over to Demi's side,

"You see Ms. Williams everyone has a signature sign, for some they want it to be found, because they know they can never be caught." Demi explains.

"And you found her signature sign I'm guessing." Casey says scanning over the files. "No, but I found this." Demi says bringing up a hologram image of an article on a large purple gem, called the Amethyst of Galaton.

"She's already on her way to steal the Amethyst?" Hyda asks.

"So it would seem, where is this Demi?" Casey asks.

"Falaux." Demi replies while grabbing a cup of tea from Tiny.

"When did you ask for tea?" Casey says confused.

"Is she always this slow?" Demi asks Tiny whilst taking a sip,

"Oh you have no idea." Tiny says.

"I'm starting to regret bringing you on board." Casey replies.

"Trea! Take us to Falaux!" Tiny yells.

"Yes Ma'am!" She yells back over the COM.

The Phoenix comes out over a red and yellow planet with a green-ish aura around it. The ship descends down into the atmosphere, it rocks back and forth as is banks down, but inside nothing moves. Once it breaks through, there are many landforms floating in the sky, the ship dodges left and right then slows down as it reaches a city on a gigantic floating plateau with many rock formations floating above the city.

Alabor, some call it the Anti-Gravity city. The Phoenix lands near the edge of the city and a group of mechanics run out to the ship and hook up fuel hoses to the underside of the thrusters. Casey exits the ship alone, and pays a man for the parking as she leaves the docking area.

"Ms. Williams are you sure about this? Going alone I mean, she is a Katharac and will most likely kill you in a heartbeat." Tiny says over the COM,

"Thank you for the vote of confidence, as always. Yeah, I would rather do this one on my own." Casey replies.

She continues through a tunnel and a few gates then comes to the last gate that opens on its own to reveal a city like nothing Casey has ever seen. It is divided with one half of the city attached to the floating rock formations that are suspended above the plateau. There are neighborhoods with people walking and kids playing right-side up on their side but are upside down from Casey's point of view. Casey continues to walk looking up with amazement until someone bumps into her. She focuses her attention on the road ahead of her that stretches all the way down the length of city. Further down the road, the buildings get larger and with a more corporate look. As Casey continues down the street, the two suns begin to descend. She walks up to a semi large building, a museum with four roman pillars in the front and a statue of a Groutarian (a very large red hairless gorilla-like creature with saber tooth fangs) holding a staff. She walks up the flight of stairs to the main doors before it gets completely dark outside and the museum closes. Once inside, Casey hides out away from the employees and guards to wait for a full close, but she is not the only one waiting.

On the third floor, there is an exhibit in the far back past the Lazarus void exhibit and the Hierigan bridge exhibit. It is the Amethyst of Galaton, the Gem of Power and it is about to be stolen by one of the best and most invisible thief in the galaxy. The thief is a Katharac, an up right walking cat race, with the strength of fifteen humans and the ability to blend in with their surroundings making them practically invisible. The thief walks from one of the pillars in the exhibit. As she begins moving, she becomes more visible in the moonlight that shines down into the room through the skylight windows above. She approaches, but stops about ten feet from the gem incased in a glass box. She pulls a small metal sphere from her belt, kneels down and rolls it to the case. The sphere silently opens up and places two little metal legs on the floor. It spins around to reveal one purple eye.

The device begins climbing up the case to the top. At the top of the glass, it releases an EMP blast shutting off all security lights and defenses around the case. The thief walks up to the case, grabs the device and pauses.

"Rayza." A voice comes from behind her. She turns around quickly with pistol in hand. Casey is standing a few feet away from her, aiming her rifle and a flashlight in her direction. Casey puts the gun down.

"I'm not here to fight, or stop you." Casey says while putting her weapon away. "Smart, but I guess have to ask what are you doing here, and how do you know who I am?" Rayza asks.

"I need your help, to basically save the galaxy." Casey says.

Rayza smiles and begins laughs a little. She turns back to the case and begins opening it with her very sharp claws, using two of her nails to carve a circle in the glass. "No offense, but the galaxy doesn't need nor want me to save it." She says as she works on the glass.

"Well technically we would be saving a Dr. Teyach, a human scientist who has a very powerful item, that if fallen into the wrong hands, could cause the end of the galaxy." Casey explains. Rayza stops right before grabbing the gem.

"Dr. Teyach." She says under her breath.

"Do you know him?" Casey asks as she takes a half step closer.

"I don't think there is a race in the galaxy that doesn't know him." Rayza says.

"So, will you help?" Casey asks.

Rayza grabs the gem and puts it in a metal container.

"No."

"Can I ask why not?" Casey asks.

"Because human problems are human problems." Rayza says as she begins walking out of the room, Casey stands in her way.

"Right now it is a human problem, but I guarantee you it will become everyone's problem."

Rayza looks up into her eyes with her large forest green eyes. Rayza's calico fur shines bright in the moonlight. She is short but the way she stands is intimidating. Her outfit matches her career, dark navy blue military vest with black pants and combat boots. She has many gadgets and daggers on her belt, but only one pistol.

"I need your help Rayza, and I will help you with anything you might need or want to steal." Casey says to her while taking one step back in case she decides to attack. Rayza looks at her weapons, two of them with a Galactic Alliance insignia on the handle.

"There is one thing I do want, that you might be able to help me with, Lieutenant." Casey is confused at first but then realizes Rayza has made that deduction from her pistols that are only issued to Lieutenants.

"So tell me how I can help you save the doctor and then I will tell you what I need." Rayza says.

"I need that gem to trade for the help of a very large and very mean Groutarian." Rayza looks at her like she is crazy. She looks at the box with the gem in her hands. Rayza sighs.

"I think I might know a way to get you, your Groutarian help and still be able to keep this. If you're interested?" Rayza asks.

"Anything to keep what you steal." Casey says with a smile,

"Well that, and there is this guy I know who not only can speak Groutarian but can also go toe to toe with one. Thing about Groutarians is, that if bribes don't work, a good fight is always a fair trade. The Groutarian would have just killed you and taken the gem."

"And where is this guy?" Casey asks.

"Not sure. He moves around a lot, but I do know someone who might. Lucky you she is currently in this city." Casey takes a step closer to her and extends her hand out.

"Well Rayza, my name is Casey."

"Nice to meet you Casey!" Rayza says shaking her hand in agreement. Her fur was soft and clean for a Katharac Casey thinks.

The alarms go off in the building with flashing red and green lights.

"Looks like that is our cue." Rayza says attaching the box to her utility belt and removing a pistol. She runs and jumps up fifteen feet out of the skylight and on to the roof of the building. Casey quickly follows suit as she hears the guards coming. She jet jumps off the gem case and barely makes it to the skylight, Rayza helps her the rest of the way and they both run down the roof. The guards run into an empty room.

Rayza leads Casey south into the city; the crescent moon is bright enough to light up a majority of the city. They continue down the main road and head toward the entertainment side of town, mostly bars and nightclubs. Rayza stops Casey across the street from a bar, called Emparedado, which is Spanish for sandwich, but right below there is a sign that says, "No humans allowed."

"Really?" Casey says in confusion and aggravation.

"Yeah, I know, but the Greys own this building, so let me check and see if she is here; just wait here okay." Rayza says before she heads over to the entrance.

Casey walks up the street just a few steps before noticing a hooded person following her in a reflection of a mirror hanging off the outside of another bar ahead of her. Casey takes a few more steps then turns down an alleyway.

She runs behind a dumpster, readies her rifle and waits for the person. She checks her wrist radar, to see if she can pick up the target coming in, but nothing shows. She hears the sound of a shoe scrapping dirt against the ground coming from the rooftop in the alley.

She looks up, to see two energy axe blades on a chain hurdling toward her; she dodges both, each one landing in the wall on both sides of her. She aims her rifle and fires a couple fire-bolt shots (a mix between hot molten lava and energy) but they hit the persons' light shield creating a small smoke screen. The assassin retracts the axes. One of them clears the smoke from the impact of the shot and the other one breaks through Casey's shield. It slits her shoulder slightly as it retracts quickly. The axes go back to the person's hand easily and they are ready for another attack. The attacker is stopped by an unusually long energy dagger placed swiftly across the neck of the hood and Rayza holding the handle of it.

"That wouldn't be a very wise choice, Cassandra." Rayza says with confidence

"Don't you already have enough key chips?" The assailant asks,

"A woman can never have too many key chips but what is the human worth to you?" Rayza asks.

"Five hundred quil." Cassandra states. Rayza's eyes widen

"What the fuck did you do?" Rayza asks a wounded Casey,

"I uh sort of..." Casey stammers.

"She killed the human president, blew his brains right out that pretty little skull of his." Cassandra adds.

"What?" Rayza says shocked by the news.

"Who put out the bounty?" Casey asks while fixing her cut with a medical gel that seals up the gash instantly by multiplying cells and any organic tissue.

"The Galactic Alliance, and if you bring her in alive you get a full pardon from them. You killing him made the bounty of the year." Cassandra says to Casey.

"No, I got accused of killing him!" Casey corrects her right before pulling out her pistol and fires two rounds at Cassandra. She dodges them after kicking Rayza to the side. Cassandra flies through the air and lands down a couple feet away from Casey. She sprints at Casey, but Casey blasts upward to avoid her. Cassandra almost slams into the waste bin, but instead she flips off the side of the dumpster. Casey descends and lights up an energy blade just as Rayza drops down between them stopping both of them from proceeding.

"As much as I would love to see her kick your ass Cassandra, we just need to know where Angel is." Rayza says.

"I can't believe this! You're just going to collect on my bounty!" Cassandra explodes. "Oh if you don't like it you can go cry to your sister! Now where is he?" Rayza asks.

Cassandra takes off her hood, revealing her jet-black hair and light purple skin.

Cassandra is a Nexus and although she didn't control the elements when fighting against Casey, she is able to do so. Her outfit is that of a typical bounty hunter, aside from her all green tactical armor. She has many different weapons and a light shield all under her hooded black trench coat.

"How should I know? The guy literally moves through time." Cassandra says relaxing and putting her axes away on her back.

"Okay, for one you know that's not how it works, and two, I know you know because your sister stalks him all the time." Rayza explains.

"I'm going to tell her you said that." Cassandra threatens with a smile.

"Go ahead, its not like I'm scared of her." Rayza says shrugging it off.

"Last I heard he is back on Phazel somewhere in the vast Larex Forest. Why are you looking for him?" Cassandra asks.

"It's above your pay grade, tell your sister I said she still owes me four million." Cassandra scoffs, pulls her hood over her face and exits the alley.

Rayza turns to Casey,

"Looks like you might have a little trouble helping me get what I need after all." Rayza says. Casey shuts off her blade with a concerned look.

"If its some sort of clearance in to an Alliance base, I can still get you what you need! They accused me of killing him and right before he died and he told me to take the ship I have now with three practically insane R A T S and get everyone on a list to help me save a scientist and get some crystal that could potentially save the universe." Casey runs on then takes a deep breath. Rayza walks up to her and puts her hand on Casey's shoulder

"It's okay Casey, I have a feeling you're good for it. How about you show me this ship of yours." She says with a big grin.

THE LAREX FOREST

CASEY IS RUNNING THROUGH A DAMP THICK FOREST. THE
tree trunks are blue and ooze a dark purple puss, yet the leaves remain
green. She is sprinting and dodging the large overgrown roots emerging
from the ground. Something large is chasing her, crushing the roots under
their feet with large red claws. Casey continues out of the forest to a large
open field in the shape of a circle, but as she makes her way to the middle
she trips over a piece of protruding earth that wraps around her leg making
her fall. She smacks her face against the ground causing a mini knockout.
To think how the fuck she even got to this point baffles her. To recap we
will go over the three hours prior.

HOUR # 1

The Phoenix comes out above Phazel, a large purple planet with streaks of
red in the gaseous looking atmosphere. Phazel is a curious planet, mainly
for the many pocket universes that are connected with this universe. A
"Pocket Universe" is how it sounds, a small part of an alternate reality that
is hidden in plain sight on our plane of existence. Each pocket universe
on Phazel has its own village or city with different skin colored Nexus
and slightly different creatures and plant life. All pocket universes work

together with each other to keep a stable community; Phazel is a planet of many worlds.

The ship descends into the sky quickly, but slows down once two medium size Nexus fighter ships come up behind it. The ships have an old school human jet plane look but have six wings with heavy fire power. They send a hailing to the Phoenix, suggesting that they follow them or receive a couple shots of heated Mynanium (green acidic energy shots most Nexus military ships use). Trea follows the two fighter ships down to a landing zone, slightly out of the main city of Kastrie. The main capital of Phazel is a city floating above a large lake that is surrounded by five mountains, one larger than the other four. The largest mountain has a white and gold castle embedded in the front of the mountain over looking the floating city. The city spreads across the entire mountain range and even on the lake below, most buildings have red, white or gold paint to match the color of the banners hanging from the city hall building. The Phoenix touches down on the landing zone near the edge of the city, making for one long walk. Casey, Rayza and Hyda exit the ship and make their way out of the docking area.

"Alright, so I don't know exactly like how to get to the Larex Forest, considering it's located in one of the pocket universe, somewhere near the eastern mountains." Rayza says as she leads them through the city pointing off in the direction they need to go.

"So how do we find it?" Casey asks as she keeps her distance from the natives. Casey has never had too much contact with the Nexus; they can control elements. Guess you could say she is a little worried.

"Well lucky for you guys, I know a few higher ups, so if I were you I wouldn't show your fear or racism when we enter the castle and that means you, Hyda." Rayza says walking ahead of the other two.

"I'm half Nexus!" Hyda exclaims, Rayza stops and turns around to face him.

"Yeah and they don't take kindly to the mixed races in the castle and I know how you are toward them, toward everyone, you're a mercenary and you don't know how to negotiate. So do me a favor and let me do all the talking." Rayza explains.

"You're the one with the biggest mouth, so by all means." Hyda replies then walks past her. Rayza gives him a fake smile then falls in step with Casey after him.

They walk down to a small boardwalk at the edge of the city, where there are sky-boats that will take any passenger to the castle on the mountain. The castle has a magnetic force field that not only protects the castle, but also could vaporize anything that touches it. It only opens a small hole for the boats to get through.

The three of them get on to the gondola shaped boat. It slowly takes off across a sea of clouds with one Nexus man at the helm. Casey looks down and sees the large lake below the clouds and the bird-like creatures flying in between. The scenery is something Casey would never expect, her eyes light up as she continues to look on both sides of the boat like a kid excited to see everything. The mountains, the color of the green and blue trees, the beauty is unlike anything she has ever seen and the stories from other alliance soldiers didn't do it justice.

"So Ms. Williams, do you really think those gloves Tiny gave you will actually work?" Hyda asks as the boat makes it halfway.

Casey stops looking around, and grabs the two pairs of gloves from her jacket pocket. She thinks back to when Tiny gave them to her.

"Ms. Williams, I have a gift for you." Tiny says stopping her from leaving the ship and opening a box in her hands.

"Gloves?" Casey says confused as to why she would give her a pair of fingerless black gloves that have what look like tiny diamonds embedded in the palm.

"As always Ms. Williams your powers observations serve you well, but one thing human brains can never overcome is that things aren't what they seem." Tiny says. "So what do they do?" Casey asks. Tiny smiles at her,

"You will find out, soon enough." Tiny says.

Casey pops back in from her thought,

"I still don't even know what they will do, but I hope it's something good." Casey says putting the gloves away as the boat begins docking.

They get off the boat, only to be stopped by a two eight feet tall Nexus guards wearing ceremonial red and white armor plates. They are holding large spear- like staffs. A Nexus woman with a gold energy bow over her shoulder pushes between the guards. She is dressed in a green and black Nexus uniform with a gold chest plate and green armor shoulder pads. Her long hair sits elegantly and is a jet-black color, along with her eyes. She is a very beautiful woman considering her skin is a pinkish almost red, which differed from all the green and blue Nexus they have seen in the city.

"What the fuck are you doing here Rayza?" the Nexus woman says with her arms crossed and a pissed off look.

"Ethereal! How are you my favorite over tanned Nexus?" Rayza says as she tries to go in for a hug but gets stopped by an energy light blade being held by Ethereal's hand.

"I'm going to ask you one more time before I have you and your two strays arrested and thrown into a dungeon with Kalites!" Ethereal says.

"Hey now, we had some really good times together." Rayza says with a smile.

"You left me in an alternate universe with Crystal! Do you have any idea how annoying that woman can be?" Ethereal asks.

"Oh you made it back just fine, plus you owe me from me saving you from that shit bag, Tartoroc." Rayza says. There is a momentary pause, before Ethereal puts her energy blade away and signals the guards away.

"Alright fine, what are you doing here, and with a human exile no less." She says looking at Casey,

"Bad news travels fast in a small Galaxy, Ms. Williams, give it a day or two and everyone who's anyone will know who you are. Lucky for you Nexus don't look for a pay out. Well, unless you're Angel." Ethereal says.

"Which is why we are here my friend, do you know how to get to the Larex Forest?" Rayza says while getting closer to her with puppy dog eyes.

"For one, we are not friends and two, yes I do, but no one is allowed to enter Estiel, due to a couple of meteorites crashing down carrying Humanity's fuck up." She says once again looking in Casey's direction.

"Look at me again bitch and see what happens." Casey says with a couple fingers on her pistol, Ethereal attempts to makes a move but gets stopped by Rayza.

"Hey now, she's just had a bit of a trying couple of days. Let's all just breathe and let's go talk to the Maiden maybe she can give us permission to go there and you can take us and that will be it, we will be even." Rayza says keeping her calm, Ethereal backs up and begins going up the flight of stairs.

"Follow me and if Casey tries anything, rest assured the bounty on her head will be the least of her worries." She says as she leads them up.

At the top of the stairs, there are large maroon steel doors with two gold rings for handles. The doors open slowly. Ethereal leads them down a long open hallway with a red carpet in the middle, eight gold pillars on either side and guards standing next to each one. There are three thrones at the end of the hall, one smaller than the other two, only two of them are filled, the smaller one and what appears to be the King's throne. In front of the King there is two Nexus soldiers expressing concern about the virus spreading into the mountains. The King seems disinterested in their conversation. The King of Phazel is a "fat lazy piece of shit" in Ethereal's words. The Maiden does more for Phazel and Universal relations.

The King notices Ethereal with the others.

"Leave us." The King says in a deep powerful tone.

The soldiers turn around and leave with a pissed off look. The King stands up. His robes make him look like Santa Claus and not the jolly kind, more like the homeless Thor kind. They are ceremonial, but there is never a ceremony.

"What is the meaning of this Ethereal?" The King explodes as they approach the thrones.

"Your highness, I seek an audience with the Maiden." The woman in the smaller throne stands up and cuts off the king before he begins to yell.

"Father, stop." She says grabbing his arm; the king walks away with a distrustful look. Casey stares at the beautiful Maiden as she walks forward. Her hair is a dark blue and put into a ponytail. Her eyes have a green tint but a shine that gives them an almost gold look. Casey's excitement at meeting the Maiden of the Nexus made her nervous and speechless.

"What is it Ethereal? Rayza? Is that you?" The Maiden asks taking a few steps down the stairs toward them.

"It sure is your majesty! How are you? Long time no see." Rayza replies.

"I'm doing alright Rayza. Yes it sure has been!" the Maiden says.

"Lena, I need your permission to send these three to the Larex Forest, they are looking for Angel." Ethereal says.

"Angel? He's here?" the Maiden asks.

"That's what Cassandra said." Rayza adds in.

" Your majesty, if I may, I know Leafa is keeping close eyes on him, we could just contact her and..." Ethereal says.

"No, Ethereal take them into the Larex Forest and find him. Please bring him to me, I must speak with him." Lena says cutting off Ethereal

"Wait, you want me to take them?" Ethereal asks.

"Yes, you know where he will be and besides I just saw Leafa, she just left with Crystal." Lena says.

"Lena, you know how I am about Estiel." Ethereal says.

"Which is why I am sending you, it's about time you bury the hatchet, is what the humans say, right, Ms. Williams?" Casey looks up at the beautiful light blue skinned woman in her ceremonial dress with an amazing design and color combination of gold and maroon.

"Yes, your majesty." Casey manages to whisper out.

"Please call me Lena, I wish you luck on your mission, for it is one that could not only change the fate of the galaxy, but the fate of this universe as well." Lena says. "Thank you, Lena." Casey replies lowering her gaze.

"You will do great things, Ms. Williams, but I also believe it will not easy." Lena says as she walks closer to Casey then lays a hand on her shoulder.

Casey looks up from the rug, now more nervous than ever before.

"Trust in the universe, and it will trust in you." Lena says then turns to Ethereal. "Now Ethereal, please take them to the passage up north, all others have been blocked off to ensure the city's safety." Lena says right before she walks away meeting up with two of her servants.

"Well looks like you're coming along for the ride! We just became universe saving buddies!" Rayza says giving Ethereal a hug.

"Fuck off Rayza!" She quickly says shaking Rayza off and storming off to the entrance.

Casey and Hyda smile, then follow suit. Casey looks back one more time at the Maiden and waves goodbye. The Maiden waves and smiles at Casey.

Outside the atmosphere of Falaux, the Guillotine docks with a small fueling station. On the board, Stephanie walks on to the bridge; Gussie walks up to her with a holopad.

"Sir, we were able to pull this feed from one of our cameras in the city." She shows her the video of Casey and Razya walking through the city.

"How long ago?" Stephanie asks.

"Well, this was four hours ago, which depending on where they went, they could be two days ahead of us, but I was able to pull some audio, they mention something called Larex Forest." Gussie replies.

"Angel." Stephanie says under her breath.

"Sir?" Gussie asks in confusion

"Alright, once we are fueled up, head back to Omicron, I have feeling, I know where she will heading to next." Stephanie says to the pilots

"Yes sir." The four pilots reply continuing to work.

HOUR # 2

Back on Phazel, Ethereal leads Casey and company to a ledge up above the castle. Once they arrive at the top, they see Arkarians waiting, which are basically pterodactyl like creatures that the Nexus use to travel between this universe and the pocket universes on the planet. Casey stops and assesses the situation of riding one of the sharp teethed blue bird-like monsters.

"Yeah, I don't know about this. Isn't there some way we can just walk there? Or another one of those lovely boat rides?" Casey says keeping her distance while the others get ready to mount up.

"Sorry Ms. Williams, but the only way to travel any of the three pocket universes is on the back on of one of these beautiful creatures." Ethereal says while petting one and climbing on it's back.

"But, I will say if these things worry you, than perhaps going into the forest, is not a good idea." She adds as she turns the creature toward the edge.

"It's not the creature that scares me, it's falling off of it." Casey says backing up from her ride.

"Don't worry, if you fall it will be a very quick death, besides what are those boots for if you can't save yourself from a little fall?" Rayza says ready to go and looking down at her boots.

"Oh it's not a little fall, we are going above the stratosphere for the first one, now hurry up, we better to do this while we still have sunlight." Ethereal says lifting off the ledge with the Arkarian's large wingspan. Casey looks at her ride face to face then sighs. She gets on it slowly, almost falling off twice.

Once she's mounted, the four of them fly off into the clouds above the mountaintop. They continue to fly until they reach above the clouds, once there, the view is like nothing Casey has ever seen. She sees two suns, a blue and green sky with red clouds under them along with the view of many mountains and green plains in the distance. Casey looks down, there isn't much of a sight, they were currently too high off the ground to even calculate how far of a drop it may be, and she slightly loses her balance, but regains it quickly.

"Watch it!" Rayza yells over to her.

"I got it, just a little distracted that's all!" Casey yells!

"Quite a sight isn't it?" Rayza asks.

"Okay get ready here we go!" Ethereal yells back to the others.

"Wait what?" Casey asks right before all four of them dive downward at a neck break speed into the clouds below.

Once they descend into the red clouds, instantaneously they are transported into a lushes green forest and fly in line down a curving river. Casey looks back and only sees more forest, no clouds and no skyline. She looks ahead and dodges a low hanging branch. The Arkarians continue down the river swerving left and then right. The river ends running through a large rock wall. Ethereal flies straight through the rock, then Rayza right after. Casey closes her eyes in fear of what is on the other side. She flies through next emerging on the other side inside what appears to be a volcanic cave, with another river, but this one is pure lava. It is much larger than the one in the forest. Once all four of them are through, they fly in unison along the river. Casey notices off to the side there is a semi large red dragonfly on a rock, as they fly by a large bullfrog like creature hops out of the lava and it's tongue wraps around the dragonfly.

The four of them continue to end of the cave and come out above a village surrounded by three mountains. The village is wide spread. Many buildings stand with one large church-like building in the center at the back. There are three flights of stairs leading up to two statues, one of a female Nexus with clothes of a bounty hunter and the other of a male Nexus with the clothes of the royal family. They circle over the village, then fly down straight through the main dirt street dodging many villagers on their way up to the center. They make one final circle over the building and then land down in the front at a quickened pace. Everyone remains on his or her Arkarian, except Casey whom is flung over the front.

Two Nexus males, look like priest officials come out the double doors.

"What is this? We told the king, no more crossing over, there is no way we can contain the virus from getting to Kastrie!" One of the men says to Ethereal as she dismounts.

"This is an exception, and a matter of universal importance, passed down from the high Maiden herself." She responds as she walks over and picks Casey off the ground.

"What does that mean?" The Priest asks.

"It means I am taking these free loaders to Larex Forest, do we have a problem?" She says putting her hand on one of her blade hilts on her belt.

"Just take the mountain pass, but we will be closing the gate once you go through." The man says pointing off to the left.

"It's ok, if all goes well, we won't be coming back here." Ethereal says sending off the Arkarian to fly off back the way they came.

HOUR # 3

Ethereal leads Casey and company down the stairs and to the gate. Two guards open up the heavy gate only enough for them to squeeze through and then close quickly once they are on the other side. Ethereal pulls up a mini map of the forest on her wrist device. She moves it around over a mountain and marks it with a small blue beacon. She touches the tip of her right ear and a small visor materializes around the one eye, allowing her to see a pathway to the beacon she set up.

"Alright, stick close, this place isn't as friendly as it looks." Ethereal says as she arms herself and leads them into the vast dark forest.

They continue for about four miles, the humidity is almost unbearable along with the smell of rotting corpses coming from the black goo oozing from most of the trees. Ethereal stops and Rayza bumps into her.

"Hey, why did you stop?" She asks as she looks ahead of her.

There is a ten-foot tall red creature. Kalite, stand like a gorilla and have three large claws on both of its feet and hands. Its head is similar to that of a crocodile with six-inch teeth that drip black ooze from its jaw. It growls like a dog protecting its land. Ethereal reaches for her blade slowly and Casey readies her rifle.

"No offense to you, Ms. Williams, but I don't think your rifle will do much work here." Ethereal says as Casey changes her shot on the rifle to one called "Big Bang" then takes two steps in front of everyone aims up and fires a huge gold colored energy blast at the creature, causing it to fly back far into the trees. Casey proud of what she has done, she turns around to gloat only to see that the others are facing off against three more Kalites.

"Oh fuck!" She says quickly getting her rifle set up with a different shot called "Sunshine", but as she aims two more Kalites come from behind. She uses her boots to fly backwards. They slam into one another and Casey fires two green orbs that push the two knocking them back past the three that Ethereal, Rayza and Hyda are fighting. Once the green orbs are behind the Kalites, the green orbs explode vaporizing some trees and at least two of the Kalites. Two of the remaining three Kalites got on their feet and begin running at Casey. She panics, puts her rifle on her back and runs away as the two Kalites chase her. Which in case you forgot, is where this chapter started.

Casey awakens from a face planting into the ground and a forty-two second daze. She slowly attempts getting up when she turns and sees the two Kalites coming from the forest. Casey begins running with a slight limp, but gets cut off by the one she hit with the "Big Bang" emerging from the forest in front of her. Half of the creature's body is melted off but has been rejuvenated by the same black ooze in its mouth. The structure of the body is there, but it is now mostly made up of a black tar-like substance.

Casey has seen this before; it is the Phazaren Virus, a virus that humanity is solely responsible for by fucking with dark matter and temporal crystals. They opened up a doorway to some fuck hole shitty universe and allowed a small portion of the black shit through that infected everything it touched. This caused the deaths of billions of humans, along with the loss of the Earth and the rest of the Sol solar system. Why was it here and how is that the planet isn't gone yet? Questions for another time Casey thinks as she backs up toward the center of the open field. The Kalites surround her. The circle gets smaller as they close in on her; she draws a weapon. An opening rift of time and space pushes Casey to the ground.

The aura emitting from the opening is a purple black color and at the center of it is an image of another part of the forest. It's almost like looking through a window. Once it dissipates, there is a person in a shredded hooded and cloaked outfit standing between Casey and the Kalites.

"The hooded look is getting to be repetitive." Casey whispers to herself.

The person's hands rise into the air. Their skin is a dark deep blue. There are strange symbols of purple black fire on the back of the hands. There is a wind like energy radiating from his palms slightly holding the

Kalites back. They growl and claw the ground getting ready to pounce. There is one Kalite behind Casey. It jumps at her but is ripped into a void like a ship into a black hole. The Kalite is thrown out of another portal above the rest of the Kalites.

The person slams their hands onto the ground now that all of them are in a line. They regroup and pounce, but are immediately vaporized by an extremely powerful black and purple energy blast rising beneath the earth. It moves forward flowing like a wave and covers ten feet wide and twenty-five feet high. It continues for about thirty feet. Casey watches in awe as the purple black flame engulfs everything and quickly extinguishes as fast as it starts. The field and part of the forest are nothing more than dirt and ash. Casey stares long at the damage, that she completely misses the person leaving. She looks to see where they left to, but no sign. She feels eyes on her back and scuttles forward then draws the pistol on the person who is holding a hand out to help her up. She hesitates at first but then puts down the pistol and reaches for the hand. It is obvious to her that this person must be Angel. He is not going to hurt her after that display, but of course she also knows that there would be no stopping that from happening.

He pulls her up; she looks into his purple eyes with red and black pupils. He removes his hood to reveal his clean-shaven dark blue head. He has no tattoo symbols on his face like the other Nexus,

"Are you alright? I'm sorry about tripping you earlier, but I needed them to catch up with you." Angel says his voice deep but comforting. The sun is setting right between both of them, the light hitting his face gives him a rugged handsome look, but it also is causing Casey to feel strange as though an excessive amount of Déjà vu has just overwhelmed her.

She becomes lightheaded and starts seeing some sort of vision. Angel is wearing silver armor with a red sashes and is shouting on a ship that is in distress.

Casey begins to shake and Angel tries to help her, she suddenly stops and passes out in his arms. Angel stares at her face. It is familiar to him, like someone he met before.

"What are you doing?" Ethereal yells from a distance.

Angel quickly drops Casey's unconscious body on to the grass.

"Nothing." He says quickly as though he was guilty of something.

Ethereal, Rayza and Hyda walk out from the forest.

"What are you doing here Ethereal? And what the hell are you doing here?" He asks while looking at Rayza.

"Why do I always get that reaction from people?" Rayza says

"Because no one likes you. Now what did you do to Ms. Williams?" Ethereal says getting her blade ready.

"Williams" Angel says under his breath looking down and finally connecting the dots to why she is familiar. He worked with her sister before and remembered the mother. He bends down to pick her up but gets a blade to his face before he can.

"Don't you dare touch her, you pervert!" Ethereal says moving the blade to his throat.

"What is your problem?" Angel asks.

"Don't you have a wife? Where's the red head? Does she know about your human fetish on the side?" Ethereal continues to question Angel. Angel waves his hand slightly, the earth begins to wrap around Ethereal, disarming her and lifting her upside down by the feet. Hyda gets his blade out and Angel gets ready, but Ethereal yells out

"No wait!" most likely to stop Hyda from making a big mistake.

Angel's eyes are glued to Hyda, and only once he hears the charging of a blaster pistol and feels the cold crystallite metal on the side of his temple does he relax and lets Ethereal go. Hyda puts his weapon away; Angel turns to see Casey shaking only slightly as she holds the gun to his head.

Despite her fear, she could and definitely would put up a fight. Angel looks in to her eyes for about thirty seconds before asking

"Why are you here?" Casey keeps the gun on him and responds

"I need your help convincing a Groutarian to join me for an off the books mission to save a scientist, Dr. Teyach, from the Rebel Militia." Angel backs up and walks a couple steps away; Casey realizes she is still aiming at him then puts it away.

"Look I have a fast ship, we can just go convince him real quick and then drop you back off here." Casey says.

"Tell me, Ms. Williams, what do you know about the Nacarous?" Casey's heart sinks like a boulder in a pound,

"Why are you asking about that ship?" she responds with a slightly angry tone.

"I know your mother and I know she is still alive." He says.

"What the fuck did you just say?" Casey says raising her gun again.

Angel looks at her. She is terrified, but would definitely hit her mark, scared or not.

"I will help you save the doctor and can ensure your safety for as long as it takes, if you help me get some information from the Galactic Alliance to prove your mother is still alive." Angel says as he walks up to her.

"I can take care of myself, thank you very much." She says relaxing her hand.

"Why are you interested in the Nacarous? Or my mother being alive?" Casey asks. "I'm not interested in the ship or your mother, I'm interested in their cargo. I assumed you want an answer as to why she hasn't tried to contact you." Angel says. Casey doesn't say anything instead, walks toward the other three.

"I assume you have a plan for taking down Tartoroc? Sierens and Katharacs are a dangerous mix, pure strength and an elevated mind that could hold you where you stand." Casey stops and turns around, she knows he's right

"Fine, but if there is no proof and if you try anything, I will kick you off the ship and it won't be near any planets." Casey says.

Angel smiles slightly and walks up to her.

"So, we have a deal then?" Angel extends his hand; Casey shakes it and responds

"Deal."

"Angel, would you be so kind as to get us back to the fucking palace now?" Ethereal says pointing her hand to the open field.

Angel walks past her and waves one hand in a circle twice then pushes his hand forward and a purple light appears in the middle of the field. As though he took a knife to the universe itself, it is a tear into time and space. He then uses both hands to open it up with out even touching it. Hyda and Casey's jaws' drop as they can clearly see Kastrie in the window he made. Ethereal goes first, then Rayza; Hyda clenches his hilt than braves the portal. Casey checks both sides of the portal. It looked like a floating mirror, but the inside image is the city on both sides. She is dumbstruck with how it looks and how it is even possible to do such a thing and not fuck up different timelines.

"Ms. Williams, whatever happens from now on, it would be wise for you to stand firm, face your destiny without fear." Angel says staring at the portal.

She nods in his direction, takes a deep breath and goes through the portal. She stands at the stairs of the palace. Angel comes through shortly after and then closes the portal by bringing the energy back to his hand. Ethereal leads them into the palace and all the knights bow as they walk in. They walk up to the thrones, but only the maiden is currently on her throne.

"You have all returned! Angel my brother, how are you?" Lena says excited standing up from her throne.

"Brother?" Hyda and Casey both say simultaneously and confused.

"Yeah, sadly Lena is related to this raggedy lazy piece of shit." Ethereal says walking up to be at Lena's side but Lena stops her from reaching the third step.

"So, have you decided to help Ms. Williams with her quest, brother?" Angel doesn't say anything instead nods in agreement.

"Oh how I wish I could join you on this adventure!" Lena says.

"You are always welcome to your highness!" Rayza yells out without consent from Casey.

"Oh no little one, I have much work to do here, but don't you worry, Ethereal will be going with you!" Lena says.

"Wait, what?" Ethereal says.

"You heard me, I do not need your protection as of right now, but I do need for you to keep an eye on my brother and to show Casey that she is not alone in her quest to save the galaxy! Protector her and help her, that is my wish." Lena says putting one hand on her shoulder.

"Lena, I beg you to reconsider this, I am not Crystal or Leafa, I can't travel with these morons!" Lena looks at Ethereal, she doesn't acknowledge her, but instead says

"Well Casey, I wish you the best of luck and as for the galactic alliance, if they come snooping we will send them off the trail." Lena says with a smile then a slight nod at Angel, who does the same back to her. Ethereal straightens her self up then storms out of the castle. Casey and the rest of them follow her.

THE MOST POWERFUL
SOMEONE IN
THE GALAXY

THE PHOENIX TAKES OFF FROM PHAZEL, NOW WITH TWO
extra companions. Angel is walking around the ship with his hands behind
is back. His outfit is different now His long coat with black and purple
lining matches with custom-made boots. The shielding strips on his pants
and arms are new tech, which means Angel has money. He paces around
the main cabin with Ethereal and they introduce themselves to Hyda, Tiny,
Jo and Trea, but Demi doesn't acknowledge them. Angel then walks up to
the projector where Casey is about to set a course for Koreno, Groutarian
home world.

"Actually, Ms. Williams, if I may, I know someone else you might
want to get, in case things go south with the Groutarian." Angel says.

"Are you telling me you are scared?" She responds. Angel scoffs

"No, but I am telling you that I know this person, here." He says
while moving a file on the projector to a larger image of a blonde haired
Sieren with a big smile.

Casey looks at the image, cute and innocent as she might look;
Sierens are the most powerful race in the galaxy. They stay away from all

other races. There are only a few that get exiled and those are the ones you have to be careful with. All Sierens are fox humanoid creatures with cute ears and cute foxtails and regular human hairstyles, also the ability to kill anything. They can melt a human brain, before you even know what's happened. The more powerful ones can sense anyone up to about two hundred feet away. Most exiles get caught, killed, skinned and eyes plucked out, which incidentally make nice necklace jewelry on the black market. Off topic, but all these facts go through Casey's head. Angel nudges her, "It will be fine. She is actually quite nice, unless you try to be hostile toward her of course, then she will kill you." Angel says.

"Wait! Hold on, if you know her, why don't you talk to her and convince her?" Casey asks.

"I'm not here to do your job, besides it's just a suggestion, considering she's powerful." Angel says while moving boxes with the purple black aura into a chair formation. He leans back on them suspended slightly off the floor.

"How do you do that?" Casey asks,

"It's a long complicated story and I'm not much of a story teller." He says.

"Yeah, Crystal loves to tell stories, you should ask her when you meet her." Rayza adds in while helping Tiny.

"Who is this Crystal?" Casey asks.

"It's his wife." Rayza says.

Casey looks back at Angel.

"You're married?" she asks.

Angel just stares at her.

"Do you not know what marriage is?" he responds sarcastically.

Rayza laughs, Casey mocks Rayza with a stupid laugh.

"I understand if you're worried about Nikket, Ms. Williams, but I promise you, she will kill you the instant she thinks you're a threat and you won't feel a thing." Angel says laying back.

"That's super Angel! And here I thought I couldn't be anymore freaked out." Casey says.

She knew she couldn't get the Groutarian fully under control without Nikket. Casey looks at the image of her smiling face and changes the course to Omicron, Trea receives the coordinates and the ship warps out into space.

Outside Omicron's atmosphere there are many Galactic Alliance ships waiting for the arrival of the Phoenix. The Guillotine, gave them the tip but the Guillotine is currently on the other side of the planet with two others.

The Phoenix arrives between the two sides of the planet being watched and flies down quickly. It breaks the sound barrier as it enters the atmosphere. The Phoenix comes to a stop about a mile from a very old hospital building. Casey jumps off the Phoenix slowing her fall with her boots, the ship flies off into space. Casey walks toward the entrance of the building. The hospital is from a time before the Grey War, a war between humans and the grey aliens that experimented on them, Casey remembers the pictures from her old history books of buildings on Earth. She has no idea why this building is here on Omicron about thirty miles from Farses. She comes up to the main entrance; the name St. Mary's Hospital is all that's left on the open glass sliding doors. The rest of the glass is on the floor mats along with ample amounts of grey dust. The main lobby has dust mounds everywhere some large some small. Casey takes a few steps into the lobby.

"There are three different paths to take, each will lead to the same place, but some exits are further than others." A woman's voice says to Casey.

She turns around quickly and looks behind her. The voice is as clear as day.

The woman laughs

"I am telepathic sweetheart, I don't have to be anywhere near you to talk to you. Now, choose a path or I will choose for you." Casey looks left then at the other two hallways. She heads down the left path,

"Good choice!" the woman says excitedly. She continues down the hallway steering clear of old rusted wheelchairs and gurneys.

"You're getting warmer." The woman says with a creepy laugh at the end. Casey walks to the end of the hall, pieces of metal and glass float up and form an arrow pointing at a door for the stairs. She goes into the stairwell; there are two flights down and one flight going up, the rest of the stairs going up are mostly gone. Casey takes one step down,

"Burr freezing." The woman says.

Casey backs up and heads up the stairs arriving at another hallway. She continues down the hallway, more dust and more wheelchairs.

"It's a shame really, all those humans vaporized instantly and turned into dust when the entire building decided to make a jump to somewhere it shouldn't be."

The woman says with no pity. Casey passes by a nurse station and sees more objects pointing to another stairway. She stops because music starts playing, she looks around at the speakers on the walls, but they are not making the sound.

"Oh don't worry, it's actually in your head, if it gets louder you are on the right track. Now put some hustle into it Ms. Williams." The woman says humming along with the tune. Casey recognizes the sounds of the instruments.

She has heard the song many times before from Stacey's music collection. Something Stacey's family took pride in, keeping all the music of Humanity's history, but how is Nikket playing an extremely old song? Casey continues up the stairs to one final hallway to one exit to the roof. The music becomes very loud. She tries the door, but it won't budge. She walks away from the door and turns back around. Casey sprints to the door and knocks it down.

On the roof, Casey sees an old boom box stereo; next to it are lockers, wheelchairs and a makeshift bed. There is small light pink skinned female Sieren lying back on a beach lounging chair with a large newspaper covering her face. The Sieren folds the paper in half showing her face wearing sunglasses and her hair is pinned up with a silver and red barrette. Her furry fox ears on top of her head twitch as she leans her head down slightly so that her sunglasses slide down just enough for her to look at Casey standing up brushing her self off.

"You better fix that door, this building is an antique." The Sieren says. Casey sets the door against the doorway and walks over to her

"You must be Nikket Terlarous?" She says as she stops two feet from her chair. Nikket folds the paper, tosses it and levitates up from sitting. Her outfit is summer ready, wearing blue shorts with her furry foxtail poking through and a green tank top with the words "Milky way Slut" in red across the front. She floats toward Casey and she steps back as Nikket gets close. Nikket begins to dance to the music playing from the boom box. Her dance is a mix between salsa and ballet. She finishes her dance with a beautiful ballet spin and a quick stop.

"Now that's an entrance!" She says with her hands on her hip.

Is she crazy? Casey thinks.

"You know I have been waiting for a long time and no I'm not crazy. Why didn't you come for me first?" Nikket asks,

"You are the mind reader, you tell me. I assumed the answer would be obvious." Casey says.

"You know you are by far way prettier than I thought you would be, you're like a solid nine." Nikket says staring deep into her eyes.

"Thanks? Are you always this random?" Casey asks.

"Random to you maybe, it really comes down to how you perceive things, Ms. Williams. Those who think you are random just don't think the way you do." Nikket says as Casey stares at her eyes.

She couldn't look away, they are mesmerizing, the stories or even the holocharacters didn't compare to seeing the real thing. The galaxy in her eyes is massive, intricate and yet familiar. The only thing more magnificent than her eyes; is her cute furry fox ears. All Sierens look human except for the fox ears and foxtails and the whole mini galaxies in their eyes. Their eyes contain imprints of galaxies or nebulas. It is said they draw their power from the stars and planets in those galaxies. Nikket snaps her fingers right in front of Casey's face. She comes back to reality.

"Stare off too long and you will owe me dinner and between you and me I'm not cheap." Nikket says floating toward a slightly higher part of the roof. Casey follows her, but stops at the three steps that lead to the higher part.

"Do you know where or when this building is from?" Nikket asks.

"Can't say I do." Casey responds.

"It's from a different timeline, a time where Humanity made technological advances quickly over the years, unlike the one we are in now. You see, recently a universe like this one suddenly collapsed and merged whatever it could into this one." Nikket says lifting something off a table, into her hand and turning around.

"Okay is that supposed to mean something?" Casey asks her as she backs up from Nikket flying over slightly then walking up to her slowly.

"Not every little thing in this story will be answered in seconds, but if you must know it means every universe is connected, Casey. There is no telling what could happen in any universe, but sometimes there are similarities between the two. An example would be, we met before in the other universe, but in a different situation." Nikket says. "Why are you telling me this?" Casey asks.

"You have to understand what's at stake, or else we will have a trilogy situation on our hands. You know where the third story always flops or a remake with a younger cast and you just *know* it's going to suck." Nikket says.

"I don't follow." Casey says while Nikket flies off and looks for something in a pile of scrap metal from a space satellite.

"If you have an understanding of what is at stake, you will take a different path and the timeline will not see the same fate. No one's going to give you a map, you have to walk your own path." Nikket says,

"I guess I understand." Casey says.

"You're a little slow aren't you, Ms. Williams?" Nikket asks rhetorically.

"Well, first off, what happened to the other timeline? And second, I was always under the impression that Sierens are not affected by time, so why care what happened in another timeline, or this one?" Casey asks.

"Humans are stupid, never focusing on the whole picture." Nikket says then flies over to another scrap pile and pulls out a silver necklace.

"Sierens may not age like everyone else, Ms. Williams, but we can die. I like being alive to see the beautiful things this universe has to offer." Nikket continues as she searches through a couple lockers and picks up a small shard of a crystal.

"Oh hey, by any chance did you have a headache this morning?" Nikket asks as she flies behind Casey.

"What?" Casey says then exhales after instantly feeling a small amount of pain throughout her body. Her eyes widen and a chill goes down her spine, she can feel her digging in her mind. It felt like a stabbing migraine, as though Nikket was scratching her brain with her somewhat sharp fingernails.

"Stop fucking with my head." Casey says out of breath as Nikket reads her mind easily,

"You will see your sister again, don't worry too much about it." Nikket says.

"I thought you were only able to read minds. Are you telling me you can know what will happen too?" Casey asks clenching her jaw due to the pain.

"No, I can only see my future, and only in like tiny bits." Nikket stops messing with her and begins flying around Casey.

"So, are you going to join me? Or just keep giving me cryptic warnings." Casey asks as she walks away from her flying around like a shark circling its prey.

"Well of course, I need more friends believe it or not." Nikket says.

Casey thinks about her crew.

"Yeah, they are not the best people to be friends with." Casey says to Nikket as she floats to the ground.

"Some people grow on you, Ms. Williams." Nikket says looking up at the Alliance ship outside the atmosphere. Casey stares at her from head to toe; she is about five feet tall, which instantly made her cute in Casey's eyes.

"Oh hey, off topic but did you see the guy with the red eyes? God dammit, what the fuck is his name?" Nikket says putting her hand to her chin.

"I've seen him twice. Who the fuck is that creepy fuck and why is he following me?" Casey anxiously says.

"He is a corrector of time, whatever the fuck that means, but I don't remember his name, Angel might know." Nikket says.

"So, why is he following me? And how do you know Angel?" Casey asks.

"Oh Angel is a sweetheart! We teamed up several years ago, but I have to say I believe he is following you to kill you and is waiting for the right moment. I mean, if he wanted to he could show up at any point and kill you; like a gouging gruesome type of killing too. Nothing to worry about though." Nikket says.

Casey takes a step back, her head feels heavy and her body is going through a draining and faint like feeling. She puts her hands on the concrete wall that goes along the edge of the whole roof and leans on it, taking deep breaths.

"Do you need a drink, I have Whiskey, I found it in one of the lockers. Although I'm not to sure if it's any good it being there for centuries and all." Nikket says patting Casey on the back. She waves her other hand in a "no" motion while shaking her head and turning toward open fresh air. Casey knew that the creepy red-eyed fuck meant bad news, by just the vibe he put off. Casey stands up straight, and then rubs her eyes. She remembers the vision of Angel when she was in the forest.

"I saw that vision in your mind, those are memories from another timeline or a warning of the future, hard to tell you with time and a multiverse." Nikket says as she leans on her shoulder.

"Yeah well, I had a seizure when it happened, so I don't want them in my brain."

"You will handle it better as things become more clear, besides you never know, Ms. Williams, they could be useful. It could keep everyone you know from dying, or on the other hand it could get everyone killed." Nikket says then holds out a necklace with a small crystal shard on it. Casey remembers seeing the crystal it, it belonged to her mother, but why did Nikket have it? She grabs it from her hand and examines it. "I hope you are ready." Nikket says pulling Casey's gaze.

"Ready for what?" Casey asks.

"For the shit storm that is about to rain down on you." Nikket says flying over to an old locker where a pink and white backpack is hanging.

"I'm sure I can handle Tartoroc." Casey says as she puts on the necklace.

"Oh god no, you're clumsy and reckless, I will be doing the killing of that dumb ass baboon, while you will be hanging back and watching mama work." Nikket says as she changes her outfit Casey looks the other direction.

She looks up and sees the Galactic Alliance ships firing shots off, most likely trying to hit the Phoenix that is creating a diversion for Casey.

Outside the atmosphere, the Guillotine charges toward the other ships firing at the very fast and very hard to hit Phoenix.

"Cadet, ready the tracker!" Stephanie yells to one of the pilots.

"Yes sir!" the pilot responds while getting the weapon ready. The Phoenix continues dodging the other cruisers fire with figure eights and twists and turns. The Guillotine moves closer and launches a semi large missile at the Phoenix. The missile flies through space quickly, it then splits into fifteen smaller rockets. Three of the missiles hit the Phoenix, none of them cause any damage and only one of them latches on a small tracking device. The Phoenix flies up, the outer shell of the ship opens up, revealing four large wings that spread from the center. The wings light up with a translucent red and blue crystal energy-shielding tech. The Phoenix's wings flap causing the ship to move vertically at a neck breaking speed. The bird-like ship then blasts down to the planet, passing too quick for any of the other ships to react.

Nikket finishes changing into what looks like a black skin-tight flight suit with a red and black pleated skirt and a red leather jacket with a blue shield trimming down each arm and a pair of black converse sneakers. She grabs her backpack and walks over to Casey.

The Phoenix descends next to the roof of the building with its wings closed.

"How did you get this?" Casey yells over the sound of the Phoenix's thrusters while holding up the necklace. The Phoenix's hatch opens, Nikket stares at Casey up and down.

"It was given to me by someone. Casey, I will travel with you, but until you prove to me that you can be strong enough to survive on your own, I will not be helping you much. Maybe, I don't know, I'm just so excited." Nikket yells back with a smile.

"Then why are you coming along?" Casey asks.

"Because I am very important to the plot later on and I need friends. Also I do whatever the fuck I want." Nikket says walking toward the open hatch.

"Oh and call me Nikki, it's a comfort thing for me." She yells back.

Casey puts on the necklace then follows her on board.

The Phoenix closes up and blasts out to space, dodging oncoming fire and swerving past the blockade.

On board the Guillotine,

"Sir the tracking device is working and should continue to work for a couple of hours." Gussie says.

"Can you tell where they're headed?" Stephanie says.

Gussie uses her holopad to throw the image of a blinking red dot slowly traveling through a map of the galaxy.

"It looks like they are headed to quadrant four, so maybe Rounon or Koreno? However none of those planets would provide fuel willingly. Their best bet would be to head to Ohyron. Gussie explains.

"Then we will cut them off, take us to Ohyron. Gussie I need you to send the image we took over Phazel to Casey, think you can do it through the tracking device?" Stephanie says.

"Yes, Ma'am…I mean sir!" Gussie stutters as Stephanie leaves the bridge.

THE GROUTARIAN

NIKKI WALKS INTO THE MAIN ROOM THROWING HER BAG IN A corner and looks around the room. She scans the crew, Angel passed out on some crates, Rayza and Hyda playing a card game. Tiny is working on the projector and her tablet and Demi is drinking tea while going over emails. Ethereal is the first to notice Nikki.

"Well I'll be damned, Nikket Terlarous." Ethereal says. Nikki looks at her, smiles and flies over to Ethereal.

"I apologize, I don't seem to remember you, but I bet that you and I shared a great adventure at one point." Nikki says smiling and extending her hand out.

"We did, a couple years ago, I'm Ethereal." She says shaking her hand.

"Nice to re-meet you then!" Nikki says with a smile.

She floats over to Rayza and Hyda who are playing Karta Rite, a card game, over a crate.

"Damn it!" Hyda yells throwing his cards down and giving cash to Rayza.

"Let's go again, I'm going to win it back." He says.

"Good luck." Rayza says with a smile counting her winnings.

Nikki interrupts her by floating five inches from her face.

"Can I help you?" Rayza asks staring at her hand and the cards on the table. Nikki hugs her without losing altitude, causing Rayza to slightly loose balance. Rayza flips her and slams her into the wall. Nikki looks at her with a smile and says

"Oh I like it rough." then winks at Hyda.

"Look, I don't care who you are, never interrupt me when I'm counting my winnings" Rayza says releasing her from the wall.

"We are going to be best friends, Rayza, I can tell." Nikki says.

"Do me a favor don't ever read my mind." Rayza replies with an attitude.

Nikki pats her on the head then floats over to Hyda,

"And who is this handsome young daring warrior?" Hyda extends his hand but Nikki pushes it aside and hugs him instead.

"I'm Hyda." He whispers to her. She smiles then says,

"It's a pleasure to meet you." She flies over to Tiny and gives her a big grin.

"How is the hardest working person of this group doing?" She asks floating in a lying down position, like a kid who watches cartoons in front of the T.V.

"Well, at least someone notices and you can't even read my mind like the meat sacks." Tiny replies while still scanning information on her pad.

"Well you are doing a great job, keep up the good work!" Nikki says excitedly doing a back flip and floating toward Angel who's sleeping in the corner.

She floats up to him and pokes him several times. Angel's entire eye sockets become engulfed in a bright purple flame and he tries to attack her, but stops as soon as sees her face.

"Ms. Terlarous." Angel says grinning with purple flame in his eyes.

"Angel!" Nikki says giving him a big hug with extra squeeze to put his fiery eyes out. "It's been too long, how is Crystal and Leafa?" Nikki asks.

"They are busy, but other than that good. So, tell me what are you doing all the way out here?" Angel asks pulling her off of him.

"Well, after helping you out, I left Typhas. My family was being complicated, so I came here, seemed as good a place as any to just sit and wait." Nikki says.

"And what is it that you are waiting for, Ms. Terlarous?"

"You mean besides for you to split with your wife and marry me instead?" Angel rolls his eyes as she smiles with puppy dog eyes.

"Believe it or not I was waiting for her." Nikki says looking at Casey as she walks up to Tiny.

Tiny hands Casey the pad she has been working on. It is a message from her sister with a picture,

"The Alliance isn't the only big group hunting you." The picture is of the Rebel Militia's flagship, the Blood Serpent outside of Phazel. The Blood Serpent's maroon and jet black color is intimidating along with its massive amounts of weapons that can put holes into most Alliance ships.

Casey only heard the stories about Tartoroc, the half Sieren, half Katharac and his rebel army of miss-matched aliens, not to mention his assassin followers, Serenity and Corbus. Serenity is a Slithian, an immortal race of humans with reptilian features like razor sharp teeth, snake eyes, super strength and a forked like snake tongue. Her kill count is high like astronomically.

Corbus is a Therox, a race of giant vampire bat hybrid creatures that have the ability to travel through black holes and can use time to change an outcome. Corbus had once destroyed three planets as a demonstration, which is most likely the reason why Hyda is seeking his head. Tiny pulls Casey away from ear shot of the rest of the crew.

"Ms. Williams, if I may, they couldn't have known we would have boon thoro." Tiny whicporc.

"Unless we have a rat." Casey finishes the sentence for her.

"Someone on this ship is not who they say they are." Tiny continues.

Casey looks back down at the pad, but Nikki flies in and puts her face between Casey and the pad.

"It will be entertaining, if you end up living through all of it." Nikki says cheerfully, Casey pushes her aside, after handing Tiny the pad.

"Do me a favor, sit down somewhere and relax until we get to Koreno." Casey says annoyed with Nikki's glee.

"Whoa, okay buddy, dial it down, I'm on your side." Nikki says.

Casey ignores her and walks over to a crate that has "rations" stamped across the front. She opens it up, Nikki hovers over her shoulder and her eyes light up.

"Oh my Cortex! All that beautiful human food!" Nikki exclaims while hovering over the crate. Through Nikki's eyes the food radiated with color as though some sort of magic had created this bountiful blessing. Casey grabs some snacks, hands some to her and walks over to the couch in the room. Casey eats at a slow pace as she watches Nikki devour the food quickly, and grabs a few more things out of the box. Casey lays back, she feels more relaxed now that Nikki is with them, and even after everything she said.

Casey didn't want to think about it; it literally just caused a headache.

It's been a week on Omicron since she left and that is three months time frame on Earth. It didn't feel like it to her, but it also didn't matter considering all the different planets she had been to and would be going to. Time is almost impossible to keep up with she thought, especially when you have a ship that can travel light speed. Other vessels that have to use crystals usually take about half a day or two to reach anyplace, where as the Phoenix had taken them to two different planets in two days. Her eyes get heavy and just as Casey begins to fall into deep sleep on the couch; Tiny shakes her.

"We've arrived at Koreno."

The Phoenix slowly lands about fifteen miles outside of the Da Rukion, the capital of Koreno. Tiny walks into the center of the room and drops a small crate

"I only got four of them, so try not to lose them." Casey pulls out a grey metallic cloak and puts it on.

"They are called clandestine scarfs. Clandestine for short and they make you invisible. They're not cheap." Tiny explains while Angel, Nikki and Hyda put on the other three. The Groutarians weren't known for having any spaceship-detecting tech, but they didn't take kindly to, any race in the galaxy. Hiding themselves is the best option at the moment. They exit the ship and begin making a very long walk to the city.

Da Rukion is one of a kind; the city is built on the side of a small mountain. All the buildings are made from a mixture of the red rock of the surface of the planet and other resources. The red rock, if molded correctly, is said to have a mirroring effect and can deflect any damage done to it. The Groutarians use it on most of their creations like the six large anti-everything turrets flanking the twenty-five foot high wall surrounding the city. The buildings behind the wall are spread out, but the space in between is occupied with very large vines that have a special trait making them rare in the galaxy.

Casey and her company, stop at a rock formation that looks a lot like Stonehenge back on Earth, just outside the front gate. There is a large boulder between them and the city.

"Okay, we are definitely not walking through the front door, so do your portal thing and get us in." Casey says to Angel while crouching behind the one of the rocks.

"What makes you think I'm just going to open one for you?"

"Come on Angel we don't have time for this." Casey says more serious this time. Angel gives her a look with real shock el look.

"There is no way that you won't get caught." He explains.

"So, why not just get caught?" Nikki adds in the middle of
his explanation.

"I mean the guy you are looking for stays in the coliseum. So, if you
were to get caught that's where they do their executions, you know by like
any means, poison, stabbing, maybe just a good old fashion decapitation."

"Okay, yes thank you for the horrifying imagery." Casey says stopping her from becoming even more morbid. Casey moves closer to Angel.

"How does she know about the Groutarian?" Angel asks,

"Yeah, How do you know that?" Hyda asks Nikki.

"Yeah, I was wondering that myself, if you don't mind filling me in
too." Tiny says over the earpiece coms in everyone's ear.

"Oh my Cortex Everyone shut the fuck up! Angel send me in, then
you guys come in after me and *please* don't show up late." Casey says
emphasizing please as she readies her weapons.

"I would recommend using the gloves, Ms. Williams." Tiny chimes
in, Casey mocks her with a movement of her mouth and rolls her eyes as
she puts the gloves on.

Angel looks at Nikki, she winks and blows him a kiss. He steps away
from the rock, passes by Nikki and turns around. He raises his hand and
stretches it. Symbols in purple and blue fire appear on the back of his hand.
A portal begins forming on the surface massive boulder in front of them.

"How do you know where they go?" Casey asks staring at the portal.

"I don't, but when I open it with my hands, it usually ends up somewhere solid." Casey gives him a serious look. He stares back with a smile.

"That's not funny." She says shaking her head walking away from
the portal.

She runs toward it and jumps into it.

The portal spits her out to the side of a building; she grabs the roof before falling into an alley. The entire alley is a hole but filled half way with red and blue vines that have thorns. Casey climbs up to the roof as the vines move to grab her leg. She jet jumps up to the roof of the next building. There are three turrets pointed at her from rooftops of buildings across the street. She quickly unzips her jacket. She pulls out one pistol, fires three shots each one hitting a target. The turrets explode without even getting a shot off. Casey runs across the rooftops dodging blaster fire coming from the streets below by somewhat smaller sized Groutarians that stand at about eight feet tall. The red hairless ape-like creatures are surprisingly organized despite their large stupid ogre look.

They manage to boost a Groutarian soldier up to the roof she is on. He tries to cut her with an energy battle axe, but Casey slides under his attack and cuts his rib, then drives the blade into the back of his neck. She pulls it out, rolls over him swiftly and easily kicks him off the roof into the alleyway with the vines. The vines instantly wrap around the soldier's body pulling him down. The thorns that touch his skin begin to dematerialize him into nothing. She jumps over to the next building, then fires off a couple more shots and takes out two more turrets before one of the larger one fires a long shot destroying the building underneath her. She falls with the rubble, but recovers quickly, only to get knocked out in one punch by a much larger Groutarian.

Casey slowly regains consciousness. "Casey, hey buddy time to wake up!" Nikki shouts in her head telepathically. Two Groutarian guards dressed in gold and maroon damaged armor drag, Casey through a couple of heavy cast iron gates. Her vision slowly returns

"Consider yourself lucky, Ms. Williams, and if you were trying to prove yourself to me, that was a terrible attempt." Nikki adds telepathically as they drag her out into the center of a large coliseum.

All the seats above the arena are filled with many Groutarians and Crilack (a race of aliens made up of rock and crystal). Casey is dropped to her knees in the center of a ring of many Groutarian warriors. They let her keep her weapons; they probably want her to try and escape.

She looks around at the screaming angry gorilla-like monsters in the bleachers, when she notices three hooded figures atop the coliseum wall.

"Yeah, we're here, but I'm not sure about an escape plan. You might want to get him to join you the nice way, first." Nikki continues saying telepathically.

Casey gets up on her feet, as a very large Groutarian steps in from the shadowy side of the arena. She looks up at the fourteen foot Groutarian.

His fists alone were almost the size of Casey. He has infinity symbol tattoos on both arms; they are Nexus marks. They can protect him from any elemental attack made from a Nexus. His head is clean-shaven with a bit of stubble on his face. He has three scars, two on one side of his face and one on the opposite side right over his bright orange eye. He has two fangs from his bottom jaw that pass over the upper lip. Casey is dumbstruck. His muscles are massive and his teeth look like they could shred through anything easily. He steps out into the sun, wearing an old Groutarian general's armor with desert sand colored cloak that drapes down like a king's cape. Casey breathes deeply then yells the words

"Alrook Coroc Delmora." It's Groutarian; it means "I seek time with the Champion." The Groutarian slightly tilts his head in confusion. He takes two steps toward her and she steps back with a hand on one of her pistols.

"Guren Tooro Katese Morendo Hacon." The Groutarian says pacing to the right causing Casey to step further away from him. Her Groutarian is limited; she translates his statement into something about his name being Gorog, the future Champion and King.

"Casey, listen to me, you have to use the gloves, when he makes his move, open your hands and let him have it." Tiny says over the COM.

"Let him have what?" Casey whispers while walking away from him.

"Why are you here, human?" Gorog says in his language.

"I need your help, the galaxy needs your help." Casey responds in Groutarian.

He stops pacing, so does Casey.

"Do you take me for a fool, human?" Gorog thunders.

"No! Listen to me! There is something coming, something we need to work together to stop and I need your help." Casey yells desperately this time in English.

Gorog clenches his fist causing a green glow around it.

Angel readies him self to pounce, but Nikki places her hand on his wrist.

"Wait, I need to see this." She says to him keeping her eyes on the area.

"She will be killed." Angel says staring at her. She doesn't acknowledge him.

"Enough!" Gorog yells jumping up and striking down toward Casey with the green glowing fist. Casey holds her open palm hands out at the fist and closes her eyes.

The gloves light up and shoot a blue energy beam out blasting Gorog into the force field around the area. He falls to his knees then looks up. The crowd goes wild; to see anyone even touch the champion is a nice change of pace.

Casey looks down at her gloves

"Bitchin." She says with a smile and quickly looks back up at Gorog.

"Ms. Williams those gloves only had one charge. You will have to charge them again by blocking any amount of energy thrown at you, they will also fire automatically when a threat is near." Tiny explains over the com, Casey gets ready to dodge Gorog's attack, which could be almost impossible, considering his reach. Gorog's hand lights up with Nexus symbols, he conjures a green fireball above his palm and throws it at Casey. She raises her hands to block it with the gloves, the force of the fireball pushes her back but it is instantly sucked into the gloves. Gorog roars and sprints to attack Casey, but he is stopped in his tracks by a bright purple light. Angel drops down between him and Casey. Gorog makes a move toward them, but Angel blocks his hit with his hand using an energy wave (the same technique he used on the Kalites in the forest). Gorog strikes again only to be blocked again, Angel opens a portal behind him then pushes him into it with his abilities. Angel chases him through the portal, closing it right after, leaving Casey all alone in arena.

All the warriors stare at Casey as they ready their energy blades and axes. Casey holds out her hands out with a surrendering gesture.

"Now wait a minute!" Casey says right before two of the warriors charge her. She quickly shoots them down with her pistols, one in each hand. Two more come from behind her; she jets up above them and shoots both of them directly in the head, the impact of the shots cause their heads to explode. Casey flies backward to avoid getting brain matter on her. Two more knock her feet up, causing her to backflip behind them and land on her feet. She shoots both of them in the leg, another warrior grabs Casey from behind and one more comes from the side. She shoots the one coming in the head. She elbows the one that grabs her face to free a hand. She shoots two more in the head that are rushing her. Three more come running but they are cut in half by a double bladed blue crystal energy sword. The bodies collapse before they can get within ten feet. Casey finally shoots the one holding her in the foot, then through the jaw and two more times in the chest once she becomes free. Hyda drops down into the arena through a hole in the force field that Nikki is making. He rolls when he lands and catches his double blade sword when he stands up. Four different warriors run at him, one gets shot up by Casey. Hyda stabs one and cuts the arm off of another. He moves quickly on the third. Hyda's speed causes the last one to lose his head in the literal sense.

Somewhere in the city, Angel is being thrown through a wall of a large mansion. Gorog walks through the wall and grabs him; Angel retaliates with a fireball causing Gorog to let him go. Angel trips him with the earth by forming it into a pillar and lifting Gorog's foot making him fall on his back. Angel opens another rift, goes through it and comes out above Gorog. Angel punches him down through another rift that he opens up underneath Gorog's body.

They are now falling from five miles above the city, fighting and wrestling on their way down. Angel manages to get on top and they crash down into a house somewhere in the southern part of the city.

Angel is launched out of the house, crashes through two houses and stops at the wall of the third house. Slightly dazed, he tries to get up, but falls back down. He knows he can't keep this up much longer. He is out of shape so the only option is to hit him hard and to get him back to the arena. Hopefully, Nikki comes to his aid. At least that's what he's hoping for. He gets up, having formed a solid plan in his head.

He looks through the hole he just made to see Gorog tearing through making a B line for him.

Angel sighs, "Shit," he says before being engulfed in Gorog's attack.

Casey and Hyda are holding off against ten Groutarian warriors left in the arena. Hyda is being held by one of them as he kicks another one. Casey shoots one in the knee and another in the arm; she takes a light blade dagger and stabs the wounded arm warrior in the heart.

Nikki's eyes widen, she turns her head to see a massive Katharac battle cruiser beyond the city abducting the Phoenix with an old ray of light technique.

"So, guys we have a slight problem." Tiny says over coms.

The battle cruiser has the shape of an elongated pretzel with small and large red domes in particular spots. The red domes are weapons, of pure crystal that when charged, emit a very powerful laser. This very large vessel is now making it's way to the arena. The turrets protecting the city, now light up the shields on the mammoth of a cruiser. The cruiser's shadow covers seventy percent of the city. It begins to slow down, as it gets closer to the arena. Nikki stands with a scared look on her face as she looks down at the arena.

Casey kicks a warrior away from her and a portal opens up in front of her. Gorog comes flying out and slams into the wall of the arena; Angel hops through and closes the portal; his hands and eyes engulfed in purple flame. Angel gets ready to attack again, but is cut off by the ray of light from the battle cruiser. It forces amounts of gravity down on to Angel, Casey, Hyda and Gorog, along with two Groutarian warriors. The ray of light triples the amount of weight of a person, or an object and pushes that augmented amount on to the subject. The ray of light begins to pull them up into the ship, Nikki flies up after them and grabs on to Casey. The light pulls them into the ship quickly and it flies out to space.

HALF WAY THERE...

THE MASSIVE KATHARAC BATTLE CRUISER IS TRAVELING through a hyper speed wormhole. On board, in the cellblock district, (yes district, as in this ship is so massive it has districts.) After being relieved of her weapons two guards push a bound Casey to the floor of a cell. Most of her crew is being held here in this large roomy and somewhat comfortable cell made from a glass/crystal mixture. There are orange lights fixed above the cell, giving the room a very half luminous look. There are benches, two beds and one bathroom inside the cell. Across from their cell is one almost identical where Angel and Gorog are chained up across from each other. There is another prisoner with them also chained up. The prisoner is a Halox, a race of lizards that stand up right and have the ability to not only breathe underwater, but can control it as well.

Gorog growls at Angel as he struggles to get out of his restraints.

Angel wakes up, sees his situation and sighs.

Casey, Tiny, Nikki, Hyda, Rayza, Demi and Ethereal are in a cell together, but not restrained. Rayza is yelling for the attention of the guards, given they are her same race, she is thinking they might let her go.

"I am clearly a Katharac and not involved with these people, so how about you guys open this up and let me out." Rayza says once she has their attention for a second. They quickly turn around and continue to ignore her.

"Most advanced ship in the Galaxy, has wings like a bird and you couldn't do anything." Casey yells at Tiny.

"That ray had some sort of gravity flux! It threw off the sensors!" Tiny yells back. Casey sits on one of the benches next to Tiny and Nikki.

She stares at the Halox prisoner. Right off the bat, she could tell that the Halox is a male, female Halox have teal colored skin. His is more a dark green skin color. His face has scars and from the looks of his whited out eyes, he is blind but still aware. His outfit is that of an assassin, it is maroon with metal hoops, perhaps to hook lines to. She continues to stare at him, until she notices him looking in her direction. Casey turns her head slightly to stare at Gorog.

"Tiny have you found out where they put our weapons?" Casey asks not moving from her position.

"They are about a mile or two in that direction." Tiny replies pointing.

"I still haven't found a way out, I'm a little more concerned about Trea and Jo and why they are not with us." She replies with worry in her voice.

Casey feels her concern but with no weapons there is no point in moving, at least not until Tiny maps out the ship to find them. Casey knew she had one charge left in her gloves but there is no guarantee that it would break the glass. The orange lights hanging above prevented Sierens, Nexus and any other race from using their abilities. The trick of the orange light is in the light bulb; it's made up of frozen solar flare shards from an aging star called Jakhi, somewhere near the edge of the galaxy. It sucks being trapped in a cell with some of the strongest beings in the galaxy and they can't do anything because of some orange crystal Casey thought. She looks down at the ground and instantly has an idea. She stands up and walks over to the glass. "Hey!" she yells in English to Gorog, he turns to acknowledge her.

"If you want out, we can help, but you have to help me with a mission and once the job is done, I will take you back home." Casey says. Gorog stares at her, then at Angel. "Why do you fight for the human?" Gorog asks in his native tongue.

"The human can help me get what I need." Angel responds back in Groutarian.

The Halox clears his throat and says in English

"One with clipped wings cannot be a chooser."

"The blind lizard has a point, but I understand. I was going to give you the Amethyst of Galaton." Casey replies.

"Whoa, wait a minute, Ms. Williams. Back it up, you will give him what?" Rayza asks with disapproving tone in her voice.

She stands up and takes two steps toward Casey.

"I agree Casey, you giving him that gem could have devastating consequences." Nikki adds.

"We're doing it. We need his help. He needs ours and we're taking the Halox with us." Casey says not looking back at them. Casey understood Nikki's concern of Gorog getting a hold of that Amethyst. Nikki wasn't the only one that was worried; she could see the disapproving thoughts of Ethereal and Hyda. Casey unzips her jacket and pulls out a bright orange crystal and holds it up. Rayza lets out a gasping shriek.

"I tried giving it to you before, but you wanted a fight instead." Casey says to Gorog. "You're a pickpocketing piece of shit!" Rayza yells,

" And you're a thief Rayza." Casey says back to her.

"That's not even... well at least, I have some class when I steal things!" Rayza yells then sits down. Gorog roars, speaking in Groutarian

"I will help you for the gem and once I have it, the deal will be done."

"Once the mission is complete. Agreed?" Casey asks. Gorog nods his head.

"Probably not a smart idea." Nikki says filing her nails. Casey puts the crystal away turns around and walks up to Nikki.

"I honestly don't give a shit what you think of my actions "Miss I'm not going to help you until you're ready;" I'm not making these choices to help you. I'm doing this because I was given this mission by someone who trusted me to get it done. I have to finish the mission and in order to finish the mission I have to rely on other races and somehow have everyone on the same side. So, if I give up a crystal that probably belongs to his grandfather and the Groutarian people, then I will do as I please, and you won't do or say shit." Casey finishes calming down and taking in a deep breathe. She walks over to Tiny. Nikki sits down without say anything. Casey knew it wasn't a nice thing to say, but she was sick of the negativity.

"Do you mind telling me what your plan is?" Tiny asks,

"I will, but first I need you to do me a favor." Casey holds up her hands, still wearing the gloves.

About ten minutes later Tiny finishes tweaking the gloves with built in tools from her left arm and hands them back to Casey. "Okay I changed the output levels on the return pads. Now they will put out more energy and use less, but I'm slightly concerned you won't have enough energy." Tiny says as Casey puts them on and heads to the center of the cell.

Everyone stares at her as she kneels down and places her hands flat on the metal floor. The gloves light up and most of the floor in the cell disintegrates beneath the crew.

Everyone falls down about two stories to the level below. They land on a cargo holding level of the ship. Everyone has a hard landing aside from Casey and Nikki. Tiny gets up first,

"I will admit that I may have made a slight miscalculation." She says.

"You think?" Ethereal replies.

"A little more warning next time, Ms. Williams." Hyda says slowly getting up,

"My bad." Casey says landing softly as she slows herself down with her boots.

The cargo hold is massive, it almost seems like it goes on forever. Casey looks ahead, there are large crates and boxes on either side, giving it a familiar warehouse look, like one she saw in an old movie.

She looks up at the hole then over to the floor below the other cell.

"Nikki can you get them out of there?" Nikki is still hovering in the air with arms crossed and a pissed look on her face.

"Look, I'm sorry for what I said, but I really need your help right now." Casey says, looking back to see a couple of guards running down the pathway toward them.

"Nikki please!" Casey begs while getting behind one for the crates for protection. "Oh Fine! I can't stay mad at you, bestie!" Nikki says excitedly.

She aims her index finger like a gun at the floor below the other cell and shoots a bright pink beam. She cuts a large portion of the floor beneath the cell. Gorog, Angel and the Halox dangle from their restraints. Nikki breaks them free using telekinesis.

They fall to the lower level, all three landing on their feet. Gorog stands fist clenched and stares down at Angel. He stares up at Gorog with his hands engulfed in purple flame. The blind Halox stands between both of them with his hands behind his back. "Hey!" Casey yells from behind the cover of the crates trying to shield herself from the hail of laser bolt shots from the guards.

Gorog runs and slams one of the large metal crates into the attacking guards crushing them between the two crates. A few more shots wiz by Gorog's head from three more guards rushing down the walkway.

A portal opens up above the group of guards and Angel drops down on one of them. He blasts another into a crate with purple fire and kicks the last one with a force that sends him bursting through the metal crate.

Gorog turns around and tries to attack Casey. Nikki holds his claw inches from her face; Casey is not fazed by his attempt.

"Now, I thought we had a deal?" Casey says with a smile.

Nikki flies in front of him.

"I like you." Nikki says.

"So, please don't make me kill you." Nikki ends with a big innocent smile.

Gorog relaxes and Nikki lets him go. Casey walks up to Gorog,

"You have to learn to trust me." She says. Gorog nods his head as the blind Halox approaches Casey with his hands still behind his back.

"Thank you for freeing me, as a reward for your kindness, I will take you to where they are holding your weapons and your ship."

"Show us the way." Casey says eagerly.

"You're really going to take directions from a blind lizard?" Nikki asks floating with arms crossed.

"There is an elevator at the halfway mark of the cargo hold and then a little walk will take us to the armory." the Halox calmly says.

"He may have lost his sight, but at least he didn't loose his manners, Ms. Mind Reader." Casey says.

"Oh! So, you and this old blind reptile are best friends now?" Nikki asks.

"Well yeah, him and I are… I'm sorry what's your name?" Casey asks the Halox

"Fade." He replies.

"Fade! More like fog." Nikki says.

Demi laughs.

"Why do you care if I trust him?" Casey asks

"Because HE IS BLIND!" Nikki says elongating on the word blind.

"You *love* pointing out the obvious." Demi says.

"Fuck you Demi." Nikki says.

"Being blind isn't a reason not to trust someone." Casey says.

"My father was blind. He navigated around pretty well, especially when he walked out on my mom." Rayza chimes in with useless information.

"That explains a lot." Tiny adds in.

"Fuck you!" Rayza yells back at Tiny.

"Anyway!" Casey cuts in.

"Fade, pleasure to meet you. My name is Casey and just ignore them, they're idiots."

"That would explain why I am always detecting very low intelligent levels." Tiny says trying to map out the ship with her right arm internal computer.

"Oh my Cortex! Shut the fuck up! Fade, please lead the way we are right behind you." Casey says to Fade. He sprints off past Angel.

Casey chases after him and everyone else follows suit. They continue down one path until a squad of Katharac guards fire at them and stop them from proceeding. Fade continues to run at them while dodging blaster fire. He pounces on the squad to disarm one of them by breaking an arm. He snaps the neck of another and quickly grabs the blaster rifle and hits the last two in their heads. Fade drops the weapon then looks back at the group. They stare in disbelief at what just happened. He begins running again and the group runs after him. Casey picks up a blaster rifle and follows the rest down the pathway.

They were only about a fraction of the way through cargo hold. It seemed like they had run forever through the massive ship. Fade leads them up a couple flights of stairs to a higher plateau. There are crates stacked up on both sides of the path, but now there is a drop off. Once on the plateau, they stop when they see a large group of guards with four

Machinoc colossal Mechs blocking the pathway. Machinoc is the leading Katharac Company in armor and weapons.

The Mechs themselves are outfitted with a low grade combat A.I.

They are whopping ten feet tall and have multiple firearms including missiles, ion blasters and even a harmonic ray that can incapacitate any Sieren.

The group takes cover, except for Gorog who towers over everyone including the Mechs. He isn't feeling the whole 'take cover and cower in fear' thing, instead he rushes them with red glowing fists. Fade, Angel and Hyda run after him. Gorog takes on two of the Mechs, while getting shot by bolt laser shots, which do nothing to him. Gorog's skin is like the red rocks of his home world, meaning his hide is almost impenetrable. Which is why he doesn't hide from a fight. He embraces it instead; Angel runs through a rift and appears above one of the other Mechs. He lands on top and begins trying to pierce the Mech's armor. While Hyda and Fade run interference on the guards, everyone else stays back behind what cover they can find.

"Rayza go help them." Casey says peeking in and out from cover and firing a couple shots at some of the guards with energy shields.

"*Yeah,* I'm not going to get in bad with my own people, besides, why don't ask you ask Nikki to do something?" Rayza replies while she cleans her cat-like claws.

Casey looks up at Nikki floating.

Nikki winks at Casey.

Casey didn't want Nikki to feel like she needed her help.

Casey smiles and goes back to providing cover fire.

Hyda slides up to a small group of the guards dodging their shots. He opens up his hands and a slightly visible force pushes them into an empty crate. Hyda pushes the empty crate into another Mech and a couple more guards. Fade fights a small group coming up behind Hyda. He dodges their fire as one of the guards using a light blade claw tries to land. Fade disarms him and stabs into his chin with the claw. He takes a pistol from the guard who is choking on his own blood and shoots four shots each hitting another one of the guards. Angel blasts through the head of one Mech with a purple energy beam that emits from his palm and throws a small purple fireball down into the circuitry and then hops off. The Mech explodes from the inside out; Gorog rips the arm off of one of the Mechs and smacks the other with it. He punches straight through the center of the one armed Mech and rips it in half. The other one decides to aim at Casey, but Gorog slams down on his arm diverting the hail of bullet fire down to the ground. He strikes his head three times and turns the gun on him blasting its head off. The last Mech shoots at Angel. Fade runs and launches himself off Angel's head with his arms still being behind his back. He summersault kicks the head clean off the Mech and lands on his feet.

Suddenly a large hologram screen appears above them through the railing of the light fixtures. A female Katharac, dressed in what looks to be armor of the royal family appears. The Katharac royal family is made up of only three, a king, a queen and a prince. She is definitely not a king and seems too young to be the queen.

"Stop this once! There are civilians on this ship, Ms. Williams I apologize for the way we detained you. It was to ensure that some of your party members would not attack my people." The Katharac woman says staring at Gorog.

He roars at loudly at her, "Gorog!" Casey yells and he lowers his roar to a snarl.

"Who are you and why the hell did you abduct us and where the fuck are my crew members?" Casey bursts enraged as she steps toward the hologram screen.

"They are safe, Ms. Williams, I will allow you and your crew mates to retrieve your weapons and ship, if I have your word that no harm will come to my people."

"As long as I get my crew back."

"Of course you will. Take the service elevator to the floor above. I will have my assistant take you to your weapons and then to my chambers to discuss why I picked you up in such haste." The hologram dissipates and the remaining guards back up and point them in the direction of the service elevator. Casey walks up to Gorog,

"I need you to calm down and not kill anyone, yet. Do you think you can handle that?" Gorog squints his eye, and nods at Casey. He does not fully understand why she is willing to trust so easily.

Casey walks past him making her way to the elevator. Angel walks next to her.

"Ms. Williams, take precaution, the princess is not as nice as she might seem." He says.

"I don't know she seemed nice besides going on a killing rampage wasn't something I particularly wanted either. Have you met her before?" Casey asks.

"Once and she was a lie back then."

Casey stops right before the elevator.

"Are you saying that the woman I just talked to is a guy?" Casey asks.

"No, Ms. Williams she was a guy." Angel replies as he gets on the elevator.

"That's not very PC." Rayza says stepping onto the elevator.

"Hey Nikki, I notice the blind lizard was right about the elevator." Rayza says.

"Shut up Rayza, it's clearly a lucky guess." Nikki replies.

Everyone steps onto the huge elevator that is spacious enough to hold everyone comfortably.

"Hold on, why would she, I mean he do that?" Casey says. She's the last one to get on. "It's an unusual universe Ms. Williams, why not just ask her yourself." Angel says as an orange gate closes and the elevator begins to rise.

On the upper level, three guards and a tall pale blue Nexus ambassador are waiting for them. His attire is of royal silk from the Katharacs, and so is the sliver and ruby infused staff on his back. The gate opens Casey steps off first.

"Ms. Williams, I am Kalith, the princess's assistant. If you will just follow me I will take you and your group to the armory." His voice is slightly raspy and she notices one scar going down the side of his face. One of his bright green eyes has a broken blood vessel, causing it to fill with a red-like orange color. Kalith begins to lead them to the armory with three guards walking along side him. They walk about half a mile until they reach a door leading to the right half of the ship. The armory looks like a grocery store, with sliding glass doors and fairly large aisles, all well organized. There are computer kiosks to search for your items and shopping carts to collect what you couldn't carry. Kalith holds the doors open for them to enter. Casey and her crew walk into the armory. Gorog stays behind, because he can't fit through the doors. Casey is feeling a trap until she sees the amount of weapons they have stored. Rayza quickly walks over to one of the kiosks and begins searching for the weapons. They take about twenty minutes to arm back up and get ready. Tiny is outside the armory talking with Kalith.

"Where is the rest of our crew?" Tiny asks.

"You will see them after meeting with the princess." Kalith waves his hand in the direction of a platform.

Tiny shakes her head and walks toward the platform; Casey looks at Kalith then goes after Tiny.

"Don't worry we will get them back." Casey reassures Tiny as they walk on the platform.

Once everyone is on the platform, Kalith walks to a podium and a hologram pops up. He hits a few symbols, the platform lifts up and begins transporting them to the front part of the ship. Casey looks over the side rail and down at as the platform glides over the center of the ship. There are many civilians, houses and small businesses down below. There are parks and running rivers with actual trees growing from the ship. It is a sight to be held. The platform continues through the civilian area and then turns into military, soldiers, weapons, Mechs and vehicles. Casey looks back up and toward the crew to see if they were even slightly impressed with how gigantic the ship is.

The crew, however, didn't move from the one side of the platform, they didn't like Kalith and didn't trust this situation. Casey knew it wasn't right for the Katharac to just pick them up and jail them, but that didn't mean she couldn't enjoy the scenery, [Besides now with their weapons returned to them if they felt threatened, they could just kill everyone.] The platform finally connects with the other side. Kalith leads them to a long arched bridge that leads to a pair of double doors. There are twenty guards standing in the middle of the bridge holding trident spears made of gold to match their golden armor. As Casey and the others take their first few steps the guards turn to clear the path, now having ten of them on each side. Kalith leads them to the double doors, Nikki flies up to a couple of guards and, tries to make some of them laugh making silly faces at them. None of them move a muscle, so Nikki gives up. As they reach the double doors, they begin to open slowly. Behind the doors is a room that is like lobby in a hotel with a very long bar on the left side, couches and chairs on the right.

"The rest of you please wait here, I will take Ms. Williams to meet with the princess, please help your self to the bar and the food." Kalith says as he leads them into the room.

"Whoa hold up, why can't we all meet with the princess?" Rayza asks.

"Because the meeting is for her, not for you." Kalith says bluntly turning around and signaling the guards to leave the room.

"Now, Ms. Williams, if you would be so kind to follow me." Casey looks over at the bar and thinks how badly she could use a drink after everything that's happened. She follows Kalith to another set of double doors at the end of the long room. There is a long hallway and yet another set of gold and ruby double doors.

"Fuck really! Why do you do all this fucking walking?" Casey asks as the doors close behind them. Kalith turns to her and replies,

"Your race is lazy." He continues down the hallway, Casey sighs then follows him. The hallway is a massive, large gold pillar on one side, ruby and sapphires incrusted into the ceiling artwork of the Great War (a war between all races that happened before the birth of the current universe). Casey couldn't take her eyes from the mural. She remembered small things about the Great War from the history books. The Great War was nothing more than one large battle that ended the universe or so the legend said. There is no way to prove it ever happened, but one thing was for sure, every Species in this Galaxy was there. Casey turns her gaze to the solid gold doors still halfway down the hall. It has two carvings, one on each door, a Nexus king on the right and on the left a Katharac warrior male. The Nexus king was different from the current king, and the Katharac warrior reminded Casey of Gorog, because of how large the representation was. They finally arrive at the door, Kalith stops about five feet from the door. Casey stops next to him. The doors open slowly inward,

"You may enter, please be warned, if you try anything, you and your friends will be killed, slowly." Kalith says,

"You're not much of a people person, are you Kalith?" Casey says as she walks past him and through the small opening of the doors. The room is enormous like the rest of the ship. There is a carpet that goes from the door to a small flight of steps and a throne in the center of the room. The bizarre throne is made up from skeletons of different races and painted a blood red. The twisted bones that hold it together fascinate Casey. Behind the throne is a small oasis with trees and other plants. Casey walks toward the throne carefully staying on the rug, so as not to agitate the more upgraded and beefier guards on both sides of the room. As she gets closer to the throne, a woman dressed in a gold and black armor steps up onto the raised platform to the side of the throne. Her armor stands apart from her royal guards with various attachments and strange glowing Nexus symbols on both shoulders. She places her hand on one of the skulls protruding from the side of the throne. Casey continues to approach, as the princess stares down at her.

"The infamous Casey Williams and her band of misfits! That is what some of the galaxy is calling you and your very unusual alliance." The princess says taking two steps down the small flight of stairs to end up in front of the throne.

"That's funny, I have also heard the galaxy call you something as well, and something about you not being who you say you are." Casey says condescendingly as she stops about ten feet from the throne.

"Rumors are just rumors, I guess." The princess says as she takes a seat on the throne.

"Why am I here?" Casey says now slightly annoyed while crossing her arms.

"If I were you I would watch my tone, seeing as you are a guest on my ship."

"Do you usually pick up your guests and imprison them?" The princess smirks,

"I like the fire that burns inside you Casey, and you're going to need it if you plan to take on the Rebel Militia. I am Kitara, Katharac's military leader and daughter to the king and I'm in need of your help, Ms. Williams."

Casey changes her stance to a less aggressive one.

"With?" Casey asks,

"I need you to retrieve something for me, from a clan of Solarian slave trading pirates, I have a contact on Ohyron that has the location of their whereabouts. I need you to meet with the contact at Club Vixen. Her name is Vikara and she will give you the details. Find the pirates and take back what is rightfully mine." Casey is baffled. Why would the Katharac royal family seek her to help? It is something she never dreamed would happen.

"If you're the leader of the military, why not just go get it yourself?" Casey asks as she takes two steps closer to Kitara.

"You and I both know that the armies of the Katharac could demolish the pirates, but using such power for one insignificant thing is not the wisest choice. As much as I would like to go to war, the Solarians are not the ones to go to war with." Kitara says,

"And who are you trying to wage war with?" Casey asks. Kitara smirks

"Ms. Williams, if you do this for me not only will I pay you a very wealthy amount, I will also return your team mates." She waves her hand and activates a hologram showing Jo and Trea sitting in a cell together.

Casey draws a pistol on Kitara and the guards ready their tridents.

"Ms. Williams, if you kill me they will die, so don't be stupid. Do the job for me and I will give them back to you, safe and sound." Casey holsters her weapon.

"I need those two, they pilot the ship."

"Well, looks like you will have to figure out how to fly your own ship." Kitara says before she snaps her fingers.

A red light filled with many symbols begins to spin around Casey's vision. Casey sees the vibrant light is spinning all around her entire body. She looks down at her feet then back up, Kitara and the throne room are gone.

She is now in the main projector room of the Phoenix, the red light fades away along with the rest of the group who appeared seconds after her. Gorog is a bit of a tight fit; the cabin height is at eighteen feet. A hologram video pops up with Kitara sitting in her throne.

"We took the liberty of flying to the location you charted on your map and dropped your hideous ship off the moment you were all transferred. Good luck Ms. Williams and due try to be quick." The transmission ends.

"That fucking bitch! She has Trea and Jo!" Casey shouts.

"What!" Tiny says squeezing through the group.

"She or He asked us to help him or her to get something from some fucking pirates and stole the only two people who can fly the fucking ship as collateral!"

"Damn what a bitch! Wait, did you mention her being a man?" Nikki says slightly laughing.

"It may have slipped out." Casey says with a feeling of guilt. Nikki laughs,

"Oh fuck that's funny, and no wonder she took those two." Nikki says as she continues to laugh.

"It's not funny you space breathing freak!" Tiny yells at her while backhanding her arm. "Owe!" Nikki says rubbing her arm.

"Tiny where are we?" Casey asks as she grabs ammunition crystal cartages from a crate.

"The last location I put in was Taloc." Tiny scrolls through the holograms and finds their location. A hologram of a planet with a red dot indicating what hemisphere they are in pops up. It zooms in to the planet showing a more accurate location.

"Looks like we're just outside the village of Karusto, but this rainforest is thick, I'm going to need you to set up some beacons to get a better map of the planet." Tiny says. Casey walks up to the projector, as the rest of the crew try to find a seat and Gorog just sits down where he stands. Casey brings up two files on the console; the files contain information on two individuals, a brother and a sister.

THE TWINS

TALOC IS A RAINFOREST PLANET WITH GINORMOUS PLANTS, insects and other creatures that are larger than most skyscrapers. This extremely dangerous planet has civilization, one major city and two somewhat heavy populated villages. This being the home world of the Halox, Casey will have to take precaution mainly because they don't take kindly to visitors that are not merchants. The Phoenix releases a ramp and the hatch opens. Casey, Angel, Nikki, Demi, Ethereal and their new best friend Fade exit the ship. Tiny sticks her head out and tosses two small rods that hit Casey.

"Good luck!" Tiny says closing the door quickly. Casey collects the rods and begins leading her small shore party through the deep blue colored woods. Ethereal leads the way by cutting down many of the vines and low hanging branches with her green and red light blade sword. They walk for about twenty minutes

"Stop! Set up one of the beacons Ms. Williams." Tiny says over the COM.

Casey twists the rod, a green light appears in the center and four small legs emerge from the bottom. She sets it on the foggy ground of the forest. The legs latch into the ground and the green light turns purple.

"Angel I have been meaning to ask you, who is the red-eyed R.A.I.S?" Casey asks.

"Tarik?" Angel asks.

"Is that his name?" Casey asks.

"Yeah and he is not a R.A.I.S, his body is, but he is a different being all together. He is more of a guideline for the universe." Angel says. As they continue to walk through the forest.

"So you have seen him, and now I'm seeing him, so what does that mean? Am I the only one that can see him?" Casey asks.

"No, but to be honest if you are seeing Tarik, it means that something you are doing is off course so to speak. That's how he will put it." Angel says stepping over a root. "Off course?" Casey asks.

"Every being in the universe is on a course that takes them through life and if one person strays from their intended course, it could have catastrophic repercussions on not just the timeline, but the whole universe as well. That is what he told me years ago." Angel says. Casey stops to think what she did differently today. Ethereal nudges her to keep going, Casey snaps out of the thought.

They continue through the forest carefully avoiding the bird sized insects and python sized centipedes crawling around. They eventually come across a small village. They hide in the dark of the forest to scope it out. The front entrance is large opening with torches on either side of a cast iron gate with four guards protecting the gate. The Halox guards are extremely large and their scales are black, which means they are the Halox from the other side of the planet. They mostly live inside volcanic areas, as opposed to forest. Their armor is decent, but their weapons are nothing more than wooden spears and arrows. Casey has always believed that the less fights you start, the more allies you will have.

"Fade, do you mind taking point?" Casey asks. Fade nods and takes the lead of the group when walking up to the guards. He approaches and speaks in his native tongue "They are with me, we are just passing through". The guards show no interest and allow them to enter.

They slowly walk inside the village, there isn't much to look at, mostly homes made in trees and huts. The people, however, seem happy and content. There is music playing on drums and strange instruments that gave a familiar sound. The smell and sound of food cooking fills the atmosphere. Toward the back of the village there are a couple of metal buildings that are mostly used for merchant trading.

"We should check out those buildings." Angel suggests.

"Casey, I need you to plant that other beacon!" Tiny yells over coms.

"Calm down, we are passing through a village. It's possible someone here might have seen the twins." Casey replies as she continues to walk behind Fade, Angel and Ethereal. Nikki flies to Casey's side.

"Did you see that hideous child? Yuck, some people should not repopulate." Nikki says loud enough for people to hear.

"Nikki!" Casey whispers angrily.

"What?" Nikki asks before bumping into Angel's back.

"What's going on? Why did we stop?" Casey asks. Fade walks up

"They were here, but just left about twenty minutes ago." Fade says.

"They left the planet?" Casey asks.

"No they are hunting something. Not sure if the man said it was a Jokark or a Holark." Fade says.

"A what or a what?" Nikki says.

"Okay let's get out of here. They should be deeper in the forest somewhere." Casey says.

The shore party leaves the village and continues through the dark forest until eventually coming up to a clearing with a much brighter color scheme. They step out slowly into the clearing, a small Galactic Alliance vessel comes out of the clouds and flies right over them and lands about four to five miles from them.

"That's not a good sign." Demi says staying under tree cover. Ethereal steps out to see if there anymore ships coming when Casey suddenly yanks her back into the cover before a bolt shot hits the dirt where she was about to stand and the group hides behind the trees.

"Thanks." Ethereal says as she readies her bow. Casey peeks around her tree trunk and sees a reflection off of the sniper's scope. Another shot goes off; Casey stays behind the tree. Yellow paint splatters against the tree. Casey takes a closer look at the splatter. It's yellow color with green flakes. It reminds her of only one person who has used that color during the Galactic Alliance annual paintball tournaments.

"Angel." Casey whispers, then kicks a small rock at him, then picks one up and throws it at him to get his attention.

"Angel!" she says louder this time.

"What?" he whispers with a slightly angry tone.

"I need you to get me across the to the other side." Casey says.

"Then don't throw shit at me!" Angel continues to whisper.

"I only threw shit at you, because you didn't hear me!"

"Can you two just get on with it?" Nikki joins in the whisper. Angel waves his hand and makes a void in front of Casey. She looks into it and sees a forest below. Casey jumps into the portal, it leads to the area above where the sniper is. She falls into the trees and slows down with her boots right behind the sniper and draws her pistol. The sniper turns around and draws a pistol on Casey at the same time. The sniper, wearing a grey hooded cloak, with red and black armor plating over a skin-tight military suit and two belts of bullets, each one drooping to each side, says

"You're a little slow, Space Case."

"Well its good thing you can't hit the broad side of a barn." The sniper and Casey both lower their weapons. The sniper stands and takes off the hood.

Stacey looks different. Her hair is not completely blonde and is longer. There are streaks of red coming from the roots and her face looks worn, like she hasn't slept for a couple days. It didn't matter to Casey though, she is just happy to see her. She hugs Stacey for about ten seconds, then pulls away.

"What are you doing here? What happened to red hair being tacky? And why are you not wearing any make up?" Casey says while slightly shaking her back and forth. "Whoa! Slow down buddy! I'm here to back you up. The red is in my hair is because when you decide to help your best friend, who happens to be the most wanted person in the galaxy, you have to change your appearance." Stacey says taking Casey's hands off her shoulders.

"What about your family?" Casey asks,

"They will be fine, you know how wealthy they are."

"True! They make Craxton look poor. So is that ship that just landed your back up?" Casey asks.

"I was about to get to that, no they are not and I assume they are here for you, which leaves us with about five minutes until they get here." Stacey says.

"Not a lot of time to catch up." Casey says.

"I'm sure we will get plenty of time to…" Stacey stops mid sentence and quickly lifts her left arm behind her as Angel falls from the sky through the trees with his fist engulfed in purple flame.

His fist meets Stacey's open palm. The energy surge doesn't affect Stacey, but the impact of his hand meeting hers destroys the trees on either side of them. Angel tries to put more power into his hit, but Stacey, changes her stance to be more grounded. The energy surge is causing wind and electricity to blow past Stacey and Casey. The light that is emitting from the stand off is too blinding for Casey to look at it, not that she could anyway with one arm blocking any debris hitting her eyes. Stacey put an end to the struggle by grabbing his fist with her other hand and swinging him back over the other side where Nikki, Demi, Ethereal and Fade were standing. He lands hard causing a streak in the dirt.

"Nice job, if only we were all as strong as you Angel, this mission would be as good as done." Ethereal says with a snarky cough while clapping to mock him.

Angel slowly gets up.

"I would like to see you do better." He replies once on his feet.

"Hey, sorry about that!" Stacey says walking over with Casey behind her.

Casey is focused on the damage they caused holding off one another.

"Yeah sometimes I don't know my own strength." Stacey says as walking to the group.

Nikki and Ethereal begin laughing,

"Oh my Cortex, she is a human, and she threw you fifteen feet!" Nikki says in between laughs.

"Fuck you Nikki!" Angel growls at her.

Casey runs over to them.

"What the fuck was that?" Casey yells at Stacey.

"Damn calm down." Stacey replies.

"No shut the fuck up and tell me what the fuck it was I just saw!"

"Casey relax, I will explain everything."

A couple energy blaster shots wiz over the group's heads. Twelve Alliance Black Ops troopers are walking and firing from the forest where Stacey was set up. Ethereal uses the earth and raises a seven-foot high long wall to provide cover, so they can escape into the forest. They run quickly through the forest dodging trees and roots. Storm clouds begin to darken the sky. The forest becomes denser, making it very hard to see more than ten feet in front of you.

"Split up!" Casey yells as they run together except for Nikki who is flying next to them. Demi and Fade run straight, Ethereal and Angel run left and Casey and Stacey run right. Nikki flies up quickly and high enough to where she can see the troopers but they cannot see her.

"Casey I need you to set up that other beacon!" Tiny says over the com.

"Well you have to be patient, because I'm currently dealing with a situation." Casey says running fast through the forest toward a mountain range.

Nikki observes from above seeing the movement through the forest trees trailing in three different directions. The Alliance spreads their forces in a long line, to cover more ground. Nikki sees two more things moving through the forest at a fast rate but they are coming from the other side of the mountain range. She can't quite make out what they are. Casey and Stacey stop once they get to a wall, at the base of the mountain on one particular side.

Casey grabs her rifle and sets the shot for "Icy Hot", Stacey pulls out two old school futuristic looking magnums. They are solid black with one red rose painted down the handle from the tip of the barrel. They look like six-shooters but can actually shoot up to fifteen rounds each clip. Stacey customized them herself. They move away from the mountain, stealth is the key at the moment, so Casey and Stacey take it slow. The darkness in the forest has caused the Alliance troopers to use their flashlights on their weapons. Casey and Stacey see some of the lights coming in their direction, so they quickly hide behind two big tree trunks.

"Uh Casey, there is something large headed toward you." Nikki says over the com. "What are you talking about? From where?" Casey whispers as she checks around the tree to see how close the troopers are. Nikki flies lower to get a better look, she sees what it is causing the two trails and instantly gets the feeling of something slithering down her spine.

"So what is it?" Casey whispers in the com as she waits for the Alliance trooper to pass her tree.

"Snakes!" Nikki says terrified for them to have to deal with such disgusting creatures. Casey's heart sinks into her stomach. She hates snakes, it figures that on a mission to save the galaxy she would have to go against things she hates.

"Psst." Stacey whispers to get Casey's attention.

"What's going on? You just went pale." She whispers to her. Casey looks over to her and whispers one word

"Snakes". Stacey leans back against the tree, Casey calms down quickly once she realizes that the snakes are the reason the twins are here on this planet. Giant snakeheads go for a lot on the black market.

Angel and Ethereal run until they reach a river.

"We should head back, regroup and take on the snakes together." Ethereal says looking back in the direction they came from. Angel looks up and down the river.

"We need a back up plan, just in case things go south." He says as he climbs down halfway to the river.

He puts his hand flat on the wall line of the river and his hand glows red. A symbol of a coiled up serpent appears on the back of his palm. The serpent uncoils slowly and goes into the wall. He climbs back up,

"What did you just do?" Ethereal asks.

"Nothing, Let's head back." Angel says as they walk back into the forest.

An Alliance trooper passes by Casey. She puts her rifle on her back and quickly pulls a dagger from her back. Casey grabs the trooper in a one-arm chokehold and takes her dagger and slides it easily into the trooper's head.

The trooper sparks an electrical discharge and the body collapses to the ground. The Galactic Alliance Black Ops team is always made up of a team of highly intelligent robots, led by either one or three human Alliance Majors, depending upon the amount of Alliance troopers they have. The Majors can control up to about twenty of these troopers at once using their mind and can see what they see by wearing a helmet with a large visor. Casey takes out the other beacon and plants in on the root of the tree where she is hiding. She pulls her rifle out and signals Stacey to follow her.

A holographic window pops up from the projector on board the Phoenix. The words "activate mapping" display across the screen. Tiny puts down her tablet and begins working from the projector. A map of the entire planet begins loading up on the projector screen.

"Well it's about time, Ms. Williams." Tiny says over the com.

"Fuck off Tiny! Nikki where are the snakes now?" Casey whispers over the com while getting behind another tree. There are three troopers now headed to Casey and Stacey.

"I think I lost them, so good luck?" Nikki says while floating on her back with a tanning reflector and sunglasses.

Two troopers slowly walk on either side of the tree Casey is leaning against and she pulls her rifle out and fires two shots one at each of the trooper's feet. Their legs freeze up to the shins keeping them in place. The ice begins to glow red immediately after it spreads. Stacey runs up behind one trooper. Summersaults over it and shoots down into its head while also using the other pistol to headshot the other trooper. She lands down in front of Casey as three more troopers come running and shooting at the two of them. Casey quickly hugs Stacey and uses her boots to blast them at least ten feet further into the forest away from their shots. The ice left on the droids Casey shot begins to glow a very bright red when the troopers pass by. The ice explodes destroying the troopers.

The force of the explosion causes Casey and Stacey to land a little hard on the ground. They instantly roll away from each other in opposite directions dodging a hail of shots coming at them from another three more troopers.

On the other side of the forest Angel and Ethereal are fighting a couple of troopers in heavy rain. Angel cuts one down with his purple trident energy blade. Ethereal uses her bow to shoot down a couple of them, as well. Angel opens three small void holes, and without even looking Ethereal fires three green energy arrows into each one. At that moment three troopers running toward Casey and Stacey get shot in the head by the same bright green energy arrows that came from Angel's voids.

Casey and Stacey get up slowly then freeze at the sound of trees snapping and branches breaking. It begins to rain lightly.

"Stacey, get up in the trees." Casey whispers as she backs up slowly to look in the direction of the snapping of breaking trees. Stacey begins climbing a tree and Casey follows suit. She climbs up the one next to Stacey's. She gets up about half way in the tree then sits on a branch and waits.

"Guys, get up in the trees." She says over the com. The roar of breaking trees comes closer. Casey's heart is pounding as she sees a very large snake below slithering slowly past the two trees. The eyes are solid red with a green pupil and its scales are covered in wet moss. The dark green scales have a red zigzagging streak. It continues to slither fast in the direction of Demi and Fade.

"The body of the snake is over fifty feet long and its height of the body is about seven feet tall" Tiny says over the COM while watching the snake from the safety of the ship. She is using a small metal humming bird fitted with a camera and two poison darts. This metal bird flies next to Casey as the snake finishes slithering by.

"I would recommend going for the soft spot right between the head and the body." Tiny says as the bird flies in front of Casey then flies off following the snake. "Understood, Nikki where are the snakes headed?" Casey asks as she and Stacey climb down from the trees. The rain begins to pick up to an almost full on pour.

Nikki is still floating on her back.

"Oh I don't know. Things are much more peaceful up here." She says floating above the storm, sunbathing with sunglasses on.

Casey and Stacey begin running down the path the snake left behind. The sound of fired shots echo in between the sound of thunder and the crack of lightning. They come up to a clearing with three trooper bodies, two of them offline and the other is crawling without legs.

Stacey pulls out a pistol and shoots the droid in the head as they run up to middle of the muddy clearing. Angel, Ethereal, Demi and Fade regroup with Stacey and Casey in the clearing.

"Tiny, do you think you can find the other snake?" Casey says touching her ear and looking around to make sure the other one didn't sneak up on them. The com line makes a static sound,

"Tiny? Tiny come in." Casey says franticly.

"Coms must be down, they probably have a cloud." Stacey says looking ahead.

"Fuck!" Casey yells tapping her wrist device.

"What's a cloud?" Ethereal asks

"A device that cuts off communication." Demi explains while twisting a small disk in his hands then throwing it into the center of the group. A small energy shield emits a cover with a thirty-foot circumference.

"This should give us a break from the rain." Demi says taking out a handkerchief and whipping his face and hair.

"Not sure what the point is, this storm is going to be around for a little bit." Stacey says kneeling down over the droid she shot.

"The point is no matter what horrible place we end up in. I will always look better than you!" Demi retorts. Stacey gives him a dumb look. Angel begins to walk over to Casey but stops half way when they hear the sound of a couple of branches snapping, they all look in the same direction.

Casey readies her rifle and shoots the droid bodies, between the group and the path of where they hear the other snake. The troopers bodies freeze and begin to glow red. The snake slowly pushes its body through two trees enough to coil and to lift its upper body into attack position.

"That's a big fucking snake." Demi says while Casey keeps her rifle fixed on the snake. Ethereal lights up her sword, and Stacey pulls the hammer back on her magnums.

The snake turns it's head toward Stacey. The ice, now bright red, explodes. Angel opens a couple voids redirecting the blast to surround the snake. The ball of fire dissipates down to just a couple of bushes and trees as the voids close up. The energy shield flashes and then shuts off. Casey puts her weapon on her back.

"Okay lets go get that other one." She says turning around to the others. She quickly turns back around to see the snake slowly rising up out of the flames.

The body has been badly burned, but it has not penetrated the indestructible scales of the snake. Casey freezes like a dear in headlights. Stacey opens fire on the snake's eyes. It moves swiftly to dodge any incoming shots. Ten troopers appear from behind Ethereal and Angel. Ethereal runs straight for them as Angel opens a void and jumps through to land on top of a couple of them. Casey pulls out a small grenade and throws it at the snake. It explodes on contact. The snake turns to Casey, who already has a head start running into the forest to lead it away from everyone else.

It quickly slithers after her, "Casey!" Stacey yells shooting the tail end of the snake as it disappears. More troopers come shooting from the first snake's path, but this time there is a Major accompanying them in the fight. Demi and Fade engage the troopers. Fade uses his speed and hand-to-hand combat to disable three of the droids with nothing more than a few kicks and well-placed punches. Demi starts with hand to hand then turns on his energy rapier and skewers through the chest of two troopers. He swings them around and using his other hand draws a pistol and shoots two more troopers until they fall. He pulls the rapier out of the two and swiftly cuts off their heads.

Tiny's small humming bird continues flying after the first snake, but gets distracted when she sees ten troopers and a Major protecting a small crate. Tiny recognizes the crate. It's a cloud device.

"Ms. Williams?" Tiny says over com but only hears static. Tiny goes through a couple holograms and the humming bird changes color to a red and then flies down to the troopers. It slows down right above two of the trooper's heads who stand on the sides of the crate. The bird fires the two poison darts into the head of one of the troopers. The darts stick out of the helmet; the droid looks at the humming bird and opens fire. The bird flies up and down to dodge the shots, and then accelerates to attack the droid. Once the bird makes contact with the trooper, a small seismic explosion destroys a couple troopers and the crate.

Casey continues to run through the forest, using her boots to give her an edge to outrun the snake.

"Ms. Williams! I lost the other snake, so stay sharp!" Tiny yells over the COM.

Casey slows down to a complete stop after checking behind to see if the snake had caught up. She hides behind a tree and takes inventory of what she has to put the fucking thing down. Her heart is racing; why would she volunteer to lead the slimy fuck away from everyone else, she thinks.

"Anyone got any suggestions on how to kill these things?" She asks over the com. "You need to hit it from above, get to high ground." Angel says as he tears one of the troopers in half.

Casey looks forward and sees a small plateau protruding from the mountainside. Lucky for her, it is somewhat close, but unfortunate because the snake has caught up with her and is currently in striking position. She turns her head just in time to see it attack. She boosts forward to dodge it. The snake's mouth wraps around the tree she was just leaning against.

The boost only threw her forward on to the ground. She gets up and runs. She sprints for about half a mile, when the forest comes to an end and she finds herself in a field of tall grass. She tries to continue running using her boots to speed her through, but they have begun to overheat. The snake forces it's way through the forest and into the field. Casey runs as fast as she can as she looks back then ahead.

In front of her, a man appears out of nowhere wearing a gas mask and a strange type of armor. The man slowly walks toward her and the snake as he materializes a huge and powerful looking chain gun into his hands. The gun starts up quickly with a thunderous roar it begins firing at Casey and the snake. Casey instinctively throws her hands up to block her face. Only two shots hit her shield, and nearly disable it. More heated laser shots wiz past her, as another gas mask is teleports in between the shots and tackles her. They fall down in the middle of the clearing where Angel, Ethereal, Stacey, Demi and Fade are fighting the last remaining droids and two majors. Nikki watches from above as the gas mask wearing man shreds through the snake's body and face with heated golden plasma shots. Not much is left of the snake.

"Bitchin." Nikki says in approval.

Casey squirms around on the ground as she feels like a bunch of tiny little needles stabbing her body all at once. She initially checks her body for any wounds and then looks up at the gas mask wearing person who just tackled her.

It is one of the twins, from the looks of it, the female. Her name is Ayeka Corolite and she is a Golomite, an intelligent race of spirit or gas like beings that can inhabit any other species. To get around from place to place they use particular suits that provide a body for them allowing them to teleport up to a distance of sixty miles. Ayeka extends her hand to help Casey up on her feet. Casey pulls out a small CPU chip from her wrist device and hands it to her.

"Thank you." Casey says relieved as she hugs her. The sound of four-mortar shots echo through the now partly cloudy sky and come crashing down as fireballs all around the clearing. They knock everyone to the ground and destroy some of the Alliance troops. Nikki sighs looking down at the others on the battlefield. A little further north of the battlefield she sees the other Golomite teleport behind the human mortar troopers and the last Major.

"This should be interesting." Nikki says finally flying down to the area.

The Golomite stabs a couple of troopers through the back and shoots down the other three standing behind the Major. The Major turns around to face the Golomite, who is wearing an advanced Tycoon suit. The Mech suit increases speed, power and have many different settings to take down multiple races.

"I will be a gentlemen and let you make the first move." The Major says grounding him self for a fight.

"I hope you boys don't mind me coming in between." Nikki says winking and floating down right in the middle of the two.

The troopers from the mortars run over to back up the Major and aim their weapons at Nikki and the Golomite. Nikki slightly waves her hand. Instantly, all the troopers are shredded into pieces and flung far away. The Major doesn't flinch. He presses a button on his arm, raises his hand and fires out a short-range energy wave. The wave brushes over Nikki, immediately rendering her unconscious.

The Major draws a pistol to shoot the Golomite and as it discharges a wall of the earth rises up and blocks the shot. The wall moves to push the Major, knocking him back. He breaks the wall with one punch.

Angel drops down on the Major from one of his portals.

The Major catches his punch and throws him across the small clearing.

The Golomite teleports in front of the Major and attempts to stab him, but he grabs the Golomite's hand before it can penetrate. The Golomite tries to teleport away but because of the Mech's abilities he can't.

The Major hits the Golomite several times, breaking his gasmask. The Major is interrupted by a couple blaster shots hitting his energy shield. He turns around to face the attacker.

Casey stands with a look of surprise to see the Major.

"Shane?" She says as she lowers her pistol.

"There she is." He says in a hopeful but creepy tone while letting go of the Golomite. Casey hesitates and then quickly continues shooting her pistols. Shane holds up his Mech arm to block his face then uses his other hand to a fire lime green energy beam at Casey. She drops her pistols and uses the gloves to absorb the energy. She fires it right back at him, but he dodges it by boosting using the mini thrusters on the back of the Mech suit.

His left Mech arm turns into an SMG. He opens fire, but a purple void opens up behind him and the earth beneath him lifts him into the portal. Shane is spat out from the sky to the ground from a different portal.

He slowly gets up. Two of Ethereal's arrows hit the Mech suit in one of the knees causing it to lock up. Shane presses one of his fists firmly into the ground, the Mech suit reroutes energy into the dirt. The dirt and rocks begin to rise up around him then drop quickly. An earthquake follows. Casey pulls out her shotgun, but the quake stops her from moving forward. Stacey, Demi, Angel, Ethereal, Fade and Ayeka rally around Casey's side. Four large metal tentacles come out of the ground and protectively surround Shane on four sides.

Ayeka teleports and picks up both her brother Boroc and Nikki before the broken up land consumes them. Ayeka leaves them on a stable piece of land. Boroc grabs her wrist before she tries to take off.

"We must leave." He says in his native tongue.

"No, we must help them." Ayeka says as she rips her hand away.

"Why?" Boroc says wheezing through his broken mask.

"Because we need to trust people again and she can help us." Ayeka says flicking the CPU chip that Casey gave her to Boroc before she teleports back to Casey's side. "That pussy bitch would use the Arcane project." Stacey says factiously getting her shotgun ready. The Arcane project is a black op project that was supposed to be scrapped. The fifteen-foot tall tentacles are attached to a circular metal pad underneath Shane. They protect the user from any harm. The plate underneath generates a shield if needed.

The four mechanical arms stop spinning and an energy shield generates from the plate. The tentacles' tips bend and fire highly intense red lasers down at Casey and her fellowship. They spread out dodging the lasers and Shane's sub machine gun shots. Ayeka goes in first, teleporting in between lasers and bullets. Once she is close enough to grab Shane, an electrical surge comes from the plate stopping her in her tracks. Ayeka manages to grab a small metal stick from her belt. She jumps at him with the stick and plants it on his shield. The stick releases an electrical surge that shuts down the energy shield but electrocutes her in the process, temporarily shutting down Ayeka's suit. Her body falls over.

Casey and Stacey are sneaking cover behind a couple trees; the lasers disintegrate the roots and tops of trees.

Angel opens a portal for Demi.

He jumps through with his rapier and ends up on top of one of the mechanical arms. Demi stabs it a couple times; it shuts off with a small explosion. Demi tries to jump away.

Shane fires a forcing wave from his Mech suit's wrist shooting Demi into the forest. Ethereal runs at Shane firing rounds but the tentacles block all of them. She lights up her sword and continues to charge at him.

Shane presses a button on his wrist, a small turret activates on the back of the mech. It fires a tank size bullet that explodes into a net and pins Ethereal to a tree. She screams as the electrocution surges through her body until she passes out. The net holds her body up to the tree.

Fade and Angel run at Shane, once Casey and Stacey begin firing at him to cover them. Angel opens a portal and jumps into it.

He comes out above Shane and attempts to strike him, but is stopped by two of the three mechanical arms. His fist makes contact with the tentacles. but doesn't make a dent. One of the arms wraps around Angel and rips him away from Shane. Angel fires a purple fire beam from one of his hands at another tentacle.

Fade sprints and kicks Shane in the face with both feet. Shane stumbles back, but quickly recovers and tries to punch him. Fade dodges, it and uses his tail to balance him from falling back completely. Shane tries again. Fade dodges then climbs on Shane's back. He pulls out a small dagger and stabs the Mech suit a couple of times.

Shane tries to grab him off his back, while Boroc teleports behind Shane, picks up Ayeka and teleports away from the battlefield.

The other two lasers focus fire on Casey, who is running away, so Staccy can shoot the tentacles with her high-powered sniper. She fires a couple of shot destroying one. Angel's eyes and hands glow as the tentacle is flailing him around.

The ground begins to shake as Casey runs toward the Arcane struggle. Suddenly, the ground underneath Shane explodes, destroying the Arcane plate and shutting off the lasers. Two more explosions send Shane flying forward as he detaches himself from the Mech suit. One last explosion sends Fade flying far out into the forest. Angel is blown away but still restrained by the tentacle. The force from explosion bends the trees back and flings Casey away into one tree knocking her out.

A huge dragon made of purple fire emerges out of the explosive mess for about ten seconds then dissipates. Debris continues to fall from the explosion.

The battlefield is covered in smoke with blazing trees adding to the haze. Stacey rises up first. She manages to push a very heavy tree that has barricaded her in. The ringing in her ear from the explosion is infuriating and obnoxious. She squints to see through the smoky battlefield for Casey.

A groan comes from the distance. Stacey follows the sound and takes out her pistol. She coughs as she makes her way through the thick smog. Stacey takes a partial facemask from under her cloak and puts it on. It covers her nose and mouth allowing her to breath easy.

As Stacey gets closer to the sound, she sees a bag on the ground. Sensing danger, she turns around, but Shane tackles her, before she can get a shot off. They struggle on the ground. Shane throws her pistol away and punches her twice. He stabs Stacey's right leg with a dagger. She screams and retaliates using her left arm to disarm him. She dislocates his shoulder.

He screams in pain kicking her away. She falls back and scrambles to get her pistol. She picks it up and aims, but Shane is gone.

Stacey aims in different directions, blinded by the smoke. She touches the top part of her ear and a visor materializes in front of her eyes. The visor aligns perfectly with the facemask allowing her to have Thermal, X-ray and Ultraviolet vision. She gets up still aiming the pistol.

"Why are you even helping her?" Shane's voice radiates through the smog. She can't pin point his location, but she continues to point the gun in any direction.

"You're in over your head, Maze." Shane says from the smoke.

Stacey pulls out another pistol while walking and constantly turning around.

"I know you strongly believe what you're doing is right, but you will fail and her death will always be on your conscious." Stacey steps over pieces of debris keeping her cool.

"Come on out, you pussy." Stacey says trying to antagonize him.

"Does Casey know?" Shane's voice echoes throughout the area.

"Know what?" Stacey asks as she continues to back up.

"Where you really come from." The voice is behind her.

She stops, but before she can spin around, Shane emerges from the smoke. He punches her twice causing the half mask to fall off and she drops a pistol. She punches back twice, but Shane counters and puts her into a submissive hold. She breaks away for a second, but he gains control again when he takes out a silver scarf and pulls it over Stacey's face blocking her vision and airflow. He kicks the back of her knee causing her to fall. He pulls tightly stopping any possible airflow and to keep her from tearing it. She struggles.

"This is not your universe." He says pulling tighter; her resistance weakens as she runs out of air.

"If you couldn't save your own universe what makes you think you could save this one?" He continues. Stacey's hands drop and Shane gets ready to finish her off when an energy blast hits him in the back. The shot breaks two of his ribs. He lets go and falls over. Stacey gags and coughs gasping for air. Casey approaches slowly, He jumps up and lights an energy blade.

"Tell me something Casey, why did you kill him? After everything he did for you."

"I didn't kill him." She says pacing cautiously. Shane kicks Stacey in the ribs knocking her down. Casey's gloves light up firing a blast that destroys his sword, right out of his hand. She runs and punches him hard across the face. He tries to retaliate, but Casey has always been better at hand-to-hand combat. She blocks his hands easily and elbows his face. He stumbles back, but manages to grab her and put her in a tight headlock.

"Maybe you killed him because you felt he betrayed you, about your mother."

"I did not kill him." She mumbles as she struggles to get out of his hold.

"You killed a good man, and now you are going to get everyone else killed, your friends, your sister."

Boroc reactivates Ayeka's body, Demi comes stumbling out of the forest. Nikki slowly wakes up while Ethereal cuts through the net and falls to the ground.

"They will all die and your failure will consume you."

Casey looks down at Stacey. Trying to kill Stacey was enough excuse to put him in the ground and maybe rip his fucking guts out.

"I DIDN'T FUCKING KILL HIM!" Casey yells.

She boosts both of them into a tree. She elbows his ribs then his face to get out of his hold. She rolls away from him and picks up Stacey's pistol. He pulls out another sword, but Casey already has the drop on him. He stops and waits for her to pull the trigger.

"Are you really going to let your entire race die for these freaks?" Shane asks as he readies himself to attack.

"I'm trying to save every race you idiot!" Casey yells.

"Why bother? Once everyone else sees what's coming, there will be no point." Shane says.

"It's at least worth trying!" Casey yells.

Shane flips his sword one more time

"Don't make me kill you Shane."

"You will never make it to Masaton." He says.

"What? How do you know where I'm going?" Casey asks right before he rushes her. He tries to stab her, but they struggle and fall to the ground. Shane is on top pushing the blade closer to Casey's face, She holds it far enough away, just enough to move the pistol on him.

"You don't have what it takes." Shane says pushing the blade closer.

Casey knows he is not going to quit, so fuck it.

"Fuck you, Shane." She whispers as she fires a shot through his right eye socket.

The blood showers her face. She pushes the body off, stands up and puts six more shots into to him. Casey drops Stacey's pistol and begins shaking. She looks at Shane's bloodied corpse and instantly vomits. She is light headed and weak in the knees. She crumbles over and vomits again, there isn't much the second time around. It's unbelievable, the death of Shane is something she wanted and hell he deserved it, but not for her to be the one to do it. Casey has never killed a human before; it is something most humans vowed not to do with so little population left. Casey screams and sobs as Stacey walks over to comfort her.

THE 82ND FLOOR

"MS. WILLIAMS! WE GOT TROUBLE, LOOKS LIKE THE REBEL Militia has finally caught up with us." Tiny yells over the com.

Casey doesn't listen; at first her thoughts are elsewhere. Killing aliens is easy, but humans, something that looks likes you in some similar way she thinks. Someone she once trusted, sure she wanted him to die, just not like this. The whole thing is a mess. Casey knew this was not going to look good. She looked innocent before, but now after what just happened, her chances were not looking good. Casey's sight blurs through her tears and her breathing slows.

She looks up from the dirt and sees a large vessel come out of a bright red portal high in the sky. She looks at the battlefield with wreckage everywhere and she sees Angel walking over with Demi and Boroc walking with Ayeka and Fade.

"Ms. Williams!" Tiny screams over the com. Things become clear for Casey.

"Hey Space Case, time to go." Stacey says trying to get Casey on her feet. Ethereal walks over with a very weak Nikki.

"Ms. Williams, I need you to get back here, you're the only one who has decent flying experience." Tiny continues to yell over the com.

Casey stands and begins walking back toward the ship. Everyone falls in step with her, but once they reach the edge of the battlefield Casey stops. She can hear trees breaking and falling behind her. She turns to see the very large snake that Tiny had lost. It has decided to come back as it slithers slowly into the battlefield.

"Give me a fucking break." Casey says right before Stacey pulls her to run. The snake begins to follow fast; everyone but Stacey and Casey casually walk up onto the ship. Angel walks on the ship,

"Where is Casey?" Tiny asks standing near the entrance,

"She should have been right behind us." Angel says. Tiny and Angel look outside the ship and see Stacey running with Casey as the snake slithers quickly after them.

"Oh fuck." Tiny says reaching for the door controls to close it. Angel looks over at her "Seriously?" he says.

"Look at that fucking thing!" Tiny yells, not feeling guilty at all. Angel shakes his head then uses his hand to open a void in front of Casey and Stacey. The void opens up in the main cabin of the ship. They jump through and the portal closes right after. The snake slams into the ship, without making a dent in it. Tiny runs into the main cabin.

"Ms. Williams, cockpit now!" She says grabbing Casey and dragging her to the cockpit. Stacey joins Nikki on the couch. Stacey rubs her fox ears. Nikki leans on her shoulder and begins to fall asleep. Casey trips as she walks into the roomy cockpit, with two seats, one facing the windshield and the other facing a wall of holograms. Tiny pushes her in further and closes the hatch to the cockpit.

"You take the seat up front and I will be the co-pilot. Between the two of us we should be able to get out of here." Tiny says taking her seat. Casey sits in the cockpit chair. She finds it to be comfortable in spite of the stiffness. The chair moves closer to the console. There is a strange steering wheel in the center and two analog sticks with buttons on either side. Holograms of two maps and the ship appear behind the steering wheel.

"Okay, so I should be able to make the flight system easier for you.

Let's start by at least getting it off the ground.

Try pressing the two green buttons on the left side." Tiny explains.

"Wait, your left or mine?" Casey asks.

"What? It's the same left you idiot!" Tiny yells.

"You know your words hurt more than you think and it's not getting this ship any closer to being off the ground." Casey responds.

Tiny sighs and calmly says.

"Casey press the only two green buttons over there, please."

Casey presses both buttons and the ship disengages the landing system and begins hovering. The snake scurries away once the ship starts up.

"Okay now, what you want to do is pull back on the steering wheel, nice and easy, but you want to be holding down both…" Tiny gets flung out of the chair before she can finish her instruction.

The ship blasts forward through the forest at a diagonal angle. Everyone in the main cabin is at the same angle, however Demi is flung across the room. Tiny climbs back to her seat and reaches for a lever next to Casey and pulls it down locking it into place. The main cabin returns to a more normal angel, as the ship continues to fly on its side.

"You have to hold down the two buttons on the steering wheel to ascend!" Tiny yells. The trees are blown apart as the ship blasts through them. Casey holds the two buttons down and the ship does a strange flip that sends the ship flying up quickly and past the Rebel vessel just scrapping a little bit of the paint job off of it as it blasts straight into space.

"Holy shit that was close." Casey says,

"Jo is going to be really pissed about the paint." Tiny says as she inspects the damage in a hologram.

"Okay, so how do we set a course for Ohyron?" Casey asks looking over the entire console for the magic button that solves all problems.

"Use the map behind the steering wheel, pick the place you want to go and the ship should do the rest.

"Wait seriously? Why couldn't you have flown the ship then?"

"Because the ship uses a duel calibration system, meaning there has to be two people in this cockpit. Not only that, it's coded to your DNA for some fucked up reason! That allows you to access everything, up until now we have just been accessing the basic functions." Tiny explains as she works.

Casey spins the hologram of the galaxy around, and then picks a planet toward the top half. The planet becomes enlarged the name OHYRON above it in big letters. Some facts about it like population, weather patterns and animal life display off to the side. Underneath the planet, there is a question

"Do you wish to travel to this place?" and under the question are two hologram buttons both in a different language, but green meaning yes and red meaning no, is the logical way of thinking. She pushes the green button and the ship's engine begins to light up along with the entire cockpit. The Phoenix blasts out into the vastness of space.

Just outside of Ohyron, the Guillotine awaits for the Phoenix to arrive. In the cargo hold of the ship, Stephanie is currently taking inventory on the ammunition and vehicles they have. Gussie runs up to her

"Commander there is a ship arriving! It's Heathrow sir." Stephanie walks quickly through the closest door.

She walks fast down the hallway while Gussie tries to keep up.

"Sir, what are we going to do?"

"Just put Heathrow up on the helm." Stephanie says walking onto the bridge and taking a seat in her chair. A hologram screen pops up with Heathrow's ugly robot mug.

"General." Stephanie says with a calm smile on her face.

"Where are they, Williams?" He asks firmly.

"They haven't arrived yet, but just so we are clear, I will be handling this."

"No! You are out of time and I will be taking over. No offense Ms. Williams, but you are too close to this." Heathrow says.

"General, it would be advisable for me to take the lead on this. I have her trust and you do not. There is no need to fight." Stephanie says trying to placate to him. Heathrow looks off to the side for a moment, then back at Stephanie.

"Fine, gain her trust, invite her in and hand her over to me."

"Copy that." Stephanie says closing out the call.

She uses the panel on the chair to open a wide broadcast across the ship.

"Alright everyone listen up! This is the time where we find out where your loyalties lie. We are about to make contact with The Phoenix, the rogue ship that had escaped Terra. They will be docking with us for a short time, because Heathrow wants to take them. But, we will not be handing them over! This is my call. Those of you who do not wish to follow my orders. You may leave the ship with no tarnish to your record the moment the Phoenix is in the clear. As for the rest of you, bring the ship to combat ready." She ends the broadcast and turns to Gussie,

"I need you to send a message." Stephanie whispers to her.

Gussie smiles and begins to work on her pad.

The Phoenix continues through hyperspace, Casey looks around the cockpit. There are many different switches and lights up above the steering wheel.

"Casey, I'm sorry for what happened back there."

"Alliance soldiers are taught to deal with death." She replies automatically.

"That doesn't mean you have to be okay with it." Tiny says looking toward her.

"I never said I was okay with it." Casey says focusing on the controls of the ship.

"I need to know Casey, do you even plan on getting Trea and Jo back?"

Casey turns to Tiny

"I promise you Tiny, we will get them back."

Tiny looks into Casey's eyes and sees determination, anger and pain.

"Now, is there anyway to put this on auto pilot?" Casey asks looking over the controls.

"Yeah I can do it. You can leave the cockpit, but the ship will make a sound when we are coming out of warp and the auto pilot will turn off, so make sure to come back before that happens." Tiny says.

"Understood." Casey says getting up and walking out of the cockpit.

She walks into the main room,

"So, tell me about your super human left arm." Casey says walking into the room with her hands in her jacket pockets.

Stacey stands up leaving Nikki to curl up on the couch.

"Casey, I need you to relax and open up your mind a bit, because this going to sound crazy."

"Stacey, look around you. I'm pretty sure I can handle it." Casey says.

Tiny walks past Casey over to Boroc.

She examines his mask, and then reaches for a small crate full of tools and miscellaneous items.

"Look Casey, the universe is a very difficult thing to understand."

"Oh and you know all it's secrets now?" Casey asks sarcastically

Stacey smiles then walks up to Casey and puts her hand on her wrist.

"I promise you I will tell you everything, but I can't right now. You have too much going on and I'm not trying to stress you out. Once everything is finished, then I will answer everything."

Casey looks at Stacey, she knew she meant well, but something was wrong and she wasn't going say anything, if she didn't have to. It became clear now to Casey why Stacey looked stressed and tired. This is not the Stacey she knows. Tiny manages to create a makeshift replacement filter for Boroc's mask and installs it. A beeping sound goes off in the room and a red light flashes.

"That's the cockpit, we are about to come out of hyperspace." Tiny says finishing up on Boroc's mask. Casey walks back to the cockpit with Tiny following close behind. The cockpit doors close once Casey and Tiny sit down.

"Casey hit the two switches to your left." Tiny says flipping fast through holograms. Casey hits the switches, and then holds on to the steering wheel.

"Okay here we go."

The Phoenix drops out of warp into the middle of a very messy conflict.

The Guillotine and the Halberd are currently fighting against a small fleet of medium sized heavily armored black and red ships. There are many small fighter ships on both sides scrambling around.

"Oh fuck!" Casey says firmly holding onto the steering wheel.

The Phoenix flies slowly over toward the battle.

On board the Guillotine, Stephanie keeps a calm composure while commanding her crew in the heat of battle.

"Commander, the Phoenix just arrived!" Gussie yells out while working at one of the consoles.

"Open up a channel to them." Stephanie says moving holograms that appear above the railing she is standing at. A hologram of Casey appears.

"Hey buddy! Long time no see!" She says calmly.

"Casey, you need to dock with us before Heathrow decides to tractor beam you in." Stephanie demands.

"Yeah sure, do you mind telling me who the hell you are fighting?"

"The Defiant Unknown." Tiny interrupts staring out the cockpit windshield.

A loud beep sound comes from Tiny's console.

"Commander I'm detecting another ship!" Gussie yells to Stephanie.

A massive vessel matching the look of the smaller ships comes out of a green portal that opens up next to the Phoenix; Casey to flies below it. The ship is long and three times the size of the Guillotine. The Phoenix looks like a small flying under the vessel. Two long towers stick out from the backside holding a perpetual black sun between them. Banners that bare the red hand of the Defiant Unknown are all over the ship.

"Who are the Defiant Unknown?" Casey asks as she flies below the ship.

"They are the last remaining army of the Groutarians, mixed with renegade Nexus warriors, they are lead by the Nexus zealot, Malak, the only Nexus to have defied the Nexus King and the high council. This huge thing we are flying under is his ship

'The Marauder.'" Tiny says a little worried.

The Phoenix finally finishes passing under the vessel. The underside has three small ship size triangles that are connected to the ship with a gravitational force. The Phoenix flies between two of them slowly.

"So, why are they here?" Casey asks.

"Doesn't matter, now get your ass over here!" Stephanie commands closing the channel. Casey flies the ship past the side of the Marauder and straight to the Guillotine. The Marauder doesn't attempt anything instead it remains stationary. The Phoenix approaches a docking bay and slowly passes through the aquamarine force field. Once it touches down, the hatch opens and Nikki pops her head out first. There are at least eighty soldiers lined up and unarmed.

"Oh a ceremony!" Nikki yells excitedly and attempts to run out of the ship only to be pulled back into the darkness of the ship by her tail. Casey walks out on to the Guillotine and in between the two rows of soldiers. At about the half way point Gussie and Stephanie walk out to meet her. Casey stops and salutes.

"Don't you dare! " Stephanie says.

"I'm only showing respect." Casey says.

"Really? How about you tell me what fuck is going on and whose blood is that?" Stephanie interrogates. Casey completely forgot she still has Shane's blood on her face.

"Look I get that you're mad, but I have been busy you know fighting for my life and trying to save the galaxy."

"Oh is that what you're doing? Well then, please continue to live in denial."

Casey rolls her eyes

"Don't roll your eyes at me! What happened with Sullivan?" Stephanie says with more rage in her voice.

"He gave me a strange key, told me to collect everyone and save Dr. Teyach from the Rebel Militia on Masaton." Casey says.

Stephanie is dumb struck.

"Casey, you need to realize the gravity of your situation. Now is not the time for your cute little games."

"I'm telling you the truth!"

"Oh bullshit, Casey! You ran away and didn't even try to talk to anyone."

"They accused me of killing the president, you know as well as I do, that the Alliance does not take prisoners when that happens."

"Casey listen to me, you need to take those people home and turn yourself in, so they can hear your side of the story." Stephanie says admonishing her.

"Home? That's rich! Most of them are homeless. Even the king of the Groutarians was living in a filthy arena with a bunch of dirty soldiers!"

"Casey that's not the point! Wait king?" Stephanie asks.

"Look, even if I wanted to take them back, I can't.

I made some promises that I have to keep and don't use the Mom tone with me, I'm not a kid anymore."

"Then quit acting like a child and own up to your actions!"

"You know what's shitty? Keep telling me that you care and yet you don't believe me! Ever since mom died, you have been treating me different, you care but you want to control my every move!" Casey yells.

"Can you blame me after what happened to you? Stacey and I both had to put up with your sulking depression and help you do everything! As soon as you got the boots, you blew us off and all you wanted was to get back out there.

I'm not going to loose you again!" Stephanie yells with teary eyes not caring what her soldiers might think.

Casey remains silent.

"That's why you weren't able to leave Terra, because I begged them to keep you on the station." Stephanie finishes.

Casey's sullen face changes to rage.

"You bitch!" Casey yells back at her.

Stephanie smacks Casey across the face and pulls her away from the gaze of the soldiers to a near by hallway.

On board the Phoenix, Nikki is dancing like a professional to a song from Stacey's music collection that is being played on the ship loud enough for the soldiers lined up outside to hear. Stacey ignores her and looks at the projector watching the Defiant Unknown ships leave slowly one small group after another except the Marauder.

"Why are they leaving?" she asks.

"It is strange, they have never just shown up and then just left, especially, without killing anyone and the Halberd didn't even lose shields, it is as almost if they were…" Rayza says.

"A distraction." Stacey says finishing for her.

In the small hallway away from the music and the soldiers,

"Why is the Defiant Unknown here?" Casey asks.

Stephanie sighs.

"The leader owed me a favor and I used it to get to you first." She says.

"You know the crazy Malak dude?" Casey asks.

"I saved his life before he was a crazy genocidal maniac okay! so don't judge me."

"So what? You just call in favors from the criminal side, Commander?" Casey asks mockingly.

"Sort of, besides you're one to talk picking up Angel and Nikki." Stephanie says. "How do you know them?" Casey asks.

"Everyone knows who they are! Dangerous and unpredictable!" Stephanie says exasperated.

"Yet, you just called in a favor from a homicidal maniac to cover for me." Casey says shaking her head as she takes a couple steps back.

"Casey, please just come back to Terra with me and we can figure out what's going on."

"I can't do that Steph, I gave him my word that I would save the doctor. Besides I wouldn't be literally standing right now, if it wasn't for Teyach." She says pointing down at her boots.

"Casey something about this isn't right, you have to see that." Stephanie pleads as she puts both her hands on Casey's shoulders.

"Not one thing about this entire trip has gone the way I thought it might. But even with all the ups and downs we have already had, I'm still going to see this through to the end. I'm sorry Stephanie, but I promise I will come back when everything is done." Casey says.

They walk out of the hallway to see that all the soldiers, Stacey, Angel, Ethereal and Hyda have formed a dancing circle around Nikki and Rayza in the middle dancing with two other soldiers, who are mediocre at best. Casey runs over to the circle and breaks it up quickly. Stacey turns the music off.

"Go on get out of here!" Casey says to the soldiers as she pushing Nikki toward the Phoenix. The soldiers collectively say, "awe" and walk back to their posts.

Casey throws Nikki back on to the ship, as the others walk on board.

"Tiny get the ship ready." Casey says.

She turns to wave to Stephanie. Stephanie waves back. Casey closes the hatch.

The Phoenix powers up and then slowly falls out of the Guillotine's hanger bay.

"The Marauder is still here, I wonder why." Tiny says watching the ship like a hawk as the Phoenix dives toward the planet.

"They will leave shortly, I'm sure. Regardless, it's not our concern at the moment." Casey says. The Phoenix glides until it reaches the orbit of Ohyron. Surrounding the orbit of Ohyron are several thin metallic wires with red, green and blue lights. Casey answers a hailing call from the planet

"Welcome to Ohyron, planet of fantastic endeavors." A woman says unenthusiastically.

"Follow the red dots and stay with in the line. Once you reach the inner checkpoint, head to AL's mega parking, Thank you and have a splendid time." The monotone voice says cutting out the line quickly.

"She sounded like she loves her job." Casey says sarcastically while lowering the altitude on the ship. The Phoenix flies in the line with red dots down into the atmosphere of the planet. Sixty percent of the planet is a city called Pyron. It's the largest city in the whole galaxy considering the planet is one of the largest in the galaxy. Casey looks in awe as she flies the ship down to the inner checkpoint above the city. The sight is something to be blown away by. There are skyscrapers and central plazas on different levels. Part of the city looked to be under ground, but still received sunlight and artificial air. Many light streets and many pedestrian paths are parallel from each other. There are several parks and suburban areas, some even in the heart of the city. There is even an ocean within the city borders, but still further away from the main land, of course. The size of the city alone is like all seven continents on Earth combined, three times over.

"The weather patterns on this planet are what make it even more unique. Snow, heat waves, freak lightning storms, but nothing affects the city due to the very powerful shield tech." Tiny explains as Casey looks up at the shield.

"There are races here from other galaxies! It's the most peaceful, respected city in the whole galaxy. Well, peaceful as in no wars can be waged on the surface. People still get mugged and killed in the lower levels though." Tiny says opening a channel to accept a call from the planet.

"Welcome Newcomer! You've been upgraded to the Drax Estate parking structure. Please follow the gold lights once you pass the inner checkpoint." The transmission cuts out.

"What the fuck!" Tiny yells,

"What? What's going on?" Casey asks looking around.

"Dexter, fucking Drax!"

"Who is Dexter Drax?"

"Are you serious right now? Dexter Drax is like the third most rich and famous human in the galaxy! Most of the weaponry we all use now a days comes from his manufacturing company." Tiny explains.

"How have you never heard of him? Doesn't the Galactic Alliance have a contract with him?" She asks.

"No, Craxton holds the contract and my rifle was made by Dr. Teyach." Casey replies.

"Craxton is an asshole. He only cares about money. Dexter cares about the scientific discovery of annihilating anything into oblivion." Tiny says biting her bottom lip.

"Sounds like you have a bit a crush." Casey teases her.

The Phoenix flies along the gold line. It directs them into the city and past a couple tall skyscrapers. The ship slows down as it pulls into a humongous wall that not only serves as the generator for the shield, but the docking bay for the entire city. Drax owned half of the docking bay wall, so therefore he owned half of the city. His half is prime location, and the half of the city not fully developed yet. Buildings and streets are still being built. The Phoenix is now being guided into the very spacious dock. The docking bay hatch closes once the Phoenix touches down. The entire group gets off the ship and approaches big bronze double doors. As they walk up, two lovely dressed Nexus women open up the doors.

Casey leads them through the doors with Stacey who takes her by the arm;

Tiny follows quickly with Demi talking to Ethereal.

Angel and Hyda are showing off their weapons to each other as they pass through the doors.

Ayeka and Boroc walk together in silence, in front of Gorog and Fade who are talking in Groutarian.

Finally, Nikki and Rayza looking at a new fashion line on a holopad.

A few paces in and they meet up with a very sharply dressed handsome man.

"Look who it is! The Unusual Alliance!" The man yells and laughs as he walks toward Casey and her group.

"I am Dexter Drax and I personally wanted to greet you and allow us to be friends. And from now on, you are welcome to use my docking stations as much as you like, for free!" He says enthusiastically

"Well uh, thank you?" Casey says caught off guard.

He has strong a southern Earth accent or a Terekon Australian accent; Casey was never good with accents. His brown eyes complimented his feathered brown hair that sits elegantly. He is ruggedly handsome with an inviting smile. He looks like he could handle himself in a fight, but only against another human.

"Mr. Drax sir, I would like to discuss some ship maintenance and possible weaponry ideas." Tiny says walking up to Dexter offering him a holopad of schematics.

Dexter flips through a couple of files on the pad.

"If I may, what is your name, darling?" He asks,

"My name is Tiny, Mr. Drax."

"Well Tiny, call me Dexter and when you are ready lets get together for some lunch and I can help you with whatever you need."

"Seriously?" Tiny says excitedly and almost faints but Ethereal catches her.

Dexter looks over to Casey and takes her hand. His hand is warm; He stares into Casey's eyes with his purple eyes.

"Casey I want you to know, if there is anything you and your company need, it's on me. Weapons, ammo, maybe a good shower or two, because you all smell worse than a couple of onions wrapped in shit." Casey looks back at her crew, some have dirty faces others have blood on their clothes. Not to mention the blood on her.

"Yes! Please! But, may I ask why you are doing this?" Casey asks.

"You guys are changing the universe banning together to fight the evils and injustices!" He says excitedly.

"Well, not really, but okay." Casey responds.

"Look at it this way, there are three things that make my capitalistic dreams come true, money, energy and ideas. Now, the energy you and your companions are giving off is teeming with ideas that will earn me a whole lot of money." Dexter says.

"Is that so? Why do I get the feeling I'm being bought?" Casey asks.

"Oh heavens no, I believe in ya'lls' goal and strictly a business man and would only need you to test some weapons, maybe a photo to promote business, no contracts and no funny business!" He says.

"Alright Dexter, I'm in no shape to argue or complain." Casey says.

"Regardless, this will be lucrative for me either way this goes. So, what can I do for you and your team, Ms. Williams?" Dexter asks.

"Food!" Rayza yells.

"A shower would be nice." Casey says.

"Why of course, right this way! Sarah, darling, take them to the suits on the fourth floor!" Dexter says pointing them to the way of the elevator.

Sarah is one of the nexus babes he had with him leads them over to the large elevator.

"Miss Williams I will be in touch once you and your crew have had time to relax." Dexter says as they leave.

The elevator that takes them down to a hotel built into the hanger. The doors open to the lobby. Many shops and bars surround both sides of the receptionist desk with two twisted gold staircases and the two sets of elevators behind the stairs.

Sarah leads Casey and her crew to the front desk. People in the lobby look at the Unusual Alliance in disgust and keep their distance as they walk up to the desk behind Sarah.

"Hi I need the Premium Suite, should be reserved for Mr. Drax." Sarah says as she pulls a small holographic card from her small ammo pouch and hands it to the front desk R.A.I.S. The R.A.I.S scans the card then hands it back along with a small keycard. "Take the elevator behind us, the room is ready." The front desk clerk says.

"Thank you." Sarah says then signals for Casey and her company to follow her to the elevator. Everyone boards it except for Sarah, she hands Casey the keycard for the room and waves goodbye as the door closes.

They exit the elevator into a small hallway with one pair of double doors. Casey uses the keycard until a beep goes off and the doors open into the room. As they enter the suite, they notice the living room area is extremely large and the view of the city is incredible. Casey walks over to the window to get a better look.

"Pyron is an amazing city, crime never goes above 25%, the security is tight but not over ruling, just enough to keep the peace." Rayza says standing next to Casey.

Casey looks down and sees a family having fun in a park. She realizes there is no way she could live comfortably after everything that has happened. She couldn't help but feel shitty and her eyes tear up. Rayza notices her eyes.

"You know business on bounties can not be exchanged, or even conducted here, you could say Pyron gives criminals a second chance provided they behave of course." Casey looks at Rayza and smiles, Rayza smiles back.

"Thank you Rayza." Casey says wiping her eyes.

"You're welcome Ms. Williams." Rayza says and walks away to another room.

Casey continues to stare out the window.

The Marauder flies over Ohyron slowly, then releases a small vessel that flies down to the planet. The Marauder then opens a wormhole and disappears into the black of space. The Halberd turns the ship to face the planet. General Heathrow opens a channel to Stephanie.

"Where are they, Williams?" He asks nastily.

"Not sure General, We were finding out where the Defiant Unknown disappeared off to." She responds.

"Don't give me that! I know you helped them get to the planet! We will send a shore party to find her and take her by any means necessary."

"Well General, I wish you luck! I will return to Omicron, incase the Defiant Unknown decides to attack Terra." Stephanie calmly says and closes out the channel quickly.

"Take us home cadet."

"Yes sir." The pilot responds. The Guillotine opens a portal and leaves Ohyron space as the Halberd releases two small carrier ships down to the planet.

The premium suite of the hotel is a massive room, which can hold up to thirty people easily. Nikki, Ethereal, Hyda, Rayza, Gorog, Demi, Boroc and Ayeka are all hanging out on different sofas and chairs after a shower and fresh change of clothes from the materializer in the corner. This device can literally materializes any outfit you want, if you have the coin of course. Their outfits are more or less the same, with slightly different color choices. Angel walks into the living room smoking a cigar, filled with, an alien type of weed. Stacey walks past him with a towel on her head and throws up a mini metal ball that sucks the smoke from his cigar into it. Angel puffs twice and the metal ball sucks it up instantly.

Stacey relaxes on the couch next to Rayza.

"You know there is quite a lot of us now." Nikki says looking over at Gorog who is manicuring his nails with a towel wrapped on his baldhead.

"Anyway, we have to think about getting a bigger ship, because of the nutty professor over here." She continues while staring at Gorog. Casey walks out of one of the rooms, hair still wet and a different set of under aero armor, with red energy strips embedded in the pants and sleeves of the shirt instead of the blue she started with.

She falls on a small ottoman and letting her legs dangle and her hair hang over the edge.

"A bigger ship is out of the question. The ship, what we have now, is the most advanced, and besides there is no time. It seems the Marauder has sent a ship to the surface along with the Alliance." Tiny explains as she works on a small rifle. The visor she is wearing is feeding her the information. Stacey gets up and walks over to one of the rooms.

"There are way too many things going on." Casey mumbles from her ottoman.

"Too many things? The story would be boring and plain if it only had one or two things going on. I say the more the merrier! Lets add more characters to this not at all confusing story!" Nikki says flying on her back eating a strange looking apple. "You were just saying how crowded it's becoming." Tiny adds.

"Oh that was weeks ago!" Nikki replies.

"It was thirty seconds ago." Casey mumbles again.

"Pishposh! Now get a move on Lieutenant! There is no time to waste!" Nikki says landing down quick.

She tosses the fruit behind her and pulling the towel off Gorog's head.

She walks over to Casey and lifts up her head with telekinesis.

"I'm fucking tired can't we take a break?" Casey says with hair in front of her face. "We just did." Nikki says while using her powers to stand Casey up.

"I hate you." Casey says while being suspended in the air.

Nikki smiles, letting her down and removing the moisture from Casey's hair, it's completely dry and ready.

"You were no help with the snakes by the way!" Casey yells.

"Bro, they were snakes. And like big ones too." Nikki says.

Stacey walks out armed up and ready.

"Alright I'm going to pick up some ammo and gadgets, meet up once you get the contact?" Stacey asks Casey who is tying her hair up and arming herself.

"Okay, who wants to go on a field trip?"

"I wouldn't mind stretching my legs." Hyda says standing up.

"I will join, I could use a drink." Demi says.

"Count me in, I got someone I have to pick something up from in a shop near by." Rayza says going over some emails with her wristband projecting the holograms.

"I will go as well." Ethereal says respectfully with her arms behind her back.

Casey gives her a slight nod and she nods back.

"Okay Tiny, let me know the minute the ship is ready." Casey says picking her rifle and jacket off of a pool table in the den and walking to the door where Ethereal and Rayza are waiting.

"Will do." Tiny replies as they all leave the room.

Stacey leaves with them, but separates once they make it outside the building.

Outside the hotel building there are many taxi services waiting. Casey only glances quickly at them, but is stuck in amazement by the tall skyscrapers and many different layered light roads.

"So where are we headed?" Demi asks looking around.

"Club Vixen." Casey says taking steps toward a directory kiosk. She types in the name and the directory's map pans out and shows the direction to the location and an icon appears where she is. The directory then uploads the schematic to Casey's wrist.

"Let's move." Casey says leading them to a respectable taxi driver.

They hop in the vehicle and it lifts off the ground and blasts up quickly. The driver is an Ogre, not like he is grotesque, but he is an Ogre, just fat and green with fangs, so yes, on second thought, he is grotesque. His race is mainly scattered near the outer rim. Ogres have a tendency to be very talkative at least that is the case with their driver.

"Fuck! He won't shut up!" Rayza yells in the back seat crammed with Ethereal, Hyda and Demi.

"At least, he is talking in his language." Casey says relaxed in her seat.

"That doesn't make it any better." Rayza replies.

"Why?" Hyda asks.

"Because it sounds like a gargling walrus." Rayza explains.

"How do you know what a walrus is?" Casey asks.

"Keep up, Williams." Rayza says.

Casey stares out the window looking at all the buildings and hologram advertisements gliding across them as the taxi speeds through the traffic on the light road. There are hundreds of small shops along the sides of the street and a sizable park behind them with several trees. The scene quickly changes as the taxi barrels down a light road tube, a tunnel where the vehicles can traverse on any side of the tunnel including the ceiling. The driver keeps it simple and stays on the bottom. When they emerge, the scenery is more of a recreational area. This particular area is known as the M.W. Gutter.

The taxi takes a left, then a right, and two more lefts before arriving outside the club. The opening to the club has a red glow coming from its elongated entrance and is guarded by two sharply dressed Groutarians.

"Let me do the talking. I'm kind of a big deal here in the Milky Way Gutter." Rayza says taking the lead.

"Hey guys! These ones are with me, if you don't mind." Rayza says while strolling past, but the Groutarians stop her. Ethereal pulls down the sleeve of her arm to show the crystal bracelet with a purple gem that is on her wrist.

The Groutarians back off and let them pass.

"So much for being a 'big deal'." Ethereal says.

"So what the fuck was that?" Rayza asks following Ethereal and Casey quickly. "Being the Maiden's assistant has its perks." Ethereal says as they walk into the first floor of the club. The room is huge with 2 bars in the center, plenty of private rooms on both sides and a dance floor in between both. Ethereal walks straight to the bar with Demi, flashes the crystal to one of the bartenders. The bartender is a female Oakrin, a green octopus like creature with eight pairs of eyes. She slides down to Ethereal, hears her order and makes it at the same time with her tentacles. The bartender hands a fluorescent green drink in a martini glass to Ethereal and opens a beer for Demi. Ethereal leaves a generous tip, while Casey looks around the room. She decides to take a walk around on the dance floor to get a better look. As soon as she gets to the middle area between the two bars she overhears one of the bar tenders saying to bring another bottle to Vikara's room. Casey smiles. How easy things are sometimes she thinks. She follows the waitress with the bottle to room 808. Casey stops, her heart beats fast, could it be the red eye corrector on the other side?

She continues to hesitate as the waitress goes in. Okay it is weird, but perhaps a coincidence. It's not some conspiracy, or there isn't any danger. If there is, blow its fucking head off. After about forty-five seconds of this pep talk to herself, Casey pulls her rifle out and kicks the door open, not realizing how small the room is, of course. The door knocks the waitress over the small round table spilling the drinks on the three patrons.

"Oh shit, I'm so sorry I didn't mean… I didn't know how small the room was." Casey says frantically as the waitress gets up and runs out of the room.

"Um excuse me! Are you going to clean this shit up?" Vikara asks.

Casey watches the waitress run to tell the bartender.

"Hello!" Vikara says before Casey turns around quickly aiming the rifle right at Vikara's face. The two Nexus women on either side of her get scared and leave the room. The bartender signals for guards, Ethereal puts her drink down then steps in front of the guards showing the bracelet.

"Don't worry, we will be out of your hair soon." She says to them, they nod at her and leave.

"Better pull the trigger, you human sack of shit." Vikara says slowly moving to get up. "Kitara sends her regards, I'm here to get her shit." Casey says keeping the gun on her.

"Ha! She sent a human? What in the fuck are you going to do against Solarian slave traders?" Vikara says siting back and stirring the martini.

"Do you have the location or not?" Casey asks lowering her weapon.

"Do you even know what you are getting?"

"No, She said you would tell me, which turns out she was fucking lying about that too. So, why don't you tell me what I need to know? So I can go and you can continue drinking." Casey says now agitated with her.

"You will be picking up her boyfriend, Nessarac and he will be held within the cell block. I know what you are thinking not original, but it beats not knowing where he is. Also I don't have the coordinates, I never had time to meet Zeek."

Casey could tell she is lying or withholding. When Casey was a detective a couple years before the Galactic Alliance. There was two ways to go about it, bad cop or bad cop. Casey sighs putting her rifle on her back. She punches Vikara in the face, then grabs her by the head and slams her into the table. Casey tops it off by throwing her out of the room onto the dance floor. Vikara lifts herself up slowly; Casey walks up to her, grabs her head and puts a pistol to her throat.

"Where is Zeek?"

"New Craxton building, near Stratus district. Eighty second floor. I was going to meet him, but was told not too."

"What do you mean told not to?" Casey asks keeping the pistol on her.

"Kitara said to let you handle the meet with Zeek." Vikara says through bloody teeth. Casey let's her go and walks quickly through the crowd with Ethereal, Hyda and Rayza following her out of the building.

"What's going on? Did you get the coordinates?" Rayza asks,

"No, Kitara told her to leave the meet up to me." Casey says while looking on the map for where the Craxton building might be.

"What?" Ethereal asks but is quickly connecting the dots.

"Trap." Hyda says.

"Yup." Casey says accessing her com from her wrist.

"Stacey, change of plans meet at new Craxton building near, Stratus district." "Understood. Almost done." Stacey responds.

"Ms. Williams, if it is a trap, maybe we should regroup first." Ethereal suggests.

"I think you're right but we don't have time. You think you can handle being the heavy hitter?" Casey asks checking her ammo.

"Uh, Ms. Williams I'm pretty sure I'm the heavy hitter." Rayza says.

"Yeah, right rat!" Hyda says hailing a cab.

"Fuck you." Rayza responds.

"Rayza, I need you to meet up with Stacey then meet up with us." Casey says.

"Ugh, fine, but save me some of the action." Rayza says.

A taxi pulls up to the sidewalk.

"Stratus district, don't be late 'heavy hitter.'"

Casey says teasing her before she gets in the front seat. Ethereal, Hyda and Demi get in the back. "Stratus district please." The driver grunts and the taxi flies off.

Somewhere in the Stratus district, Stacey is walking down the sidewalk looking up at the not finished sky scrapper across from the also not finished Craxton building. As she gets closer to the building, there are less and less people. Inside the building about three dozen Alliance troops are getting ready to begin an assault on the Craxton building. The Lieutenant in charge has a sniper on her back and all black armor with the letters "DC" in red on both shoulder plates. She wears a helmet to conceal her identity, but to also help with scanning wind ratio.

"Go down three levels and wait for my signal to breach." She says with a voice scrambler built in the helmet.

"Yes sir." One of the soldiers responds and signals the rest of the soldiers to move out. The Lieutenant begins to set up her sniper, as Stacey enters the building. Casey's Taxi touches down between both buildings.

Now for this next part it might be a little confusing, The Alliance is split up, but everything is happening **simultaneously**.

Casey, Hyda, Ethereal and Demi enter the Craxton building.

It is empty, no workers nothing.

They get on what seems to be the only working elevator.

Stacey runs up a staircase several flights quickly.

The elevator doors close slowly.

Stacey reaches the floor with the three-dozen Alliance troops.

"Stacey is dangerous." Tiny says gathering her things.

"Why do you say that?" Angel asks.

"R.A.I.S have a time anomaly sensors, we can see particles of matter and dark matter around objects that have moved through space and time.

And Stacey has that shit all over her, not to mention her extremely power-ful arm." Tiny says throwing shit around the room.

"Bio enhancers." Nikki says.

Stacey opens a hologram on her wrist, the word "Music" is at the top of the hologram.

"No, she came from some other timeline and she could destroy this one!" Tiny says.

The elevator begins ascending.

"Incorrect." Nikki says staring out the window.

"I know you out of all us can see it too." Tiny says walking toward her.

Nikki turns around

"She is from a different timeline or at the very least something close to it but she is not dangerous." Nikki corrects Tiny.

Stacey runs up behind one of the soldiers, jumps up on his back and stabs him in the throat. Blood spews out and the body falls. Stacey rolls for-ward, takes the same dagger and stabs another soldier under the arm and swings him around to block the incoming shots from two more soldiers.

The elevator passes the 5th floor.

"She's cunning, smart and vicious." Nikki says to Tiny.

Stacey pulls her pistol and shoots two more soldiers. The bullets from her pistol hit the soldiers in the face and explode on contact. Brain matter, eyeballs and blood fly across the room.

"She is here in our time, if I had to guess. Casey is dead in the future, which is her past, and she's here to prevent that from happening. Which is going to cause this timeline to change." Nikki explains to everyone in the suite.

Stacey flips the shot up solider onto four soldiers aiming at her. Stacey runs at three more soldiers dodging their fire easily.

Once in front of the soldiers, she shoots one of them in the leg, blows the brains out of the second one, then finishes off the wounded one with two more shots, one to the gut then head.

The third soldier tries to stab her, but she blocks his arm and shoots the soldier several times in the gut while pushing him into a support beam. Stacey turns around and shoots the four soldiers she knocked down.

One shot each head, so as not to waste bullets. She lets the body against the support beam fall to the side. Stacey hides behind the support beam from incoming fire from a couple more troops walking her way. She drops two small metal balls. They release a thick smoke giving her a perfect cloud cover, but of course the troops came prepared with Thermal goggles.

The elevator passes the 12th floor.

Casey sends a message to the crew.

The message reads, "It's a trap! Ha-ha! No seriously, it's a trap on the 82nd floor of the new Craxton building, Stratus district." Tiny, Angel and Nikki look at each other after reading the message.

"Time to go?" Nikki asks

"Yup." Tiny says as everyone grabs his or her stuff and head out the door of the suite. The smoke fills the whole floor and Stacey stays in cover. The troopers move in on her slowly. Stacey clenches her free hand, the unusually strong one. It glows blue and two soldiers push in closer only to see the blue light getting brighter. The blinding light disrupts the thermal goggles.

Stacey runs up and punches one of them hard enough to send him flying through two steel support beams.

"Holy fuck." The other soldier stutters in fear. Stacey puts the pistol in his face and pulls the trigger. Three more soldiers begin firing at her. Stacey punches the floor creating a barrier of vibrant blue electricity blocking the shots. Ten more troops join in the firing lighting up the barrier with each hit. Stacey remains calm and takes deep breaths.

The elevator passes the 32nd floor.

A taxi lands down between the two buildings in the Stratus district; Rayza exits and pays the driver. The taxi flies off just as Stacey pushes out more energy. The energy begins to shake the entire building. A massive wave of electrical energy sends thirteen soldiers flying out the windows and down to the street below. Rayza jumps out of the way of debris and bodies. She checks the bodies and finds Alliance dog tags. She looks up to see what floor they fell from but can't tell which one, so she heads inside.

The sniper quickly grabs their equipment and heads up the stairs.

The Phoenix powers up, Angel and Tiny are in the cockpit tracking Casey's location. The Phoenix slowly flies out of the docking bay.

One trooper throws an incendiary grenade at Stacey only to have it redirected back at him by her foot with a crazy flip kick. The grenade explodes on contact and he is engulfed in flame.

Two more troopers fire at her, she slides in front of them and kicks one of the rifles up into the soldiers face. The shot disintegrates his head. Stacey then sweeps the leg of the other and shoves a dagger into his skull.

Two more troopers shoot at her but she rolls out of the way. She uses another soldier as cover for a couple shots before she punches him across the room into the other troops.

The elevator passes the 47th floor.

One soldier runs at Stacey with a light blade swinging it mercilessly. She dodges his attacks, then grabs him by the throat with her special hand. She lifts him up and breaks his neck. Rayza works her way up the stairs to Stacey.

Still holding the trooper, she glares over at the four remaining troopers. The reflection of the burning body in her eyes and the blood dripping down her face gives a look of "you're next".

The troopers are shaking in fear trying to reload their weapons. One of the soldiers pisses on himself. Stacey's smile and the fire of the burning corpse in the reflection of her green eyes is enough to terrify anyone.

She drops the body and sprints at them.

The elevator now passes the 60th floor.

Rayza walks on to the floor to hear screaming of the soldiers. She walks past many bodies until she sees Stacey using a dagger to cut out the organs of the last living trooper.

"Holy shit, a little gruesome for my taste, but hey to each his own, am I right?" Rayza says surprising Stacey. She pulls the dagger out, stands up and shakes the blood off her hands.

"You shouldn't be here." Stacey says.

"Is it because you don't want Casey to know that you are a homicidal maniac?" Rayza asks looking around at the bodies.

"Rayza, I'm serious, Casey is walking into a trap."

"Yeah we know, I went to the arms dealing shop and wouldn't you know it, you weren't there. So, I decided I would just show up here and what do I find, you killing human and Nexus Alliance soldiers. I mean if you were trying to be discrete, the bodies on the street are sending a different message." Rayza says walking over to the broken window. Stacey opens up a gym bag and begins throwing ammo clips, grenades and weapons into it.

"Rayza take this bag and get to Casey, I've got one more to take care of." Stacey says leaving the bag and heading to the stairwell.

"Yeah sure, just leave all the heavy lifting to me!" Rayza complains as she picks up the bag.

The elevator has reached the 82nd floor.

The elevator doors open up, Casey exits with her pistol ready. The 82nd floor is still under construction with many tarps and equipment lying around. No walls, windows or furniture have been installed yet, making the wind a bit strong. There is what seems to be a makeshift shelter between two support beams near the edge. Casey takes a few steps toward the shelter.

"Zeek? I'm Casey, I'm here to get the location of Kitara's cargo." Casey says keeping her pistol down. Zeek emerges from his shelter like a scared cat. He hops up quick with a pistol. Casey turns her pistol stance to a surrender stance quickly to make him feel at ease.

"Stay away!" Zeek says waving his gun at Casey and company.

"Hey it's okay, just stay away from the edge, all I need to know is where the pirates are, that's it." Casey says putting her pistol away. The sniper begins aiming at her target. Stacey is still two more flights away but moving quickly. Razya with bag of weapons on her back jumps across to the Craxton building easily then makes her way up to Casey.

"They are over at Enroch, I already told this to Vikara, why are you here?" Zeek says nervously still waving the gun.

"That bitch already knew." Ethereal says.

"Which means this is just a trap." Hyda says grabbing his blade.

"Set by whom?" Ethereal asks.

"Hey! Put that away, or I will put you down!" Zeek yells. Casey takes one step closer to try and take him down, but before she can, a quick zipping sound of a sniper shot blows through Zeek's face leaving a hole the size of a cantaloupe and bounces off a couple of support beams.

Hyda, Casey and Ethereal seek cover quickly. Zeek's body falls off the edge.

"Anyone see where it came from?" Casey asks. She looks back at the others to see Demi lying down in a pool of blood.

"Demi!" Casey yells. She keeps her head down and rushes over to him. He begins choking on his own blood. Casey applies pressure to the gapping wound, but ultimately she knows he's not going to make it.

"Just hold on Demi!" She yells. He grabs Casey by her jacket and pulls her closer. "Ikaroth...Ikar...go to Ikaroth..." He says before dying. "I don't understand, what do you mean?" Casey asks as his hand falls to the floor. She looks down at the blood on her hands. Only thing running through her head is, this is her fault.

The sniper continues to look down sights for Casey, but feels a presence coming up from behind.

The sniper fires two more random shots to keep Casey down in cover, then quickly turns around to block Stacey's dagger. The sniper punches Stacey twice and then kicks her off. Stacey pulls out a pistol, but the sniper tries to disarm her.

Stacey fires three shots as they struggle; one of the shots damages the sniper's helmet. The sniper disarms Stacey of the pistol. Stacey punches the sniper clear across the room. A flash bang is left at Stacey's feet, disorienting her giving the sniper enough time to take off the damaged helmet and rush Stacey. Ethereal attempts to slowly look for the sniper, but the sunlight blinds her sight from the building across from them. She looks over to Casey and sees a black figure above her.

"Casey!" Ethereal shouts. Casey looks up quickly to see purple curved blade coming down. She moves out of the way, just in time. Casey stands up with her pistol on the assassin that is pulling her sword from the metal crate.

"Nothing personal, but I'm here to kill you." The assassin says.

"Really? Because it feels personal." Casey says backing up.

The woman smiles and turns on another sickle blade.

Serenity: one of the deadliest assassin's in the galaxy, the two sickle blades is her signature. Well that, and how she gets off on every kill she makes.

She is screwed, Casey thinks, but thankfully she brought some heavy hitters. Casey looks over to see a ten-foot Groutarian with metal arms choking Ethereal and holding Hyda off with the other hand.

"That sounds about right." Casey says to herself right before Serenity rushes her. Casey dodges Serenity's attacks, but only by a little.

The Phoenix continues flying in between skyscrapers,

"Which is illegal by the way." Tiny says to Angel who is flying the ship as best as he can. The ship glides like an eagle over the city. The sunlight shines on the Phoenix's wings turning their color from faded cobalt to a blood orange flame.

The Groutarian throws Ethereal a few feet away to try and get Hyda off his back. Ethereal recovers instantly and activates a long gold staff with a red ruby at the top that has four spikes intersecting each other. She looks over and sees Casey struggling to dodge Serenity. Ethereal moves to help, but before she can, Casey blasts Serenity across the room with her gloves. Ethereal instead rushes to help Hyda. Serenity gets up slowly as Casey walks over turning on her light daggers. Serenity makes the first move. Casey blocks it and throws her blades down, then elbows her in the face. Serenity stumbles back and wipes the blood from her lip, then grins.

"Not bad for a human." She says right before she attacks.

Stacey is caught in a headlock, but quickly breaks free by using her "hand" to electrocute the floor. Stacey crawls away and picks up a pistol, she turns around to see the sniper for the first time. Kristin Conway, the psychologist and apparently the famous black op sniper, known only as Death Cat, stupid name, but surprisingly fits.

Stacey is confused to see her; there is no mention of her being involved in the future. Kristin moves quickly, Stacey fires two shots but misses both. Kristin tackles Stacey disarming her. She punches her a couple times. Stacey catches her fist on the fourth hit and breaks her hand. Kristin screams in pain. Stacey throws her off and reaches for the sniper rifle, turns around to shoot, but Kristin is gone. Stacey relaxes.

Casey gets thrown into a beam hard, fracturing a rib. She tries to recover, but Serenity picks her up by her jacket.

Casey uses her boots to push Serenity through two beams before letting go and landing on her bad rib. The Groutarian holds Hyda high before slamming him down cracking the concrete. Malak, the leader of the Defiant Unknown, is ruthless and extremely powerful, although he has lost a step ever since Angel tore off his arms a few years ago. Ethereal remembers him well, but the question is, why is he here?

Malak raises Hyda up to slam him down again, but Ethereal runs up on Malak, flips her staff around and fires a vibrant red energy blast out of the tip into his torso causing him to let go of Hyda. The energy roars from the staff throwing him a few feet away.

"Thanks." Hyda says clearing his throat and getting up.

Serenity gets up and turns on her blade. She jumps up to slam down onto Casey, but Rayza quickly rolls Casey out of the way. Serenity slams down through two concrete floors. Rayza helps Casey up.

"Thank you." Casey says out of breath.

"Yeah, sorry I'm late." Rayza replies looking at Serenity climb up.

"Go help them Rayza." Casey says combining her daggers to make an energy sword. "What? Casey that's *Serenity.*"

"And that's a Groutarian! They will need a heavy hitter." Casey says nodding her head in the direction of Hyda and Ethereal.

"Besides, I got this." Casey says with a wink before running at Serenity.

Rayza sprints over and punches Malak in the face, before he can hit Ethereal. He stumbles back, Rayza jumps and tries to kick him several times, but he blocks her hits with his arms. When she lands on the ground,

Rayza slides under him and kicks the back of his knees, causing him to kneel. Ethereal tries to stab him with her staff, but he catches it. Hyda comes down with his energy blade onto Malak's arm in hopes of cutting it off. Instead, the blade doesn't even make a scratch! Rayza jumps on his back and claws into his skin. Malak growls loudly and pushes Ethereal. She loses her footing and falls back. Malak then grabs Hyda and throws him far enough to fly off the edge.

However, Hyda is not easy to kill. While in mid-air, he quickly uses a small hook shot device and latches it on to a beam on the floor above. He then swings back and kicks Malak in the face, causing him to crash into the elevator and the beams that hold it in place. The elevator cord snaps and the car drops down to the lobby.

The structural integrity of the building is now compromised. Casey is holding Serenity off with one blade to her two. Serenity slashes only to get one of her blades stuck in one of the larger beams. Casey makes an attempt to stab her, but Serenity wraps around on Casey's back holding the sickle blade to her throat. Casey pulls a pistol out and puts a pretty good size hole in Serenity's foot. Serenity screams and lets go of Casey, but manages to slice Casey's torso before falling over. The blade breaks clean through Casey's energy like a hot knife through butter. Casey slams against the larger beam holding her bloody wound. Broken rib, bleeding arm and now a gash on the good side, how much worse could it get, Casey thinks, trying to catch her breath. Serenity gets up on her feet and turns her blade back on.

"You are resourceful for a human." Serenity says with her sharp grin.

"You have no idea." Casey says not moving from the side of the pillar.

Serenity rushes her, Casey dodges as best as she can, but gets punched then kicked to the floor near the edge. Serenity steps on Casey's bad rib holding her in place.

Casey screams in pain.

Rayza gets thrown through two beams while Ethereal and Hyda attempt to hold Malak off, but get knocked out one punch each.

Serenity presses down on her knee putting more pressure on Casey's rib, she groans in pain. "Your pathetic race has no place in this Universe. I mean, did you really think you could take me on all on your own?" Serenity ask pressing down on Casey's rib. Casey holds in the scream and looks dead into Serenity's eyes. She smiles with bloody teeth and asks,

"What makes you think I'm on my own?" Serenity tilts her head in confusion, then looks up only to catch a quick glimpse of a bright pink orb before it hit her face with enough force to send her flying past Malak. Casey rolls over to see Nikki floating from the open hatch of the Phoenix.

"Damn girl! You look like shit." Nikki says as a purple and black portal opens up next to her and Angel steps through it.

The Phoenix remains afloat and extends the hatch to the floor of the building.

"What took you so long?" Casey asks while trying to get up.

"Well, there is a tiny ramen shop that makes the best Mu Shu Pork outside this district, so naturally I stopped the entire ship and picked us up some dinner! No need to thank me, just trying to contribute anyway I can to my team." Nikki says with her hands on her hips and a smile on her face.

"I hate you so much." Casey says,

"Oh don't be like that, silly!" Nikki says trying to help her up.

Angel opens up voids for Ethereal, Rayza and Hyda, so they can be next to him.

Casey continues to say "I hate you" as Nikki continues to say

"No you don't and that's not possible because every one loves me."

Rayza regains conciseness grabs the bag of weapons and jumps through the void coming up behind Angel.

"Glad you guys showed up." Rayza says getting on board.

Ethereal helps Hyda onto the Phoenix.

Angel walks toward Malak hands engulfed in purple flame.

Malak stops a few feet from Angel.

"How are those arms?" Angel says with a smile.

Malak doesn't speak, he sneers at Angel.

"It looks like I did you favor, I mean those are high tech." Angel says right before Malak rushes at him.

Angel blocks a couple hits, but one punch sends Angel back a few feet.

Nikki stops him before he falls on his back. Malak rushes again and throws one powerful punch at Angel. He braces for the impact, but there is no impact.

Stacey is holding back is his fist with her hand. Malak pushes, but Stacey doesn't move, instead Malak's feet slide trying to push Stacey.

Angel jumps over her and fires a bright purple beam at Malak blasting him back into Serenity. Stacey and Angel get on board as the hatch closes.

The Phoenix turns it's thrusters toward the building then blasts out to space.

The force of the thrusters causes the building to collapse down to the street.

THE LEVIATHAN

THE PHOENIX WARPS OUT OF OHYRON'S ORBIT.

On board, Casey is in the small bathroom toward the back of the ship. There is no shower, just a toilet and a metal sink with a mirror. Casey is washing her hands of Demi's blood. It won't come off no matter how hard she scrubs. Her heart begins to race, she throws water on her face and puts her hands on the sink and looks into the mirror. She sees blood all over her face, she shuts her eyes tight, but all she sees is Demi choking on his blood. She squeezes the sink tight. There is a metal crunching sound. She looks down at the sink and sees her hands have crushed the sink like an aluminum can. She looks into the mirror and sees strange symbols around the pupil of her eyes with a black and white glow to them. She gets closer to the mirror to see them better, she blinks and the symbols are gone. Casey backs away from the mirror, dries her hands and face, grabs her gloves and leaves the restroom. Everyone (aside from Angel and Tiny, who are flying the ship) is in the main cabin eating Nikki's Chinese food. Casey finds a spot to lie down on the floor. Ethereal rushes to her and begins placing pale green bandages over her wounds. Nikki places a Chinese food box with chopsticks in front of her.

Tiny walks over to Casey. "His name was Robbie." She says

Casey looks up at her. "What?" She asks.

"Demi, his name was Robbie and he worked for the Rebel militia, he was born on Seraco. He had a facial reconstruction to look like Demi, the real Demi died four years ago." Tiny says.

Everyone remains silent.

"I know it probably doesn't change much." Tiny says.

"Honestly, I never liked him." Stacey says.

Casey remains silent grabs the food and beings eating. Nikki stares at her.

"At least we found out who the mole was!" Nikki says.

"We will be coming up on Enroch soon, so be ready." Tiny says before going back to the cockpit.

"Why are we going to Enroch?" Rayza says with a stuffed mouth.

"We need to get Trea and Jo back from Kitara, so we have to get that shit from the pirates." Casey says picking around in the box.

"Spoiler alert, we end up winning!" Nikki says with a fat content smile on her face. "It would be sad if we didn't, considering the team we've established here." Rayza says throwing a shrimp up and catching it in her mouth.

Casey yawns. Stacey picks a different song from her music.

"Hey guys, I will be activating the cloaking device when we arrive, so we can make a game plan." Tiny says over com to the main room. Ethereal walks over to Casey and removes the bandages revealing her wounds have vanished.

"Good as new." Ethereal says with a smile.

"Hey Ethereal, why does Angel not have the face tattoos like other Nexus?" Casey whispers.

"Because he is a Void Walker. It's a group of Nexus that specialize in the elements of the universe rather than the elements that make the universe. Although he believes the power has a mind of its own and he is capable of many things. I once seen him teleport someone by simply touching them but he tends not to over do it."

"Why?" Casey asks.

"Because he believes it would change him" Ethereal says.

"Change him how?" Casey asks wanting to know more.

"You will have to ask him, Ms. Williams." Ethereal says.

"The Groutarian on the 82nd floor, who was he?" She asks.

"Malak, that guy is just a punk. Angel tore his arms off a long time ago and left him for dead, but I guess what I heard about the Galactic Alliance saving him, was true." Ethereal says.

"Thank you for patching me up." Casey says.

"My pleasure, Ms. Williams." She says with a smile. She gets up and walks away. Casey gets up slowly and walks over to Stacey lying on the couch.

"So, how about you tell me what futuristic world you are from and what the deal is with your arm?" Casey asks.

Stacey looks up from her wrist and smiles.

"I'm from your time, Case and my arm is an advanced R.A.I.S. tech made from a metal found on a burnt out star." Stacey explains.

"What happened to your arm?" Casey asks.

"That is story for another time." Stacey says standing up and grabbing some Mu shu pork and chopsticks.

"Why am I getting the feeling you are not telling me the truth?" Casey asks watching Stacey gorge herself on pork. Stacey swallows then sighs.

"Okay Space Case, I left the Alliance to find you right after the president, but unlucky me, I went through a wormhole and showed up at least four years earlier from now. Then, I went back through and I arrived in the future." Stacey says while eating.

"How far in the future?" Casey asks.

"Ten years, when I arrived out of the wormhole, you were already dead. I'm here to make sure that doesn't happen. It took what was left of us, at least four years, to find a way to make a viable change in the past, to create a different timeline, one, where we lose the battle, but not the war."

Stacey says taking sip of her drink and relaxes on her seat.

Casey remains quiet.

In a way, she thought she knew this was a much different Stacey, but still the same. Casey hugs her, but when she pulls away, she notices that Stacey's tattoo of a dragon lying on a diamond, behind her ear, is not there. This is cause for concern, but instead of confronting her about it Casey just says.

"Thank you and I'm sorry."

"Don't thank me yet, and never apologize Case, you know I would walk through fire for you." Stacey says with a smile while she continues to eat.

"Besides I'm just glad to be back in this time and this Mu shu pork is divine."

Stacey says to Casey as she walks over to the projector.

Gorog walks up to Casey. He stands tall and says "Take me with you" in Groutarian. Casey gives him a nod. She is glad to hear he wants to help and who knows by the end of this, they might even become friends. She turns around when she hears a semi loud beeping sound coming from the projector and the colors of the holograms and the interior lighting of the ship goes dark.

The Phoenix comes out of warp and quickly cloaks itself.

"Damn." Angel says looking out the window at the dark, large pirate ship. The vessel's elongated shape makes it look like a barbell with one end much larger than the back end. It is blacked out with bits of red and the spikes that protrude from every side except the middle portion. They are extremely sharp and act as conductors.

"That's the Leviathan, the second largest and most terrifying pirate ship in the galaxy." Tiny says going over exterior map of the ship. She taps on the com.

"Casey there is a small exhaust port on the top of the vessel, and you should be able to enter through it without causing any alarms or vacuum seal to alert your presence." Tiny says.

Casey grabs her weapons and opens a crate labeled "Space Shit".

She pulls out four medium sized silver and blue rings.

Casey hands one to Gorog, Rayza and Ethereal. Casey puts the ring around her neck then presses two green buttons on the side. The ring then conforms neatly around her neck. She presses the one red button in the front center of the ring. The necklace uses Nanites to create a black and red helmet over Casey's head. The other three do the same.

"Hey what about me?" Nikki says with puppy dog eyes.

"Nikki you can breathe in space, you don't need one of these." Casey says.

"But." Nikki says about to cry.

"Fine! Just don't break it, we only have so many of these." Casey warns her before handing it to her.

In the cockpit, Tiny flips a couple switches above her head and sits back down.

"Alright, we should be good if they decide to scan the area around them." Tiny says looking over the ship's schematics.

"I don't understand why we are even doing this. We can fly the ship to Masaton without Trea and Jo." Angel says.

"That's not the point, we need them, or do you want to be flying from now on?" Tiny says irritated.

"What are they to you?" Angel asks.

"They are my friends, my family! It's not like you would understand." Tiny says still working.

"I apologize, it isn't my intention to sound harsh. I was simply stating we could do the mission at hand first, then steal them back from Kitara." Angel says.

Tiny looks at Angel.

"And how would we do that?" Tiny asks.

Angel holds out a small disc.

"Is that?" Tiny asks but doesn't get the chance to finish her question.

"The device that teleported us off her ship." Angel finishes for her.

"I thought they all disintegrated once we were transported." Tiny says.

"I managed to hold on to mine." Angel explains.

"You're thinking we redirect it and somehow use the ones attached to Trea and Jo, if there is one, and have them teleport on to our ship assuming we are in range." Tiny says.

"Yes." Angel simply replies.

"Okay I'll bite. How do you plan on getting in range?" Tiny asks.

Angel leans back and shows Tiny a message on the dashboard of the ship.

The message reads: "We got it, now come get It." with their location added to the bottom. Angel presses a button and sends the message.

"What the fuck dude? " Tiny says hitting him.

"Relax and get to work." Angel says smiling and hands her the disc. Tiny hesitates, then takes the disc and opens up the cockpit. She rushes out to the main cabin and grabs a few bags and two small boxes then tries to return to the cockpit, but is cut off by Casey.

"Whoa, what's the rush? Is everything ready?" Casey asks but her questions muffled due to the helmet.

"You have to take off the helmet, dumbass." Tiny says.

Casey hits the button to turn off the helmet.

"Are we ready to fly over the ship?" Casey asks.

"Oh no, that's not what we are doing, you will have to get over there on your own, and use the cargo hold exit." Tiny says walking back to the cockpit.

"Cargo hold? What cargo hold?" Casey asks. Hyda pulls a lever on the wall. The floor beneath Casey begins to shift and opens up to a flight of stairs.

"I thought you read the manual." Hyda says.

"It didn't say anything about a cargo hold!" Casey snaps at him.

"Casey, you guys need to get going!" Tiny yells over com. Casey breathes in and out to calm herself and heads down to the cargo hold.

Nikki, Gorog, Rayza and Ethereal follow her down into the cargo hold. The room is very spacious, plenty of room for the whole crew. The entrance closes up and the room goes dark. There are tiny mechanical fireflies with blue lights keeping the room barely lit.

"Alright, give me a second to pressurize the cargo hold." Tiny instructs over the com. Casey and the group readies their helmets. A loud beep sound rings.

"Good luck." Tiny says right before cargo door opens quickly. The crew is ripped out into space. Nikki uses her abilities to stop the crew from straying too far. A pink aura- like bubble covers each crewmember allowing Nikki to pull them through space over to the Leviathan. Nikki guides them slowly floating in between the sharp metal spikes and lands them down next to the vent Casey opens the vent using her rifle and Gorog rips the cover off. One by one they drop in. Nikki still using the aura to move them down the vent shaft. They emerge in the engine department. There are mostly metal grates for pathways, hot molten lava pouring into a fusion core and a few computer consoles near life support systems and weapon systems. Rayza messes with a small box that beeps twice. Rayza then takes off the helmet.

"Air is good, we don't need the helmets." Rayza says putting the box away. Everyone else follows suit and turns off their helmets.

"Okay we need to find out where they keep their prisoners." Casey says looking for a way out of the engine room. Ethereal readies her bow then sees two Solarian sentries walking into the engine room.

"Hide." She says getting into cover behind the life support system. The crew stays hidden behind various machines until the unaware two guards leave the room.

"Okay, I think if we head straight, we should come up to a cargo hold and there should be a console I can get into." Rayza says checking a map of the ship on her wrist.

"Alright Rayza lead the way, Gorog, you stay in the middle and Ethereal can you cover the rear?" Casey asks.

"Yeah I got it!" Ethereal replies and takes formation. Rayza pulls up her map and takes the lead. They crew walks for about five minutes before they reach a large gold circular door. Rayza breaks open a panel next to the door and begins messing with wires.

"All good Ethereal?" Casey asks checking one more row of machines before regrouping with the rest of the group.

"Yeah, not a soul, and no cameras from what I can tell." Ethereal says.

"That's strange." Casey says.

"Not entirely. The ship wasn't moving when we showed up, so I assume they are on a lunch break." Rayza says before a spark comes from the panel and the door opens with six sections receding in a clockwise motion.

"I'm hungry." Nikki says.

"After the job is done, Nikki." Casey says passing her up and following closely behind Rayza as they enter a long dark and dripping hallway. A green slime oozes down both walls. Thorns coming from the walls make the hallway a little tight in some spots.

"Do you guys remember when I said I was hungry?" Nikki asks but no one responds. Nikki touches the slime with her finger then flings it on the floor.

"Well I'm definitely not anymore." She says looking disgusted.

The hall way ends at another corridor. No spikes are in this one and it is overall larger. Gorog is the last to emerge from the tight hallway.

"So, where are we?" Casey asks Rayza.

"Well, it would seem that narrow hallway is a security measure. This is what the actual corridors seem to be." Rayza explains as she works on getting her map to function correctly.

"Thank god! That shit was gross." Nikki says cleaning her clothes.

"Alright, we should head this way." Rayza says leading them.

Back on the Phoenix, Tiny and Angel continue working on the small teleportation device. Stacey and Demi are working on getting the music to play through the coms, when a loud beep comes from the projector. Stacey checks the console; Kitara's ship has warped on the opposite side of the Leviathan.

"That's not good." Stacey says to her self.

"Hey Case, Kitara's ship is here." Stacey says over com. Casey stops,

"Come again?" She asks.

"Guys, relax I told her we had her prize early, so I could re-engineer her teleportation device to bring Trea and Jo back. I mean just look how quickly she showed up." Tiny interrupts on com.

"Tiny! You little shit! That wasn't part of the plan!" Casey whispers angrily into the com. Rayza signals her over to a room.

"Just do what you are going to do, fast!" Casey says over com as she walks into the room. The room is more narrow than spacious. There is a large cryo-tank in the back. It has several hoses hooked up to the wall and several blue lights on the locking points. Nikki flies up to it and wipes away the fog to show an ugly bat creature.

"Oh my! He is so ugly, it's sad!" Nikki says floating down.

"Nikki, is it him?" Casey asks

"Not sure if I would classify that thing as a him." Nikki says. Casey rolls her eyes

"Is it the Therox?" Casey says exasperated.

"Its ok, Ms. Williams. I will get the tank open." Rayza says working on the panel next to the tank.

"Whoa! Hold on! Are we even sure this his him?" Casey asks.

"Well if its not, we kill him, and just so you know, this is the cell block for the entire ship." Rayza says.

"Wait really?" Casey asks.

"Pirates don't take many prisoners, unless they want something." Rayza explains. "So, why did they take this guy from Kitara?" Nikki asks.

"You can see the future, you tell me." Rayza says annoyed with answering questions.

Back on the Phoenix.

"Eventually, you will get it." Angel says to Tiny.

"Don't do that." Tiny shoots back.

"Do what?" Angel asks.

"Patronize me." She says quickly focusing only on the device.

"I don't know what that means, but I do know Rayza would have already been done with this." Angel replies' looking out the cockpit window, while Tiny gives him a death squint then returns to the device.

Rayza produces a few sparks and the cryo tank makes a loud hiss sound.

"Jeez Rayza, could you possibly make anymore noise?" Casey asks.

At that exact moment, the hinges on top of the tank break and the door slams down on the metal grated floor with a loud bang echoing throughout the whole ship.

"Well, that was loud." Rayza says with a smiling at Casey. The cryo tank is empty.

"That's not right." Nikki says taking a look inside.

"Ms. Williams." Ethereal calls out nodding her head to look above. Casey looks up, but before she can draw her weapon, The Therox grabs her with both hands and flies her into the wall.

"Where am I human?" He growls with broken English.

"On Board the Leviathan. We have been sent by Kitara to save you, but I will kill you if you don't let go of me right now." Casey says with a pistol pointed at his groin.

The Therox sees her gun and puts her down. Ethereal and everyone else relaxes as well.

"I'm Casey, that's Nikki, Rayza, Gorog and Ethereal."

"I am Nessarac and I am in your debt." He says his voice is raspy and low.

"Glad to hear it, Rayza find the escape pods and..." Before Casey could finishes a loud deep guttural scream comes from somewhere in the ship followed by the sound of many opening doors and plenty of pirates on the way. "

Fuck me." Casey says readying her rifle.

"Are you sure you want me to fuck you now, Ms. Williams?" Nikki says getting ready to take her shirt off.

"What?" Casey asks.

"I found the escape pods two levels below us." Rayza says checking the map.

"Alright, lets head out, Ethereal cover the back, Rayza up front and Gorog... Casey says turning to him. He grins and he aus down to her.

"Smash whatever you want." Casey says smiling back at him.

Gorog roars and bursts through the door to the hallway crushing two Solarians behind the door.

Four more pirates at the end of the hall look terrified. Gorog roars again and the pirates trample over each other trying to run away. Gorog chases them. Casey and crew follow him. Gorog catches up to the pirates at a hallway intersection. He grabs two and crushes them into the floor; their faces squeeze through the grate like meat through a grinder. The other two pirates ready their weapons but Casey jumps over Gorog's back with her pistol and shoots both in the head before they can fire.

"Go right!" Rayza yells catching up. Nessarac takes the lead down the hallway to the right. Casey, Nikki and Rayza follow him quickly. Ethereal and Gorog follow after killing a couple more pirates. Casey stops when they come across the next fork, the group continues down the path after Nessarac, but Casey stops. She has a feeling that someone is watching her. She looks down the left hallway and sees him.

Tarik, the corrector of time, is standing under a flickering light. He stares at her, turns to look down the hallway, he is standing in front of, then turns back to look at her before fading away. Casey knew this wasn't going to be a good idea, but she needs to know why he is here. She pulls her rifle out and slowly approaches the spot where he was.

When she gets to where he was standing, she looks down the dark hallway in the direction that he looked to see a dead end. Tarik is nowhere to be seen. She is about to leave, but stops when she notices a cryo-tank is sitting at the end of the hall. She continues down the hallway but again stops when she realizes that the walls of the hallway are cryo-tanks. There has to be hundreds of cryo-tanks throughout the ship she thinks. Casey gets up close to one of them and wipes the condensation off the window.

She sees a human Galactic Alliance soldier inside.

Nessarac reaches a big locked door; Rayza pushes through him and Gorog to get to the access panel.

"Alright, Casey I'm going to need your pistol it has a specific energy charge…" Rayza stops and turns around to look for Casey.

"Where's Casey?" she asks. Everyone looks around.

"She was right behind me." Ethereal says.

"Forak!" Rayza says, which is the Nexus equivalent to the word cunt in English, grabbing a bag and heading back whisper-yelling "Casey!"

She continues backtracking to the fork and then continues down the right. She finds Casey getting ready to break open one of the tanks with a pipe in hand. Rayza stops her.

"What are you doing?" She asks.

"They are human, Rayza! They kidnapped humans!" Casey screams irrationally on the verge of tears.

"Okay, just take it easy. Breaking them out of here won't help anyone, not them, not us and not the pirates." Rayza explains.

"The pirates?" Casey says confused.

"Don't think that was the right thing to say." Nikki interjects.

"Now hear me out. These people were captured and they are probably being transported to a group that pays for human bodies." Rayza says.

"Not any better." Nikki continuing her commentary.

Casey tries to strike the tank again, but before she can, a loud voice is heard at the end of the hallway

"Why would you hesitate to do what you have already done?"

A startled Casey jumps back still holding the pipe up ready to strike. Tarik emerges from the shadowy corner.

"You can not run from what you were always meant to do." He says.

His voice is a raspy almost broken for a R.A.I.S; his armor plates are slightly damaged.

"Casey, he is clearly trying to bait you to do something, we need to go." Rayza says trying to get Casey's attention. Nikki can feel pirates presence headed toward them.

"They're coming." She says to the group.

"Guys a Galactic Alliance ship just warped out on the other side of Seraco and Case, it's Heathrow." Stacey says over the com.

"Casey, we need to go, right now!" Rayza yells.

Casey drops the pipe and gives Tarik the look of "nice try".

"Let's go." Casey says.

"Finally." Rayza says grabbing Casey's hand and pulling her away from him.

Casey looks back one more time.

"Dread it, Ms. Williams, for your Fate is inevitable." Tarik says as they turn the corner.

Back on the Phoenix, Tiny runs to the main cabin and hooks the devices to a holopad. She presses a few buttons and two shapes begin to appear in front of her. When they fully materialize, Trea and Jo are standing there not sure of what just happened.

"Trea! Jo!" Tiny yells with excitement! She hugs them.

"Okay, not a whole lot of time to explain, but we need you two in the cockpit. Everything is unlocked on the ship." Tiny says speed talking.

"Okay, Honey, take it easy. Where's Casey?" Trea asks.

On board the Leviathan, Rayza manages to open the heavy blast doors and gives Casey back her pistol. They walk in a large dark room filled with nothing more than metal crates.

"Storage, escape pods are on the other side." Rayza says pointing them to the doors across from them. The lights turn on once they make it to the middle. At least a hundred pirates come from behind a pyramid like structure of metal crates. Some pirates climb on top. They have daggers on their belts at the hip. Others are dressed with rusted armor or a hodge-podge of armors they stole from the ones they have killed. One larger pirate climbs up to the center crate at the top of the pyramid. He appears to be the one in charge. His armor is a decent looking gold and his flail is made up of green crystals.

"Pretty cool Flail bro." Nikki says to the big guy.

"Garkag Derock!" The leader shouts.

"Speak English!" Nikki yells back. The pirates begin to run at them.

Casey pulls out her rifle and opens fire. She presses a button on her rifle that switches to "Chain" with a lightening bolt symbol. She fires three shots into three different pirates, the bullets dig into their skin then explode with a high intensity electric blast that connects with the other three then spreads to six more pirates near by. Casey continues to shoot, the pirates with the daggers jump up and throw them at Casey, but Gorog intervenes by throwing two large crates at the daggers and the pyramid. All the pirates rush the group, but before the fight could begin the Leviathan sirens go off.

The Leviathan is under attack by the Halberd.

"Casey!" a voice says over com.

"Trea?" Casey asks.

"The one and only love. Looks like you guys could use a little distraction." Trea says in the cockpit getting ready.

"I will take what you can give me." Casey says as she kicks one pirate down. A huge group of the pirates leave as the alarms continue to blare. The leading pirate stays behind, so it's safe to assume he's not the top brass. Nikki, Rayza and Gorog hold off a few, while Ethereal heads up to take out the flail bro.

"We should get to the pods." Nessarac says.

"Why? Are you afraid of a little scrap?" Casey asks with a smile. Nessarac grins, "Pirates tend to run, Ms. Williams."

The Leviathan engines begin to hum, Casey looses her smile quickly when she realizes they about to make a hyperspace jump.

"Guys! We got to go!" She yells just as Ethereal pushes her sword through the spine of the leader. Ethereal drops the body down the pyramid, the rest of pirates see his body and begin to screech, and scurry away.

"Show off." Nikki says.

Ethereal smiles.

"Guys let's go!" Casey yells to the group.

"Trea, light it up!" Casey says over com as the shore party makes their way into a long room with six escape pods.

Trea turns off the cloak of the ship, opens the four wings and blasts past the front of the Leviathan.

"I think we need some tunes." Stacey says as she hooks up her music to not only the com system, but also the outer speaker system. An outer speaker system can jam the speakers of other vessels with whatever sound you want them to hear. Not many ships have it or even use it, but the Phoenix is not like many ships.

Heathrow walks out the long walkway on the bridge of the Halberd.

"Destroy that ship!" He yells.

A shrilling voice comes in over the coms of the Halberd. The voice sings

"I don't worry, worrying don't agree."

The beat of song comes in loud with drums and trumpets on all the coms and not just the Halberd but the Leviathan and the Talo (Kitara's vessel) as well. Heathrow growls in anger.

"Fire everything at that ship!" He yells trying to mask the song. The Halberd fires many lasers and missiles at the Phoenix, but nothing hits.

The Phoenix dodges every shot with ease and the shots that get close, bounce off the wings. Its flight pattern is sporadic at best making it hard to target.

On board Kitara's vessel, her assistant runs into the throne room.

"The R.A.I.S are gone Kitara." He says.

"Obviously." she says looking at a hologram of the Phoenix dodging the Halberd's attempts.

"Fire the Halo at them!" She yells over the song that just became a little louder. The Talo's red domes all glow a bright orange, the largest red dome turns blue.

All the other red domes emit a laser that connects to a common point right above the blue dome. The blue dome harnesses all the energy and fires a monstrosity of a laser beam at the Phoenix. The Halberd also charges a laser and fires.

The Phoenix's wings hinge up to form a triangle from both sides. The music finally stops playing. Two small wormholes are formed on either side of the Phoenix. Both giant laser blasts are instantly sucked inside the small wormholes. The Phoenix's wings return to their normal outstretched span and the two small wormholes return to the tips of the wings.

The Phoenix becomes engulfed in a flame of turquoise and red.

"What the hell is that thing?" Heathrow says under his breath.

The Leviathan flies straight past the Phoenix.

Three escape pods launch from the underside of the ship and fall down to the planet Seraco; the Rebel Militia home world.

Seraco looks strangely bare, like the moon, but instead of craters, there are silver mirror looking puddles that lead you to world below the surface. The world within has it's own natural perpetual sun that rotates much like the sun outside the planet. Two cities thrive amongst plenty of plant and animal life.

The three escape pods crash down on the surface. They open and fling Ethereal, Casey and Nikki out on to the ground. Actually, Casey hits the ground while Ethereal is graceful enough to land on her feet and Nikki just floated around.

"Yeah, that's why I hate Gyros, they always throw out one passenger." Rayza says comfortably unfastening her seatbelt and getting out of the pod.

"Breathable air, so you won't be needing the helmet." Nikki says to Casey.

Ethereal and Gorog deactivate their helmets.

Casey also takes hers off and looks around as she gets up. Many Rebel militia troops are rising out of a silver lake about half a mile out. They have red and gold armor and are carry banners with their insignia. A group of larger troops are pushing what appears to be a long metal rectangular box.

"Rebels." Ethereal says readying her bow.

"Casey." Nikki says letting Casey know that The Halberd is sending troops down to Seraco. Gorog growls loudly at the Alliance ships coming in.

There is a loud crackling sound from the Leviathan. It fires a beam of pure electricity at the Phoenix but Trea flies upward to avoid the attack. The Phoenix fires a rainbow colored beam out of the tip of the beak (a few feet from the cockpit). The beam tears through one of the thrusters at the back end of the Leviathan.

"That was fucking awesome! Okay now just come down here and get us so we can go!" Casey says over COM watching the attack overhead.

There is only static over the COM.

The Phoenix suddenly implodes in on itself.

"Oh shit! Trea? Angel? Anybody?" Casey frantically calls out over com.

"What happened?" Ethereal asks.

"I don't know!" Casey yells.

"Guys, the Rebels!" Rayza says reminding them. Casey looks over to the other side where the Alliance has just landed.

"Nikki, I need you to find something big to cover us with!" Casey says.

"You got it!" Nikki responds using her ability to make a pink general's hat appear on her head and saluting Casey before flying straight up.

The Rebels open up their rectangular boxes to reveal catapult tanks that can launch dark matter.

"It just keeps getting better." Casey says under her breath while grabbing the Amethyst of Galaton.

"Gorog!" She yells and tosses him the gem. Gorog catches it and puts it away.

"In case we don't make it out of here…" Casey says in Groutarian.

He gives Casey a nod, a grin and then runs at the Rebels. They open fire on him, but Nessarac destroys their guns before they can cause any real harm. Gorog grabs one of the catapults and throws it at the other one. It smashes into the other one and they both fall down to the rebel city below the surface. Casey, Rayza and Ethereal try to slow down the Alliance. Casey uses her last few "bubblegum" shots on a couple of them, and Ethereal uses the surface of the planet to build a wall to shield them.

The Talo moves in closer to strike the Leviathan, but the Leviathan with limited power, creates a warp and leaves. The Halberd moves cautiously closer toward the planet so as not get hit by Seraco's planetary defenses.

Gorog and Nessarac are finishing off a few more rebels before reinforcements arrive. Casey and Ethereal rush the Alliance troops taking them down one by one, or two by two in Ethereal's case. Casey takes her time making sure not to fatally hurt anyone. Rayza, on the other hand shoots several of them in the head. Holding back was never her strong suit, bad business for a thief to be weak. One Alliance troop with heavy armor rushes in with a big shield knocking both Ethereal and Casey off their feet.

Casey rolls and falls into one of the small silver puddles, but before she falls to the rebel city below, a hand catches her hand and pulls her up.

It's Angel. Surprised and excited to see him, she gives a quick hug him.

"Are you okay? Where's the Phoenix?" Casey asks looking around.

"Trea is working on it. I'm not sure what just happened, I jumped and ended up here." Angel says.

"Okay. Everyone is okay though?" Casey says switching weapons.

" Yes, Ms. Williams, however without sounding callus, now would be a good time to get that information." Angel says looking up at the Halberd.

"Right now?" Casey asks.

"Yeah. We will be right back." Angel says.

"We can't just leave!" Casey yells.

"Do you trust me?" Angel asks

"No." Casey says.

"Well, you should really learn to trust people more often, Ms. Williams." Angel says.

Somewhere on board the Halberd a purple portal opens up.

Casey is pushed through and Angel steps out.

"Okay where do we go?" Angel asks. Casey quickly puts a dagger to Angel's throat "Do that again and I will kill you." Casey says.

"Where to, Ms. Williams?" Angel asks calmly. Casey sighs and turns off her dagger. "Follow me, and no killing!" She says running down a white hallway.

They continue down two hallways before running into two soldiers. Casey slams one against the wall and knocks him out with his own rifle. Angel is holding the other by the neck until she passes out then drops her. "Come on, its right over here." Casey says dragging the soldier to a door down the hallway. She takes the soldier's hand and puts it on a scanner to open the door. It's a Server room. Every Galactic Alliance vessel has server rooms, mainly for communication, but higher-ranking ships have all the good secrets in these rooms, so to speak. Angel pulls out a small storage drive device and plugs it into one of the servers. Casey guards the door pistol ready.

"What's that?" Casey asks.

"Tiny gave it to me and right now it is getting everything." Angel says walking over to a computer.

"Oh shit!" He yells.

"What?" Casey asks.

"This is a terrible photo of you." Angel says pointing at the computer.

"Asshole." She mutters.

Two green blaster shots wiz by Casey's head, she gets into cover and provides suppressive fire. Angel walks over to the device and pulls it out.

"Let's go!" He yells opening a portal back to Seraco's surface.

Casey hops through the hole then Angel.

"Did you get everything?" Casey asks.

"Yeah, we will have Tiny go over it." Angels says closing the portal.

"Hey Casey." Is whispered four times into the wind.

"Hello! Who is this?" Casey yells over coms.

"It's me silly! And I found something huge to cover you!" Nikki says over com. Angel's eyes widen as he looks up past the Halberd.

Casey turns around to see what he is looking at.

Enroch, the second moon of Seraco, has a pink aura over it and is on a direct path to collide with Seraco.

"Is that what I think that is?" Rayza asks.

The Phoenix suddenly reappears as if it was harshly spat out from an invisible mouth and lands on the surface about a quarter mile from Casey and her crew.

"Nikki put the moon back!" Casey yells over com.

"Now why would I do a thing like that!" Nikki says over com.

Angel grabs Casey and puts her over his shoulder as he runs for the Phoenix yelling

"Has Kell!" The phrase is Nexus for "run like hell."

Everyone begins running to the Phoenix.

"Nikki! PUT THE MOON BACK!" Casey yells again.

"Oh, Sweetie, gravity is like madness as you know. Once the ball starts rolling, or in this case moon, I can't just roll it back. It's no longer under my control." Nikki says over com while lying down doing her nails on top of the moon as it barrels toward the planet.

The Halberd moves quickly over the planet to get away from the crushing force of the moon.

The Talo opens up a portal and leaves.

The entire planet begins shaking as the moon enters the atmosphere.

Rebel militia troops run back to their city and Alliance soldiers desperately try to project themselves back to the Halberd, but many are left on the surface of the planet.

Angel opens several portals to the inside of the Phoenix, one by one.

Rayza falls into a portal first, then Gorog.

Ethereal jumps and rolls when landing inside the Phoenix, unlike Rayza who just face planted.

Nessarac floats through a portal and nearly gives Demi a heart attack.

Angel opens the last one for Casey and himself.

He puts Casey down once they arrive in the main cabin.

Nikki flies through the last portal that Angel made for her.

The Phoenix lifts up just as the moon hits the surface.

Seraco's surface is ripped away easily, once the moon barrels further into the planet.

There are explosions from Rebel Militia ships that bail to escape and also from the city inside the planet. A huge wave of debris and gravity pushes the Halberd, but barely affects the Phoenix. Trea sets the destination and Phoenix blasts out of Rebel space, leaving nothing, but death and dust behind.

THE
CORTEX CRYSTAL

THE PHOENIX SLICES THROUGH SPACE.

"What the hell is wrong with you?" Casey yells grabbing Nikki by her red jacket.

"What is your deal?" Nikki asks pulling her jacket away.

"Nikki, do you have any idea what you've done? You just killed billions of innocent people. You're a monster." Casey says.

"Uh I'm Sorry." Nikki says unashamedly with big smile and puppy dog eyes.

"You really don't give a shit about anything do you?" Casey asks with teary eyes.

"Oh honey! No I don't, besides that shithole planet was nothing more than an eye sore and it also belonged to the Rebel Militia. You know the same bad guys who slaughter everyone and are trying to kill you! I did you and the universe a favor." Nikki shouts as she walks away.

Casey wants to be mad at her, but it won't matter.

Casey breathes in and out a few times before Tiny tugs on her jacket.

"Ms. Williams, we need to make a plan." Tiny says tugging on her sleeve.

"Okay," Casey says refocusing her attention to the present.

"Check what we have as far as weapons. I will rally the troops."

She walks over the majority of the group.

Somewhere in the galaxy, The Blood Serpent is traveling through space.

"You have failed me, Serenity." Tartoroc says as he holds Serenity in a telekinetic hold. He clenches his fist and the hold becomes tighter.

"Give me another chance, same price." Serenity manages to cough out.

Tartoroc lets her go and walks to the front of the bridge.

"Sir, Seraco has been destroyed." One of the pilots says.

"What!" Tartoroc snarls.

"One of our ships on site says it was the Unusual Alliance." The pilot says.

"Proceed to Masaton." Tartoroc orders as he angrily stares out at the wormhole.

On Board the Phoenix, Casey is eating, but she feels sick to her stomach. Traveling with her crew is causing stress on top of the stress of finishing this mission.

"Ms. Williams, I'm ready." Tiny says.

"You have the floor." Casey says clearing her throat. Tiny walks to the center of the main cabin. She uses her pad to make a hologram of a small solar system emerge from the floor.

"I didn't know the ship could do that." Casey says.

"It didn't, I added it." Tiny says.

"Alright listen up everybody, because I'm only going to say this once. Masaton's star is going supernova, destroying the solar system. We will have little less than three hours to do what we need to do and get the fuck off the planet before turning into over cooked chimichangas." Tiny says.

"Ms. Williams, anything to add?" Tiny says nodding for her to take charge.

Casey stands up and walks over to the center.

"Okay guys, all I ask is that we work together quickly and efficiently, that means no stepping on each other toes, and no destroying the planet!" She says looking at Nikki. "Let the sun do that, we are going down to get the doctor and the Cortex Crystal. Take out anyone who gets in the way." Casey stops as Nikki raises her hand.

"Yes Nikki." Casey says.

"Two things, when it comes to the Cortex Crystal, how do we pick it up? As far as my knowledge, no one here can touch it. And two, if there are humans do you want us to kill them?" Nikki says with raised eyebrows.

"Tiny has developed a case to hold the crystal and anyone that shoots or tries to kill us at this point, is an enemy, understood?" Casey asks, Nikki nods.

"Now, when it comes to the Rebel Militia and Tartoroc, if they are there we will take care of them accordingly. If they are NOT there, then we do the job at hand and leave. We do not under any circumstance intervene with Tartoroc, if we have the goods. We pull this off and none of us have to see each other again." Casey says looking at the entire group.

"Yeah about that, Ms. Williams." Trea says from behind her.

Casey turns to see Trea and Jo standing side by side.

"What's up? Welcome back by the way." Casey asks.

"Thank you, but I think it would be wise, if this alliance remains." Trea says then nods to Boroc.

Boroc and Ayeka drag a black alien body out and drop in the center of the room.

The body wasn't of any known race that Casey knew.

"What the fuck is that?" Casey asks.

"When we lost contact on Seraco, The Phoenix made a trip to a different universe of Seraco being demolished by these things in a ship that I, or anyone has never seen." "Angel, it looks like…" Rayza begins but is quickly cut off by Angel

"I know." He says.

"Would you like to share with the rest of the class, Mr. Brooding?" Casey asks.

"There is a myth and a carving in a very old cave on Phazel about Ancient beings called Kazrin. They are world eaters and they serve a much more powerful entity." Angel explains.

"Okay and you and your race decided not to let the R.A.I.S know?" Trea yells.

"It's a myth, a bed time story." Angel replies.

"That's a fucking terrifying bed time story." Rayza says.

"That's not the point!" Trea yells.

"Whoa! Okay everybody calm down!" Stacey says

"Oh well, forgive me Time Traveler, why didn't you say anything about this?" Trea asks.

"I didn't even know who or what I was fighting, but it wasn't that!" Stacey yells. Nikki and Casey stare intently at the body.

Its skin is armored with a dark black that shined almost like the emptiness of space. The only part on the face that you could distinguish is its teeth. There are thousands of razor sharp teeth doing a clockwise rotation inside the opened mouth. Casey now sees things clearly. The president was terrified, he said

"There is something near Tiabanus." Casey's heart sinks, as the fighting gets louder. Nikki notices Casey's mood and silences everyone on the ship by closing their mouths using telekinesis.

"Would you like to share with the class, Ms. Williams?" Nikki asks.

Casey zones back in. She looks around at everyone and notices that his or her mouths are being held together with a pink aura.

"The President told me that there is something near Tiabanus and that to ensure survival, we would all have to work together. It's why we need the Cortex crystal." Casey says then looks back down at the creature. Nikki unlocks the mouths. "Tiabanus?" Trea says hands shaking.

"These things are only the beginning. The universe is always meant to end, but I think if we stand against it we might have chance." Nikki says.

"Stand against it?" Trea asks.

"Did he say how the cortex crystal is going to help us defeat them?" Rayza asks.

"No, he didn't say anything, he just gave me the device and said good luck." Casey says.

"Well that's helpful." Hyda says.

"Obviously it has something to do with this ship and I'm assuming we have to figure out how to destroy them on our own." Casey says.

"You guys seriously think we can kill them?" Trea interrupts with a headshake of disbelief. "Let me tell you what exactly happened."

About one hour ago

The Phoenix appears out of a blue and green portal above Seraco #2. The lights on board are flashing sporadically and alarms are wailing.

"What the hell happened? Where are all the other ships?" Trea yells to Tiny in the center room.

"I'm working on it! I can't seem to reach Casey on coms. Angel go to surface and check." Tiny says trying to fix overheating issues.

Angel jumps through one of his voids but ends up on Seraco #1.

"Hey what's that covering the sun?" Jo asks.

Trea looks over and sees a metallic black sheet covering not one, but both sides of Seraco #2.

"Tiny, we got a problem! How much longer until I can fly this bird?" Trea asks.

"Five seconds!" Tiny responds.

The black sheets cover the planet and waves begin to radiate through the sheets. The black sheets produce large spikes and begin to destroy the planet.

"Tiny!" Trea yells. "

Go!" She yells back.

The Phoenix's thrusters charge up and let out a blast.

The spikes continue to come down, some huge and thick, others are quick and thin like needles.

The Phoenix dodges accordingly.

The spikes get close, but nothing Trea can't handle.

"I got hostiles incoming!" Jo yells.

"Shit." Trea says before making the Phoenix dive toward the destruction of the planet. The hostile ships are fast and shaped like a bat with full extent wings.

They glide quickly after the Phoenix firing black needles all around.

The Phoenix does a couple of flips and turns a couple of times in an attempt to lose the ships.

One of the hostile's ships splits in two halves while flying to avoid crashing own ship into the spikes penetrating the planet, then repairs itself into one ship again as it flies past the spike.

"As we went further in the spikes became more erratic." Trea continues telling the crew of the incident.

The Phoenix dodges, quickly but ends up getting hit by one of the spikes.

That spike bursts through the center room floor.

The vacuum of space begins to pull the crew toward the spike. The crew attempts to hold on to anything that is tied down, when the spike falls out, but not without leaving an enemy behind. Nanites quickly seal the hole of the spike.

"We got company!" Hyda yells readying his blade.

Hyda and Boroc intervene with the Kazrin enemy. Tiny works diligently on the Phoenix. The enemy ships break off from the Phoenix.

"Show me something, Jo." Trea says. Jo activates the weapon systems.

The Phoenix fires a rainbow beam through the black goo ship providing a way out. The Phoenix blasts out, but the Kazrin ship latches onto the Phoenix like black tar onto a dying animal.

"Anytime now would be great Tiny!" Trea yells trying to move the ship.

Tiny works faster trying to reconnect all power to the thrusters.

The Kazrin on board get close to stabbing Tiny, but Hyda pulls her away and blocks the Kazrin. Boroc appears behind the Kazrin to hold him in place. As soon as Boroc has a firm grip on the Kazrin, it turns into black liquid goo and re solidifies behind Boroc.

The Kazrin kicks Boroc into Hyda.

Ayeka tries to stab the Kazrin with her daggers but fails to leave a mark.

The Kazrin grabs Ayeka by the throat and pushes her into the wall.

The Kazrin's gooey arm sticks her to the wall of the ship.

Stacey punches the Kazrin to the wall. She strikes it several times before it blocks her attack and kicks her away. Hyda tries to slice it, but gets thrown into the wall. Hyda rushes the Kazrin, but the Kazrin over powers him, but not before he stabs it with his energy blade. The Kazrin pushes

Hyda down onto a pile of crates. He holds the Kazrin blade inches from his eye. The blade begins burning his hands.

The Phoenix struggles to keep from being pulled down into the void. Tiny finally finishes the sequence.

"Give it everything you got!" Tiny yells.

Trea and Jo punch in coordinates and activate hyper drive. The Phoenix begins to glow and the wings begin to burn away the black tar. The Phoenix then repeats its bright disappearing act.

"Then we reappeared and lucky we did, because that thing just turned off when we came back." Trea says pointing at the Kazrin body.

"So, its not dead?" Rayza asks.

"Get rid of it." Casey says,

"I don't want those things tracking us through this."

"You heard her, lets drop this shit off somewhere." Tiny says to Trea.

The Phoenix comes out of warp, dumps the body and warps back out.

"Are you sure this crystal will help us defeat them?" Casey asks Tiny.

"It's going to take time, but I have already begun working on a plan." Tiny replies. "Keep me informed." Casey says walking away.

"Everyone get ready, we're about to arrive." Casey says loud enough for everyone to hear. Angel looks around and decides to answer for them.

"Understood, Ms. Williams." Casey smiles.

"One more thing! I recently was able to access a new way of landing a shore party. It's molecular cloud dispersal; it will look like smoke to others, but can safely transfer anyone who stands here in the center to the ground. It will not make your limbs appear on someone else! It is safe and secure. We will be using it when we land." Tiny says as everyone walks away looking unimpressed.

"Idiots." Tiny says shaking her head.

Masaton is a class four planet, with temperatures as high as 2000 degrees Fahrenheit. This planet, is not all lava and dry deserts, there are several strange eco spots where the atmosphere is different. Allowing for cool temperatures and even plant life. The spots have dwindled down to about three on the planet. Masaton's star is to blame for the loss of eco spots. The star has reached supernova. It will explode destroying any planet within its reach. The planets that are not within the boundary will freeze off into extinction.

The Phoenix launches out above Masaton and begins descending to the surface.

"There is a large base, it takes up most of the eco spot. Where should I put her down?" Trea asks.

"Use the EMP to scramble their turrets and communications and land right in front." Tiny says packing a satchel and putting a small tube on her back. Everyone on board gathers into the center aside from Trea. Jo walks up and cocks her shotgun. Casey gives her smile.

"Oh I'm not staying on the ship for this and Trea is coming too." Jo says.

"Nice." Angel says.

"Ms. Williams!" Tiny yells trying to get past everyone.

"I have been going over some of the information that you and Angel obtained from the Halberd." She says.

"'What did you find?" Casey asks. Tiny holds out the pad with the information.

Casey grabs it. She looks over the pad and sees a Temporary Alliance Treaty with the Rebel Militia, with signatures from Sullivan and the senate, but one name stood out, vice president Hogan. The data had documents of covert operations between both of them. There are tabs with plenty of information on the Cortex Crystals and the Nacarous.

"Teyach found this ship on some moon covered in sand. He and the rest of those idiots assumed it was trash they were only interested in what was inside the ship." Tiny says.

"The Cortex Crystal." Casey finishes her sentence for her.

"Precisely! They didn't realize that this ship is already capable of harnessing the power of the crystal." Tiny explains.

"How did they not notice what the ship could do?" Casey asks.

"A simple over look I guess, what I can't understand is who brought this ship from the future and why would they remove the Cortex Crystal and put it in a cargo container to make it look like simple treasure on a strange ship? My hypothesis would be that Sullivan somehow figured it out and I assume the Doctor wasn't acting like himself, or else he would have told him." Tiny finishes her theory.

"Which is why he gave it to me." Casey says handing her back the pad.

"That and whoever gave him the pyramid key knew it went to the ship and had your DNA coded to it. But I do believe he knew you were the only one who might be able to help the doctor, to see what he's done wrong." Tiny says.

"In other words, kill him before he hurts anyone." Casey says.

Tiny could hear it in her voice. Casey is sad about the news of Teyach.

"Well, looks like we have a new plan, get the crystal away from Teyach." Casey says.

"Casey, one last thing, I found some information on the day Sullivan died. There is a large amount of money being withdrawn from an account connected to the Galactic Alliance and put into a private account. I would have to do more digging, but I bet this could lead to something." Tiny whispers.

"No." Casey says.

"What?" Tiny asks,

"They don't know that we know, lets keep it that way for now, I don't want my sister being in the middle of this." Casey explains.

"Oh okay." Tiny says slightly confused by her answer. Casey tries to walk away. "Casey wait! Take these." She says handing her four small grenade discs.

"I don't need grenades." Casey says.

"You will need these ones." Tiny says.

"Why?" Casey asks.

"Let's just say they are anti-Sieren grenades." Tiny whispers.

She drops them into Casey's palm.

"Thank you Tiny." Casey says.

"If you get the chance, Ms. Williams, don't hesitate because something tells me he won't." She whispers.

Casey nods in agreement.

The Phoenix closes its wings and flies straight down through the atmosphere at an easy Mach 7. When it arrives above the front gate of the base, the Phoenix opens its wings and creates dust to cover it. There is an electromagnetic pulse that comes from the Phoenix disabling weapons and communications to the base, but not the power.

Four soldiers and a Lieutenant gather at the front gate. Most of the dust has settled, but there is still a grey smoke coming from the ship. The grey smoke expands and the soldiers get into position.

"Come out unarmed, or we will open fire!" The Lieutenant yells.

No response, just the sound of footsteps. Casey emerges from the smoke with hands on her gun belt. She takes three steps out of the smoke and stops. Her hair is down and she has a comfortable smile.

"Hi" she says cheerfully raising her hand for a quick wave.

Two figures rush out of the smoke on either side of Casey causing her hair to look like she is in a wind tunnel.

Before the Lieutenant can say anything, his head hits the ground, while his body still stands. Blood spews from the neck like a broken fire hydrant. Hyda kicks the body over. Ethereal gives the four soldiers a similar fate but instead of losing their heads...

"It cost them an arm and a leg." Nikki laughs standing next to Casey.

"Terrible joke." Casey says tying up her hair.

The smoke dissipates and reveals the rest of the crew.

Trea is not with them. She is on top of the Phoenix. There is electricity surging through around her hands from the ship. She runs and jumps up as two mini rockets fly up from her legs and suspends her in the air. She uses the electricity she charged up to fire beams of bright blue lightning at all the turrets simultaneously destroying each one. After, she descends to the ground.

"Turrets are down, except for the big one in the back, I need to get closer for that one." She explains walking up to Casey.

"Understood, I will go with you, Tiny get us a map of the compound and find the doctor." Casey says.

The Unusual Alliance walks toward the first building.

Tiny begins hacking the access panel of the building.

"Plenty of contacts further out in the compound, a couple tanks and Mechs too. Good news is they will be in a bottleneck to you, There is not a whole lot of room for the full battalion" Stacey says looking through the scope of her newly acquired sniper from the assassin on the 82nd floor.

Stacey is perched up on the roof of one of the buildings the Phoenix landed on.

Fade, the blind Halox, is oddly enough also perched up with a sniper on the opposite side of Stacey.

"Map is up." Tiny says.

"Rayza, Boroc and Nikki find the doctor and then get the crystal to the ship; everyone else run offense." Casey says.

Tiny hands a small cylinder to Rayza.

"Uh, how big is this crystal?" Rayza asks.

"It gets bigger." Tiny says pointing at the red button on the cylinder.

Boroc grabs Rayza and Nikki's arm.

They disappear and reappear inside the base. Rayza and Nikki shake off the pain of teleporting.

"You are not fun to travel with." Nikki says to Boroc.

"Alright, my turn." Rayza says as she grabs Boroc and Nikki's arms.

All three of them become camouflaged as the same color of the walls of the base.

"Oh my." Nikki says looking at herself.

"It doesn't last very long, so let's get moving." Rayza says.

She checks the map and leads the way.

"Well, so far so good." Tiny says standing next to Casey.

A large explosion knocks Casey, Tiny and Hyda to the ground.

Two tanks and several soldiers make their way toward them.

Angel walks out of the smoke from the crater with a cigar in his mouth.

"You boys are the unlucky first wave." He says with a smile.

The soldiers raise their weapons; Angel grabs the cigar out of his mouth and points up, behind the tanks.

A portal opens up and Gorog lands down on top of the tank. He slams down twice, then grabs the tank by the barrel and swings it around until it hits the other tank. The other tank rolls over the soldiers and is sucked into a portal before crushing Angel, as he puts the cigar back into his mouth.

Around the corner, Casey and Ethereal are waiting on opposite roofs as the two Mechs and more soldiers walk past them.

The second tank is thrown out of another portal and into the Mechs.

Casey and Ethereal open fire on the soldiers from above, while Jo and Ayeka attack from the ground level.

More soldiers begin charging them, but are stopped by Hyda's blade as it plunges into one of the soldier's chest.

They attempt to open fire on him, but several of their heads explode due sniper shots coming from Fade and Stacey.

Ayeka gets pinned to a wall by a trooper, Casey jets down to the ground and pulls him off and shoots the trooper until he falls.

Ethereal does a summersault off the roof firing multiple arrows into several troops before landing safely on the ground.

More soldiers and Mechs march toward the battle.

A void opens up before them, Angel, Trea, Nessarac and Gorog with Tiny on his shoulder step out of the portal.

Tiny pulls out a small canon that transforms into a much larger one as a couple soldiers frantically try to ready their weapons.

Fade shoots them with his automatic custom-made rifle. The rifle has bullets that track the target and is loaded using the feeding belt system. Stacey looks over at Fade as he holds the belt of bullets and continues to fire many shots, not missing any of them.

"Show off." Stacey says to herself.

Gorog roars as Tiny fires a massive blast from her cannon destroying two Mechs. Debris flies in all directions.

Trea goes hand-to-hand with a couple soldiers, along side Angel. Trea breaks the arms of the soldiers, and then tosses them to Angel who finishes them off by a simple touch that ignites them into purple flame.

Nessarac flies straight into a couple of soldiers, picking them up and as he rises, he twists and throws them down to the ground.

Casey, Jo and Ethereal try to catch up and help with the fight.

Ayeka teleports with Hyda into the middle of the battlefield, he falls to his knees, due to the pain.

"You really need to find a nicer way of traveling with people." He says to Ayeka as she helps him up.

Gorog rushes past them into the crowd.

Tiny jumps off and rolls.

A soldier puts a weapon in her face, but Trea cuts off his arms and electrocutes him until he falls over.

"We have to take care of the Turret!" Tiny yells over the sound of a mini war.

Trea helps her up and they both run to the giant Turret in the center of the compound.

"It's not active yet, let's make sure it stays that way." Tiny says running up to the command panel.

Trea runs over to the side of the turret and begins ripping off panels.

"Okay, I'm going to activate it and when I do, give it a little shock inside. That should make sure all parts on the inside get fried." Tiny says working.

"Understood." Trea says struggling to make an opening.

A couple soldiers come running to attack Tiny and Trea.

Casey shoots one in the leg, runs up and kicks him with her boots in the face. Ethereal stabs the other, before he could run away.

"Okay ready?" Tiny asks.

Trea slips her arm inside as far as she can.

"Ready." She responds. Tiny activates the turret, it begins to hum and glow. Trea fires her electrical charge from her hand. The turret short-circuits and shuts down. The discharge sends Trea to ground, Tiny rushes to her aid.

"You good?" Tiny asks.

Trea twitches with a static spark.

"Good." She replies twitching.

Inside the base, Rayza, Nikki and Boroc take down a few guards protecting the door to the labs. Rayza uses a security card to open the door. The door opens to a long dark hallway with a light at the end of it.

"Queue the ominous music." Nikki says as they begin to walk down the hallway.

Dramatic music plays, but the music is being played backwards giving it a very eerie sound. The doors close behind them as they continue down the hallway. Dr. Teyach is humming the tune of the music as they approach the well-lit laboratory. The lab was large, but cluttered. There are two machines on either side of the Cortex Crystal. "Hey doc, good to see you. Now let's pack this shit up and get out of here." Rayza says loudly white walking toward him. Nikki grabs her by the wrist and pulls her back.

"What the hell?" Rayza whispers.

"Look." Nikki whispers back nodding her head. Rayza looks closely at the doctor. His arm is covered in some black substance. His coat is torn and stained. He has a beard that looks several years old, despite the fact it had only been two months since his capture on Helix Prime. His skin is dry and pale. His eyes are bloodshot and the black substance has made its way to his neck. He walks up to the Cortex Crystal and touches it with his tainted arm.

"Oh I see." Rayza says.

"No not yet you don't, but they can show us the way!" Dr. Teyach says rubbing the crystal.

"They?" Nikki asks.

"Okay, well that's all good, but we are running out of time, so if you could just pack it up." Rayza says.

"Time is nothing more than a barrier." The Dr. continues.

Nikki approaches the doctor slowly. Rayza hands the cylinder to Boroc; he walks over to the side.

"There is no escape from what is to come." Dr. Teyach says turning to face Nikki. "I'm sorry doctor, but I know how this ends." Nikki says.

Outside the base, a wormhole opens up in the stratosphere. The Blood Serpent, Tartoroc's vessel emerges from the void. Casey and her crew look up,

"Ah shit." Casey says.

"Do you think he's still mad about Seraco?" Tiny asks over the COM.

The Blood Serpent charges up a laser.

Nikki eyes widen, she turns to Rayza and Boroc and covers them in a pink aura.

The Blood Serpent fires down on to the laboratory, demolishing the building in two shots.

"Nikki!" Casey screams and runs over to the destruction.

Stacey and Fade leave their post and head toward the battle.

"Rayza! Boroc!" Casey yells over COM as she runs to the rubble.

Tiny readies her cannon by hitting a few buttons. The gun expands and three legs attach to the ground making it a large stationary weapon. Tiny flips out a scope and aims for the Blood Serpent, the cannon hums then glows.

"Let's see how you like it" Tiny says to herself.

The cannon fires a massive blue beam that is so bright it turns the day to night. The light is blinding to the rest of the Alliance, but Angel puffs his cigar as the beam flies fast and hits the Blood Serpent near the front with a crippling blow.

There are several explosions through out the Blood Serpent. The shot didn't destroy the vessel, but it could have, had Tiny had a better angle.

Casey continues to call over COM as she begins frantically pulling rocks off, even though there was no way she could clear a path in time. The rest of the crew assembles at the destroyed building.

The rubble explodes open, Nikki rises with Boroc and Rayza unharmed. They descend to Casey. Nikki pulls the case containing the crystal out from the rubble. "You guys okay?" Casey asks.

"Yeah I'm good but the doc didn't make it." Rayza says taking a seat on top of the rubble.

"I'm not! Look what happened to my hair!" Nikki says pointing at it.

There isn't much of a difference; it just looks a little untamed Casey thinks.

Casey gives Nikki a quick hug catching her by surprise,

"I'm just glad you guys are okay." Casey says. Nikki smiles and hugs her back.

"Hate to break up this heartwarming fuck fest, but we have a problem." Tiny says pointing up at the Blood Serpent as several carrier ships descend to the surface.

"Seems to me they want the crystal." Tiny says.

"Corbus!" Nessarac says.

"Get in line Asshole!" Hyda yells.

"Alright, take it easy, how much time do we have?" Casey asks.

"One hour." Tiny responds.

"Ayeka can you take Tiny, Trea and the crystal back to the ship?" Casey asks.

Ayeka nods and teleports over to Tiny, then to Trea, then to the crystal and finally they reappear on the Phoenix. Tiny rushes to the cockpit to activate the cloaking and extra shielding.

"Wait a minute we got the crystal, why don't we just leave?" Rayza asks,

"Because Tartoroc needs to pay for his crimes, even if we can't kill him, we can make sure he doesn't leave this planet." Casey says.

"They have an army on the way, there is only fourteen of us!" Rayza yells.

Nikki looks at the rubble.

"Can we leave this spot?" She asks worried. Casey looks over at her.

"You okay?" Casey asks.

"Please." Nikki says. She is afraid of something, Casey could tell.

"Hey guys." Angel says looking at an army that has gathered on the hill behind the compound. Tartoroc is front and center with Serenity and Corbus on both sides of him. There are four tanks and many troops on either side of Tartoroc.

"We do this together." Casey says jumping down from the rubble. Casey and her crew walk out to the desert field between them and Tartoroc. Nikki takes one more look at the rubble then catches up with the crew. A couple rocks move in the rubble.

THE NIGHTMARE

"THERE ARE MANY THINGS IN THIS UNIVERSE THAT CAN NOT be explained. Life, death and the delusions of hope you and your friends have of saving a doomed galaxy. None of you were able to live with your own failures and so you try for redemption by banning together in hopes to run from the nightmare that haunts you." Tartoroc's voice bellows across the field.

This is what many call the calm before the storm, not a sound, but the breeze and the Unusual Alliance walking to meet the storm.

They form what Nikki refers to as a "Hero Line". Trea, Hyda, Rayza, Ethereal, Boroc, Stacey, Gorog, Casey, Nikki, Ayeka, Jo, Angel and Fade now stand side by side across from an almost impossible feat.

Casey is now beginning to realize that Tartoroc is much larger in person. Only a few Katharacs in every generation grows to his size. He is, maybe, a little shorter than Gorog. His fur is cut short and has a reddish brown color to it, or at least his arms are. Armor covers his body and shoulders, but no helmet. It must interfere with his abilities, she thinks. Although he doesn't have the cute fox ears and tail like the Sieren do, his eyes are similar. Half-breed Sierens posses the eyes, but they only draw power from a few stars, as opposed to a whole Galaxy. They are not as powerful or connected, however, Tartoroc is a fearsome opponent with nothing left to loose.

"I take it you're still mad about Seraco?" Casey yells across the field. Tartoroc smirks with anger.

"Hand over the crystal now and I might spare one of you!" He roars.

"Oh my, he sounds serious." Nikki says.

"I'll tell you what Mistoffelees, how about you surrender before we kick your ass!" Casey yells. Tartoroc and his companions laugh.

"Your optimism amuses me, however that is all you will ever amount to!" Tartoroc roars and signals his tanks to fire. Sixteen fiery mortar shots fly across the field. Stacey quickly runs to Casey's side, her hand charges up electricity.

"Hurry up, I won't be able to hold it long!" Stacey cries before she punches the ground creating a small crater.

Her arm emits an electric energy shield destroying the mortar shots. Stacey keeps her fist firm into the dirt still emitting the energy to keep the shield up. Nikki pulls Casey back away from Stacey. Everyone is huddled together as Angel and Ethereal on both sides begin using the earth to create a dome. Stacey screams as her Energy shield continues to take hits. The electricity from her fist begins to burn away the skin on her arm revealing a black metal arm with streaks of a fluorescent dark green. Nikki grabs Stacey with her ability and pulls her inside the earth dome before it closes up.

"Ready?" Angel asks staring at Ethereal with his glowing orange eyes.

"Yeah." Ethereal responds also with glowing orange eyes. Ethereal puts one hand on the wall of dirt and the earth below their feet begins to descend like an elevator straight to hell. The earth elevator stops once they are far enough away from the surface.

Nikki reinforces the dome at the surface with her ability by creating a pink dome to cover the original. More shots hit the dome and part of the compound around it. Stacey screams in pain. Her metal arm is torn from her shoulder; there are wires from the arm that have been severed and are covered in blood from her shoulder. Jo is holding Stacey's head on her lap as she checks the arm and tries to fix it.

"Jo?" Casey asks.

"I don't know this is a little out of my depth" Jo says.

"We have to move from here!" Nikki says having a little trouble holding the pink shield up from continuous barrage from the tanks.

"Okay I got her legs." Casey says lifting up Stacey's legs. Ethereal then places both hands on the wall in front of her and a large tunnel begins forming. Ethereal leads as her hands continue to glow orange, Jo and Casey carry Stacey behind her. The crew follows after them down the dark tunnel underground.

Nikki releases her hold on the dome; the tanks continue to fire a few more shots to fully eradicate their "Pathetic excuse of cover." Serenity says.

"Finish them off Serenity and do not fail me this time." Tartoroc says.

Serenity signals her troops and begins walking down to the half-way-destroyed dome.

Ethereal comes to a stop and creates a dome underground so they could regroup in it. Jo and Casey lay Stacey down. Rayza tries to help with Stacey's arm.

"Okay we need a plan because hiding underground isn't exactly heroic." Rayza says.

"Anyone got any ideas on how to deal with him?" Stacey says sitting up with a fixed arm. Gorog says something in Groutarian.

Nikki gasps.

"Whoa!" Casey says.

Jo and Trea giggle in the corner.

"You got a real mouth on you pal." Hyda says.

"That's disgusting Gorog!" Rayza says.

"You should be ashamed of yourself." Ethereal says.

Gorog apologizes and pouts.

"I have an idea." Angel says. Everyone looks to him.

"We are going to need all the explosives." Angel says with a smile.

Back on the surface, Serenity and a majority of the army move in closer to the dome. Two tanks slowly make their way on either side of the dome. Serenity activates her blade and cuts open the dome to reveal nothing, a flat surface with nothing but ash and rubble. Serenity turns around as one of the tanks is launched up and thrown twenty feet in the air. The tank comes back down quick. Serenity jumps out of the way as it crashes down onto a group of soldiers. She activates her blades and looks over to where the tank went up. She walks up to the spot slowly with two soldiers. There is a small hole in a small crater. Two small holes open up underneath the two troopers and a slimy black tentacle pierces through their bodies.

The tentacles burst through their spines and lift the soldiers up off the ground. Different colors of blood spew out of the bodies before the tentacles rip them in half. Serenity runs and tries to cut them but the tentacles recede into the ground before she can. Another hole begins to open up beneath Serenity, but she rolls out of the way before the tentacle can get her. All the soldiers direct their attention to the ground and anywhere else. An earthquake shakes the ground beneath the soldiers. The quake is short, but when it ends the rubble of the base explodes open. Fifteen black slimy tentacles rise up from the rubble. There is a black figure walking out of the debris. The body is a combination of smoke and slimy tar like dripping goo. The encumbering black smoke has a mind of it's own. The tentacles are emitting from the figure's smoke and flail in every direction. The bright purple eyes are the only features of the face that are visible.

Soldiers open fire on the figure, the tentacles block all the shots while killing a few soldiers with a quick stab through the face. The remaining tank fires a shot at the creature. The tentacles coil around the fiery shot and redirect it back at the tank. The top half of the tank explodes into tiny pieces as the driver is burning alive screaming in pain.

Tartoroc signals the rest of his army to engage the unknown foe. Corbus flies straight into the sky to lead Tartoroc's army into battle. Tartoroc heads back to the ships. All the carrier ships explode. The explosion is powerful and massive, but Tartoroc doesn't budge just puts his hand up to shield his eyes. When he puts his hand down, Angel and Casey are standing between him and the fiery wreckage.

The rest of the Unusual Alliance rises from the ground behind Tartoroc's army. "Okay everybody we do this together!" Nikki yells. Everyone turns on their weapons.

So there is no confusion, the final fight will be split into two parts both of which are happening simultaneously.

TARTOROC V.S. ANGEL AND CASEY

"SO, WERE YOU PLANNING ON LEAVING EARLY?" CASEY SAYS pointing back to the wreckage.

"Miss Williams, you and I both know you don't have the strength to kill me, unfortunately, for you I do posses enough power to kill both of you." Tartoroc says.

"You know, I told Nikki that and she said and I quote 'If I were to fight him it would be over in seconds and that's too anti-climatic of an ending.' So, you are stuck with us." Casey says with a smile. Tartoroc smirks

"Angel, I'm surprised to see you here. Heroism doesn't suit you." Tartoroc says.

Angel's eyes and hands lite up with purple fire, Casey pulls out a single pistol.

"Are we done talking?" Casey asks.

Tartoroc takes two steps forward and a small click sound goes off. A small disc rises from the ground and disperses a pink smoke cloud. Tartoroc coughs and swats the smoke away. His vision becomes blurred as though he has just been poisoned.

"Hey are you okay? You don't look so good." Casey says sarcastically.

Tartoroc focuses his vision and stands up straight.

"If you think I will need my Sieren abilities to kill you, you will be sorely mistaken." He says, as his muscles grow larger.

His claws fully extend from his hands. Katharac claws are almost indestructible and cut through most metals easily. He changes his stance to be more aggressive. Casey can almost see the orange energy aura around him.

Tartoroc roars then rushes Angel and Casey with both arms ready to attack. Tartoroc swings at them but they manage to dodge his attack. Casey empties the clips in her pistols on Tartoroc but he quickly lifts a large piece of the ground and throws it at her. Tartoroc quickly puts his focus on Angel. He tries to slice him, but Angel blocks his claws with small void tears. Angel opens a portal above and behind Tartoroc. Casey comes out and lands on Tartoroc's back.

She tries to stab his back like a psychopath, but his hide is too tough even for a blade made of light and energy to pierce through. He grabs Casey and throws her far away. Angel opens a portal to catch her while also holding back Tartoroc's attacks. Casey falls into the portal like a ball into an outfielders glove.

Her travel through the portal isn't instantaneous this time. She is floating in a space of black and purple. There are stars and galaxies on either side of her. She continues to fall, but very slowly as though she is underwater. Casey looks to her side and sees Nikki and the rest of the crew fighting something right before she is ripped forward out to reality.

Casey comes out disoriented. She takes a knee to gather her balance. Angel uses the earth to uppercut Tartoroc throwing his footing off. Tartoroc quickly recovers, but before he can attack a bright blue beam blasts him into the wreckage of the carrier ships. Casey runs to Angel's side.

"You really like those gloves don't you Miss Williams?" Angel asks out of breath. "Yeah they really give me that knock out punch, you know?" Casey says waving her hands to cool them off.

Tartoroc breaks his way out of the debris and throws a wing of the ship at the two of them. Angel creates a portal to catch it, while Casey sprints for Tartoroc with two pistols. He jumps out of the wreckage and slams down on the ground in front of Casey. She fires at him, but he blocks the shots with his arm.

A portal opens up behind Tartoroc sending the wing he threw back at him, but Tartoroc has learned from last time and cuts the wing in half and continues to attack Casey. Casey uses her boots to boost away from his claws.

Tartoroc isn't as fast as Serenity, but he's definitely a lot stronger, no time for fuck ups Casey thinks to herself.

Tartoroc gets irritated with trying to hit her, so instead he slams his fist into the earth causing a fissure that erupts the land and trips her. Casey falls on her back and looks up to see Tartoroc coming down with full force. She quickly uses her boots to boost her away from his attack barely making it in time. Tartoroc stands up slowly from the small crater his attack had made.

"This would be so much easier if you just give me the crystal." Tartoroc says cracking his neck.

"I'm not giving you a crystal so you can destroy the universe with it." Casey says. "Destroy? Ms. Williams, I plan to save the universe, free it from all things that threaten our way of life." Tartoroc says.

"Our? You mean your way of life, and what do *you* consider threatening? Your Rebel Militia slaughtered hundreds of Human and Nexus colonies, so forgive me if I'm having trouble believing you." Casey responds with anger in her voice.

"They were a small price to pay for the safety of the universe. Just like your failures will bare the death of your friends." Tartoroc says.

"I will kill you, if you touch any of them, just like your precious Seraco." Casey threatens him.

"Humans always take credit for what they can't accomplish themselves." Tartoroc bellows. His face changes and he stands tall and his eyes glow. The aura around him became more visible. His Sieren powers have returned. He raises his hand up and using his telekinesis, he lifts Casey up off the ground holding her in place. He slowly walks toward her.

"You're right, I didn't destroy your planet, but I did plant that disc on your shoulder." Casey manages to say. She uses her thumb to twist a ring on her index finger.

The disc explodes with more pink smoke right into Tartoroc's face. Casey is released from his hold as he coughs and swats the smoke away. Angel rushes him from behind while Casey takes the front. Angel hits his lower back while Casey drop kicks him in the face. Tartoroc falls to the ground.

Casey backflips to be at Angel's side and pulls out her rifle. Angel lights his hands up with his purple fire. Casey opens fire with her rifle; Tartoroc shields his face and body with his arms. She fires regular photon shots and four mini rockets that explode against Tartoroc's arm.

There is a large could of smoke where Tartoroc is kneeling. The smoke dissipates revealing Tartoroc unscathed as he cracks his neck in both directions. He roars loudly and slams both of his fists on the ground in front of him. The power of his hit created a small earthquake, Casey and Angel try to keep a stable footing, but Tartoroc rushes them before they can. He punches Angel hard across the face sending him a few feet away. He tries the same thing on Casey, but she dodges the punch only to be kneed in the gut almost breaking the rib that just healed. She falls to the ground heaving and coughing. Tartoroc grabs her, his whole hand easily wrapping around her body. He tosses her like a piece of trash in his way. Her rifle falls into a lava pit nearby as she lands hard on the dirt somewhat close to Angel.

She groans.

"Okay we need a knew plan, because *this* is not working." Casey says slowly getting up. Angel is still lying on the ground.

"Well, I have an idea but it's not that good." Angel says right before Tartoroc steps on him. Casey tries to help, but Tartoroc picks her up before she can.

"Pathetic little insects." He says putting more weight down on Angel. Casey tries to squirm out of his hold but no use. Angel's eyes light up.

Dealing with a different problem, Nikki flies up high to get a better vantage point. A portal opens up next to her when she is high enough. She looks inside the portal and sees Angel and Casey being held by Tartoroc.

Nikki charges her fist with a pink energy and fires a bright pink beam down at the back of his head. Tartoroc stumbles and looks to see where it came from. Casey manages to get her dagger and actually stab his forearm. She gets free of his hold as he steps off of Angel. He pulls the dagger out and crushes it in his hand until a pop and spark is seen. He grins and takes one step toward Casey, before getting hit by Angel's purple fire in the form of a tornado knocking him into a nearby bolder.

"I'm running out of weapons and patience and ammo." Casey says as she looks to Angel. He falls to one knee,

"Hey are you okay?" Casey asks helping him up.

"Running out of ammo." He says.

"Then it's time we finish this." Casey says. Angel nods in agreement before opening a portal for her to hop into. Tartoroc explodes out of the rubble of the bolder. His aura is visible and much larger than before.

"I would have never imagined killing you idiots would be so much fun." Tartoroc says walking toward Angel.

"Oh trust me, we're a blast!" Casey yells right before firing her rocket launcher. The shot leaving the barrel is a purple orb with a green flame around it.

Tartoroc stretches his hand to catch it. The shot explodes once it hits his hand and implodes as it should, but Tartoroc is unharmed. Tartoroc lifts his hand now glowing more green and orange.

"Oh fuck." Casey says. Tartoroc using his other hand fires a massive orange beam at Casey. She raises her hands to block it. The gloves take the energy, but the force from the blast pushes Casey into some wreckage causing an explosion.

"No!" Angel yells before his eyes light up orange. He uses the earth to grab Tartoroc's shoulders and pull him down to the ground. Angel's right eye then becomes purple. His fist light up with purple fire, he then punches him over and over. Tartoroc breaks free and punches Angel to the ground.

He tries to step on him but Angel rolls out of the way and uses the earth to make a fist and punch Tartoroc. He loses his balance a little, before destroying the earth fist and firing an orange beam at Angel. Thinking quickly, Angel makes a portal on the ground and comes out above Tartoroc with a purple energy blade shaped like a trident barreling down at him. Tartoroc puts his hand up to block the blade. Angel cuts three of his fingers before getting punched so hard it sends him ten feet away. Tartoroc growls and fights through the pain. He walks over to Angel's blade sticking out of the ground. He picks it up and slowly walks over to Angel.

"You have my respect Angel. Once I have the power the Cortex Crystals provide, Phazel will be able to live its miserable span of existence as one of my satellites." Tartoroc says stopping right behind Angel who is on his knees.

"Why don't you say that to my face?" Angel says like a cocky drunk with a bloody face. "Very well." Tartoroc says before picking Angel up by his head.

"Your own blade will be the very last thing your pathetic eyes ever see." Tartoroc says lifting up the blade to plunge into Angel's face.

Tartoroc quickly drops Angel and turns around to stop a bright green orb. It pushes him back a few feet before he clenches his fist to extinguish it.

"It's going to take more than..."

Casey uses her boots to push him into a nearby boulder to cut off Tartoroc.

His back slams hard into the boulder knocking the wind out of him. Casey uses her boots and knee uppercut his jaw before he can react. She quickly pulls out her energy whip and jumps on the other side of the boulder while wrapping it around Tartoroc's throat. She pulls tight on the whip. Tartoroc chokes as he struggles to get the whip from his neck.

Casey puts her feet on the boulder to hold a better ground as she pulls harder. Tartoroc slips one of his fingers pass the whip, he manages to get a firm grip and pulls it away from his throat. Casey tries to hold her side, but ends up letting go.

She pulls out her last two guns and jet-jumps over the boulder firing the two SMGs down at Tartoroc. He quickly covers his head from the incoming fire. The shots however rip up the flesh of his arm.

He uses his telekinesis and disassembles the two guns right out of her hands before she touches the ground. Casey pulls out a dagger and quickly drives it into his lower leg. Tartoroc roars from the pain, he punches down on to Casey disorienting her. He kicks her hard causing her to roll a few feet away; she picks up Angel's blade hilt along the way. Tartoroc pulls the dagger from his leg and drops it. He looks for Casey, but she is nowhere to be seen.

One of Angel's portals opens up above Tartoroc and Casey comes flying out with Angel's blade lit up. Tartoroc raises his hand to stop her, but is too late. Casey forces the blade down through his hand severing his thumb down through to his shoulder cutting his arm clean off. Blood spews out of his socket, some splashing on Casey before Tartoroc uses his ability to push Casey away with a lot of power.

Tartoroc holds his blood hole while looking down at his bloodied arm. He looks up and sees Casey standing with blood dripping from her hand gripping the blade hilt tightly. Her hair is covering part of her serious but scary facial expression.

The most terrifying thing is in her eyes. There're strange symbols of blue and white around the pupil of her eye. Casey changes her footing slightly not taking her eyes off of him.

"What are you?" Tartoroc says trembling.

Casey flips the sword around and sprints at Tartoroc. He uses his remaining arm to rip the ground up to stop her, or at the very least slow her down. She jet-jumps over the incoming rubble and rolls behind him.

She slices his back twice before he turns around to strike her, but she ducks under his attack and drives the blade into his gut. He falls to his knees blood pouring from his mouth.

Casey pushes it in further, "I told you. I would kill you, if you touched any of them." Casey says before pulling out the blade and shoving it through his jaw and up into his cranium. The stars in his eyes flicker before going black like a burnt out light bulb. Casey pulls the blade out and looks at her blood soak hands.

Tartoroc's body falling over startles her. She begins to look around, then back at the body. It felt like a dream to her, killing him. As if someone was controlling her, when she was fighting him. She could see it happening, but couldn't do anything about it. She snaps back into reality and looks for Angel. She sees him lying on his back on the ground a few feet away. She drops the blade and runs to him. She kneels next to him "Are you alive?" She asks.

"Sadly yes." Angel says opening one eye. Casey smiles and helps him get up.

She puts his arm over her and holds his side. They walk together back to the Phoenix, but something is off. There is no sound of a battle in that direction. Did Nikki and rest of them already finish them off? Either way Casey has a feeling that this isn't over yet.

THE UNUSUAL
ALLIANCE V. S.
THE NIGHTMARE

"OKAY GUYS, NOW LET'S WORK TOGETHER AND REMEMBER I should get the most screen time because I'm obviously the beautiful one." Nikki says fixing her hair.

"What the fuck is that?" Rayza says looking at the army fighting the black slimy figure.

The Unusual Alliance watches the army get spanked by the one person, while Serenity and Corbus run away with a small amount of soldiers to a drop ship landing down leaving a majority of the army behind.

Nessarac roars and flies toward Corbus.

"Hey!" Hyda yells out chasing him. Nikki sighs,

"I *just* said we needed to work together. Oh well, let's go!" Nikki says excited.

"Yeah I'm pretty sure Casey isn't paying us that much." Rayza says.

"Quit being a coward." Ethereal says readying her bow.

"We should probably help Hyda out and take this thing as a group." Stacey says.

"Nah, Corbus is going to get away, Hyda will get his revenge in the second story." Nikki says.

"Since you're seeing the future do we win this fight?" Rayza asks.

"No." Nikki says. Everyone looks at her.

"But we will give it our all and then things will be okay." Nikki finishes with a big smile. Everyone else shrugs and begins walking toward the crazy creature.

"Just okay?" Rayza complains.

They begin their march toward the black evil creature strangling the life out of the last few soldiers. This black slimy creature is the stuff of nightmares. There is no face, so it makes it difficult to look at. As for the body, it seems to be humanoid by the looks of it. It turns its faceless head toward the Alliance. Nikki floats down in front of its gaze.

"So you are very ugly and dangerous and we are kind of like a new thing now. You know heroes, guardians, and revenge enthusiasts. The Unusual Alliance, maybe you've heard of us?" Nikki says.

The Nightmare's face forms a mouth with razor sharp teeth and creepily says, "Bring me the Cortex Crystal."

"Gross, it sounds like he has spider webs in his throat." Nikki says.

The Nightmare raises six black tentacles around him. All six of them fly fast at Nikki but she flies up. Two of them follow her up while the other four head straight for Rayza, Ethereal, Boroc and Stacey. Before any of them could get close, they are cut in half by Hyda's double bladed energy sword flying through and sticking into a nearby halfway-destroyed building.

Nightmare turns his attention to Hyda running at him. Hyda uses his ability to retract his blade back to his hand. He twirls it around before jumping to attack; Nightmare simply pushes him back with an unseen force. Stacey opens fire with her pistols and Boroc uses his chain gun, but the shots don't do any damage. Their shots hit his slimy flesh like bullets hitting water. Ethereal uses the earth to hold him in place

"Nice! Now punch him in his stupid face!" Nikki yells. Gorog and Rayza run up to punch him in the face but are lifted up but their feet by more tentacles. Ayeka teleports above the tentacles holding Gorog and Rayza, she cuts them free and rolls when she lands.

Two more tentacles move toward her, but get smashed into the ground by Stacey's fist. Stacey pulls out a pistol and shoots his mouth with six shots directly hitting. Nightmare sends more tentacles out to grab her, but before they can Nikki fires a bright pink energy beam from her hands into the Nightmare, sending him flying about twenty feet away. Nikki lands next to Stacey reloading her pistol. The Nightmare slowly rises up. He uses his tentacles to stab into the already dead soldiers. The tentacles begin to reanimate the bodies. Their eyes are covered in a thick white smoke as the bones in their body crack and snap back into a barely standing form. The soldiers' raise their weapons to the hip.

"That's not good." Rayza says. Ethereal pulls out her staff and quickly raises the earth into a long wall to block the incoming blaster fire.

The Alliance takes cover behind Ethereal's wall. Stacey, Boroc and Rayza return fire with their pistols peaking in and out of cover. The shots they manage get out hit the soldiers, but the black goo repairs the damage instantaneously.

"Alright, Ethereal get ready to push this wall!" Nikki says before Nessarac comes flying down firing a medium sized red beam from his eyes down onto the soldiers' heads. The second the beams touch each head of the soldiers, the heads explode and the bodies drop. Nessarac lands down between Nightmare and the wall. Ethereal crumbles the wall with her staff more dug into the ground. Several symbols glow orange on the ground around her and the staff.

"Give some time." Ethereal says.

"You heard her ladies!" Nikki yells flying straight up to get a better vantage point. Boroc and Ayeka teleport on either side of Nightmare and begin shooting at him. Nessarac and Gorog rush him while he distracted by the twins or so they thought. Nightmare uses tentacles to slow both of them down. Fade drops down on top of him, using two energy daggers he stabs both sides of his neck area.

Hyda and Rayza slip pass his mess of tentacles and attempt to slice or stab him. His movements are sporadic and impossible to predict. Fade holds on tight like a rodeo clown on a bull. Rayza and Hyda take turns trying to hit him so not to hit each other. Nightmare eventually pushes the two of them away with his power while pulling Fade off with one of his extra appendages and tossing him into debris.

Stacey uses her fist to release Gorog and Nessarac from the tangle of his tentacles. Electrical energy surges through the slimy vines causing them to recede back to Nightmare. He uses tentacles to hold up Boroc and Ayeka. He throws them at Hyda and Rayza. Ethereal's staff continues to form more symbols on the ground. Nightmare takes notice and sends a few tentacles her way, but before they could strike her Jo uses a very strange energy blade to reduce them down to nothing. The blade is the shape of the figure eight and has a fluorescent purple glow.

"I'm almost ready!" Ethereal yells.

Nikki is finally high enough, she powers up her fist. They glow a bright pink, electricity circles around her and her eyes begin to glow a light blue. A portal opens up next to Nikki. She looks inside and sees Tartoroc holding Angle and Casey.

"I knew he would need my help." Nikki says shaking her head. She forms her hand into a gun and fires a small shot at the back of his head. The portal closes and Nikki dives down fast at Nightmare slamming all the stored energy she has down on him. He blocks her attack, but the ground beneath him becomes a large crater. The rest of the alliance retreats back to Ethereal's position. Nikki forces more energy down on him, the crater becomes massive, but Nightmare is unaffected.

"Nikki." Ethereal whispers. Nikki stops her attack catching him off guard and kicks his head causing it to spin before she flies back behind Ethereal.

Nightmare twists his head back around to see Ethereal spin her staff around. She slams the gem into the ground. Four thick and large cylinders made of earth slam into Nightmare holding him in place as they melt into the ground around him. He struggles to get free, but no use as the dirt creates a cocoon of mud and cement from the destroyed buildings.

Ethereal flips her staff and lifts the gem to the sky. A small black cloud quickly appears and sends one lightning bolt down onto the gem. Ethereal flips her staff one more time and points the gem now glowing bright red right at Nightmare.

A massive beam of orange and black hews fly out of the gem. The energy force exerting from the blast pushes everyone else back while Ethereal stands firm. The beam hits Nightmare sending him miles out of the compound and into a lava lake. The beam destroys everything in its path; the energy fades away and Ethereal falls to her knees using the staff to hold herself up.

Sweat pours down her face as she attempts to catch her breath. Nikki lands next to her, to try to help her up.

"Can you stand?" Nikki asks.

"No." Ethereal says.

The rest of the alliance gathers around Nikki and Ethereal. Nikki looks out over the lava lake, waves begin to form where Nightmare had landed.

"We don't have a lot of time." Nikki says.

"There is no way that thing is still alive." Rayza says.

"He is and this is the part where we lose." Nikki says.

"I'm not dying here." Jo grunts out.

"No one is dying here, Jo." Nikki replies while still holding Ethereal.

"I assume you have a plan?" Rayza asks.

"Casey will save us." Nikki says.

"WHAT! Casey! Ethereal just gave it her all and it's still alive; You gave it your all and it's still alive! You really think Casey is going to be able kill that thing?" Nikki stands up and walks over to Rayza. She places one hand on her shoulder,

"Yeah I do." Nikki says right before making her fall asleep with her abilities.

Nikki catches her and whispers in her ear before using her telekinesis to push her far away from the rest of them. She uses her ability to place her in a safe spot hidden from view of Nightmare.

"So that's it, we are going to die here." Hyda says.

"No, we just need a heavy hitter for my plan to work." Nikki says with smile turning around to encourage her team.

"We got this guys! Boroc take Ethereal back to the ship." Nikki says.

Boroc teleports to her side, but she stops him.

"No, I will continue to fight." Ethereal says attempting to stand.

"Alright suit yourself." Nikki says with a smile.

However, the sight of Nightmare slowly rising up out of the lava and making his way to land quickly takes her smile away. His form has changed, more slender and terrifying. He looks like candlestick of pure black wax and his black head is a matching resemblance to a flame on the wick. He slithers out of the lava slowly, several tentacles rise up in front of him. These ones are different, they have a red glow at the tip of each one and seem to maneuver faster than the last ones. Nikki's heart begins to race; she takes a couple deep breaths before letting out

"Shit."

Nightmare slowly moves forward forming more tentacles with red tips. Nikki flies straight up and fires pink energy beams from her hands at Nightmare. He blocks her attacks.

Boroc and Ayeka use a special technique called "Doe Jin" where they stand across from each other and they proceed to wave their hands in different directions before generating a light blue energy ball. They plunge their hands into the energy and when they pull them back the energy has now transferred to their hands. They point their fists toward Nightmare; four bright blue beams of energy knock him back into the lava. The tentacles lunge at the twins, they wrap around them and the red tips touch the back of their neck. Grey smoke clouds up their eyes and their bodies become dead weight.

Nikki flies away cutting down the few tentacles that go after her.

Ethereal cuts two down before the third attaches to her. Her eyes become cloudy with the same grey smoke as she falls to the ground.

Fade fights off four of them before falling.

Jo cuts a few a down and is almost taken, but Nessarac saves her from it. Unfortunately he falls into the strange spell.

Jo runs and re groups with Gorog who has four tentacles already attached. He continues to fight despite the spell, until the fifth one attaches to him and his eyes become grey as he falls.

Jo shoots down a few tentacles before they take her.

Only Stacey, Hyda and Nikki remain. They are back to back to back fighting off the infinite amount of tentacles. Nightmare slowly walks toward them while he ceases his attacks. "I thought you said we were not going to die" Stacey says reloading her pistols. "You're only going to wish he had killed us." Nikki says. Nightmare walks toward the trio.

"Give me the crystal and I will make sure to do it quick and painless." He says as gets closer to them.

"Well, I can promise you this will be painful." Hyda says.

His fists clench tight onto his hilt, electricity surges from his hands. Hyda swings his blade toward him and several of his appendages. He exerts his energy into his blade causing currents of energy that cut through Nightmare.

He cuts down all of his tentacles.

Nightmare rebuilds himself quickly. Hyda runs at him to deliver a final blow, but is tripped and taken down by one of the tentacles before he could reach him.

"Nikki run!" Stacey says before using her fist to fire a beam of rainbow colors at Nightmare knocking him back. Nikki flies straight up and watches Stacey get taken by this monster. He looks up at Nikki.

Nikki clenches her fist and vibrant pink aura surrounds her hands and eyes. She remains airborne as the red tentacles slowly try to climb up to her.

"Sorry, but there is no chance of you getting me!" Nikki yells down to him. Nightmare smiles, his teeth are razor sharp and resemble shark teeth.

"You pathetic creature, I already have you." He says softly.

The sky turns black along with everything else. The setting quickly changes to a black room of oozing tar that begins to close in around Nikki. She uses her energy and blasts back the goop and flies straight at him. She punches him, hard but he just smiles and fades away.

The floor turns into a marble tile; one Nikki is very familiar with. She hears heavy footsteps behind her. She turns around slowly not looking up from the tile. She feels a pit in her stomach, terrified. She knew exactly who she was about to look at. She looks up slowly scanning the man. He wore boots of high quality and silver armor with gold gauntlets. There is one red sash coming from his left shoulder. She looks up at his face. He is a Sieren, his skin tone is more on the red side compared to most Sieren and his eyes show the horsehead nebula.

He is Nikki's father, the leader of the Sierens. He is an abusive dictator.

"Your pathetic!" He shouts at Nikki. Nikki clenches her fist, but the power of the galaxy has deserted her. She runs at him, but he throws her down to the ground. She tries to get back up, but black chains hold her in place. A shadow of a tall Sieren woman appears at his side, He grabs her by the neck and throws her to the ground. Nikki screams and struggles to get free, but it's no use, this place is a hell specifically made for her.

Outside in reality, Nikki's body lies on the warm dirt with grey smoke covering her eyes. The rest of the Unusual Alliance is also in a dream like state of their own fears.

Gorog's nightmare deals with a friend who betrays him to steal the crown he is not fit for. Gorog is heir to the throne and believes that even he is not worthy of the crown.

Nessarac's nightmare is to watch his family be killed over and over again. Just like Nikki's, black chains are holding him as it happens.

Hyda's dream inflicts horrible pain as he sent to a nightmarish world, with monsters that rip him apart limb from limb, over and over.

In Stacey's dream she is buried alive in a metal coffin that continues to get smaller. Stacey is claustrophobic and this was the worst way to go for her. She punches and screams, but the container won't budge and no one is going to hear her screams.

Ethereal's fear is watching an evil black shadow creature kill the Maiden and everyone on Phazel.

The Twins nightmares both involve each other dying, but in Boroc's nightmare, he is the one to die, not her.

Fade's nightmare is watching his people be enslaved by Humans and not being able to fight back.

Jo's dream is interesting considering R.A.I.S don't have brains. She is shown a vision of Rounon, the home world of the R.A.I.S in flames and her two best friends; Tiny and Trea are hanging off of spikes. Their bodies are torn to shreds and the city crumbles before her very eyes.

While the alliance is trapped in their nightmares, Tiny and Trea are aboard the Phoenix.

"Tiny, how much time do we have?" Trea asks walking from the cockpit.

"Ten minutes at best." Tiny says messing with the projector.

She and Trea get headaches and flashes of Jo's vision begin to appear in their heads. All R.A.I.S share the information through their CPU brains. The headaches stop as quickly as they started.

"What the hell was that?" Trea asks.

"I don't know." Tiny says before grabbing her ear com.

"Hey guys what's going on out there?" Tiny asks over the channel.

No response.

She accesses her pad to hone in on one COM device.

"Casey!" Tiny yells.

"What's up Tiny?" Casey asks.

"What's going out there? I can't get a hold of anyone." Tiny says worried.

"Me and Angel are on our way to meet up with the rest of them. Just get the ship running." Casey says ending the com and holding up Angel.

Casey and Angel walk down toward the battlefield to find their comrades incapacitated with grey smoke emitting from their eyes with tears raining down their faces. The tentacles attached to the back of their heads, with a red flickering glow from within the slimy black exterior. Nightmare stands across the sea of bodies from Casey.

"Angel I'm going to put you down." Casey whispers.

"Stall him for five minutes." Angel whispers to her.

She nods and sets him down. Casey takes a few steps forward away from Angel. She walks over to Stacey, kneels next to her and checks her pulse. Still breathing, thank Cortex, Casey thinks. She sees one of Stacey's pistols lying on the ground next to her. Casey picks up the pistol and clenches it tight as she stands up.

"Let them go." Casey says. Nightmare's black goo recedes into his body; Dr. Teyach now stands in its step. His lab coat and clothes are torn and cindered probably from the explosion. His body, however, has no gashes or bruises or damage of any kind. His eyes emit a strange array of colors and his face has black veins coming from his scalp.

"Hello Casey." He says calmly.

"Doctor." Casey replies. It does not surprise her to see what he has become; his search for knowledge has always been an addiction to say the least. Even then it never hurt anybody, just ruined his life, well until now.

"How are the boots?" he asks.

"They're a little clunky." She says with a smile. He asked her how they were the first time they met, seemed only fitting for him to ask again here in the end she thought.

"I had a feeling he would choose you to retrieve the crystal, tell me how is Sully these days?" Teyach asks.

"He's dead." Casey replies.

"Pity, he had such dreams for the future of humanity." Teyach says.

He takes two steps forward.

"The Cortex Crystal however, can make those dreams a reality. It can give humanity a second chance. It will bestow power to the god Cortex himself to those who are worthy." Teyach says.

"Something tells me you are going to force this gift of power." Casey says.

He breathes in and exhales.

"Ms. Williams, give me the crystal and I will release your friends." He says calmly with a comfortable smile. Casey has the upper hand, sort of, she thinks to herself. He can't sense the crystal nor can he take the answer from her crew.

"I'm sorry Doc, I can't do that." Casey says clenching Angel's energy blade hilt in her hand. Teyach takes a step forward as the black goo consumes his body again. His face with a content creepy smile as the tar covers him slowly.

Three tentacles quickly rise up and fly at Casey, she gets ready to dodge them, but before she does the tentacle tips are cut off. The rest of the tentacles recede back into the ground. Casey looks back to see if Angel did that, but is stopped by Rayza patting her right shoulder.

"I got you, Ms. Williams." Rayza says with a smile.

"Rayza!" Casey says giving her a quick hug in excitement.

Rayza is holding four Kunai blades with a chain made of energy wrapped around her hand. Nightmare summons more tentacles and sends them at Rayza and Casey. Rayza pushes Casey back then uses the energy chains to swing her kunai blades in a defensive sphere to protect her and Casey. Rayza's speed of swinging the blades is too fast for Casey's eyes to keep up. Nightmare tries to send more to break her defense, but nothing happens.

"How are you doing that?" Casey asks in amazement.

"Ms. Williams focus, we only get one shot at this!" Angel yells over com.

Angel's hands become lit up in purple flame he waves his hands in two concentric circles causing a rift to open up behind Nightmare. The rift was open to the blackness of space. The vacuum suction begins to slightly pull Nightmare in, but he plants himself firm although struggling to hold ground he still attempts to attack Casey. Rayza switches to using one hand to swing only two of her blades.

There is a break in her defense, several tentacles make it through her slicing shield, but are pulled back to Nightmare as the rift drags him slowly closer. Nikki and the rest of the crew still unconscious are also slightly pulled toward the rift. Rayza uses her free hand to throw her other two blades into a big piece of debris from a tank. Once the blades pierce through the steel, they open up to latch above the hole it made securing it in place.

Rayza uses her strength to pull the debris and throw it at Nightmare.

Casey raises Stacey's magnum, takes aim using one eye and pulls the trigger as the blades release the debris hurdling toward Nightmare.

The magnum hammer slams down launching the bullet out of the chamber. The bullet is half the size of a .50 caliber and as it spirals through the air, it begins opening up showing a blue gel in the center of bullet. As soon as the bullet makes contact with the debris, it explodes with a bright blue hue.

The explosion is small, but enough to send Nightmare into the void. Angel shuts the rift immediately after he is pushed into it. Angel falls face first to the ground

The rest of the crew awakens abruptly gasping for air as the tentacles fade into dust. "Tiny get that bird in the air!" Casey says quickly over COM while helping Stacey up. The Phoenix's thrusters roar as it lifts off of the building it is on and slowly flies over to Casey and crew. Casey runs over to Nikki helping her up.

"You good?" She asks. Nikki stares up at her.

"Nikki!" Casey yells.

"Yeah I'm good." Nikki is able to stutter.

Casey can see it did a number on her, along with everyone else as she looks around. She sees Angel on the ground and runs to him. She checks his pulse, its low for a Nexus, but he is alive. She throws his arm over her and picks him up. The Phoenix hovers above the crew and opens it's hatch. Nikki uses her telekinesis to lift everyone up into the ship. The hatch closes as the Phoenix turns to blast out of the atmosphere. The Blood Serpent, the Tartoroc's flagship opens a wormhole and disappears into space as The Phoenix flies away from the planet.

The star in Masaton's solar system implodes on it's self, causing a massive supernova. A wave of fiery molecular energy bursts out as the implosion turns into a black hole.

Trea and Jo are in the cockpit getting the ship ready for a warp. The Phoenix's four wings burn bright against the blackness of space around as it flies as fast it can. On board the cabin is rocking back and forth due to the amount of Gs the ship is producing. Casey is standing holding onto a metal handle protruding from the wall. The Cortex Crystal is set up in it's container in the center of the cabin close to the projector. She looks around at the crew; they're in bad shape. Whatever he did to them, it cut deep. All of them have a slightly terrified depressing look, including Nikki. Casey could almost feel their pain all around her, this feeling, however is interrupted by Tiny hooking up wires and hoses to the crystal's container from the projector.

"What are you doing?" Casey asks.

"What does it look like, Ms. Williams? I'm going to use the crystal to juice us up and get out of here." Tiny says screwing on the last hose.

"I don't think that will be a good idea!" Casey yells.

"That's your problem, Ms. Williams you don't think, I do and what I think is that this is a great idea!" Tiny yells back as she finishes working on her pad.

One single hologram screen appears at the center of the projector.

Casey can't read what it says but it has a green or red bar to press.

"When you're ready Trea!" Tiny yells.

"Punch it!" Trea yells back. Tiny presses the green button and the entire ship explodes.

Casey breathes in, choking on the air. She looks around and sees everyone is fine and the ship is not destroyed. Nikki looks up from the ground.

"Casey." She calls out. Casey turns to her, but quickly turns back around when the sound of the single hologram pops up on the projector.

"When you're ready Trea!" Tiny yells.

"Wait no!" Casey screams as she reaches out toward Tiny.

Tiny hits the button, but this time the ship does not explode.

The ship and everyone in it are covered in a bright pink aura being suspended in mid air. Nikki stands up raising one hand engulfed in red and pink electricity. The Phoenix is currently being thrashed in between space and time in every direction and in every universe. Her hand shakes as she struggles to keep them in her protective aura.

She clenches her teeth as her eyes glow with a red and black hue. Stars, planets and gravity crush her from both sides. The ship begins to tear apart above Nikki, but she quickly uses her free hand to pull the pieces together, before they could separate. She screams out trying to hold everything as the ship is tossed back and forth between time and space.

A black void appears in front of Nikki. She can see giant red eyes staring at her. Silver glittering tears run from her eyes down her cheeks. The black void extends a large shadowy hand. It slowly reaches for Nikki.

Angel slowly gets up covered in an aura of purple flame; he puts his hand on the wall of the ship. Angel yells as the purple flame grows and spreads to every piece of the ship and everyone on board. Once the flame has covered everything, the Phoenix vanishes before the shadow hand could grab Nikki.

It then reappears back in normal space. The ship's power flickers as it drifts. Alarms and lights are flashing in the main cabin as everyone slowly regains consciousness. Trea and Jo manage to get the cockpit doors open and run to the main cabin to find Casey on her feet staring down at Tiny.

Casey runs over to the crystal container and rips the hoses and other wires off of it.

"I told you that thing is dangerous!" Casey yells at Tiny.

"You could have gotten us all killed!" Casey continues.

"I'm sorry." Tiny says looking down at the floor.

Casey grabs her by the throat and slams her into a wall, holding her there while she uses her other hand to put a pistol to her face. Tiny is terrified with hands up. "Casey!" Trea yells.

Casey sees the look of fear on Tiny and let's her go.

She drops her pistol and walks away from Tiny.

"I'm sorry, Ms. Williams, I miscalculated the density of..."

"You think?" Casey yells cutting her off.

Casey walks over to Nikki. She is on her knees with a terrified look on her face and tears still trickling down.

"Nikki?" Casey says slowly approaching her.

Stacey watches with her hand on her pistol.

"Are you okay?" Casey asks while putting her hand on her shoulder.

She jumps from the touch, but quickly smiles.

"Ms. Williams! I didn't hear you sneaking up on me and yes everything is fine! I will survive, for now, but I'm not the one who got us out." Nikki says exhausted putting a hand on Casey's arm and looking over at Angel.

Stacey relaxes and attempts to help Nikki up.

Casey rushes over to Angel who is lying on his stomach. She flips him over. He opens is eyes barely and smiles.

"No, not yet, Ms. Williams." Casey smiles and helps him up onto the couch.

Casey takes a look around at the crew and the ship.

"Trea, damage report." Casey asks.

"Its not good, we are definitely dead in the water. It's going to take some time." Trea says.

"I can fix the thrusters, but the life support and rations will only last us about two months at most." Tiny says.

"Is there a system near by?" Rayza asks.

"Well, yes and no. The closest system is at the very least two jumps away and with the state of the ship, a second jump is out of the question." Tiny explains.

There is a silence among the group.

"So we're stuck?" Ethereal asks.

"I have already put out distress calls, but from where we are I don't think anyone is going to pick it up." Tiny says.

The silence continues until Casey clears her throat.

"Okay, Tiny gather all the damage Intel on the ship, Trea and Rayza get the cockpit working. Hyda and Ethereal take account of all interior damages. Boroc and Ayeka work with Jo on the thrusters. Gorog, Nessarac fix up the cargo hold, I'm 90% sure its tossed around. Nikki when you are up to it, coordinate with Tiny and head outside with Stacey see if you guys can keep this thing together. The way I see it, we're not dead yet, so we're not giving up." Casey finishes.

"I don't know Ms. Williams, with all due respect, I think giving up might be a whole lot easier." Rayza says.

"So, what you're saying is, we can have your rations?" Angel asks,

"Oh that's funny, you're a real comedian." Rayza responds.

"Well, I guess now is a good time to talk about our feelings and for us to get to know each other!" Nikki says excitedly smiling at everyone.

Everyone lets out a groan and a scoff.

"What?" Nikki asks.

Everyone just ignores her.

"But, we need to build our character arcs for the next few books." Nikki says. Everyone groans again.

Nikki continues to annoy the crew as the Phoenix floats adrift in uncharted space but as news of the Unusual Alliance's success spreads throughout the galaxy, so does the greed of others. The universe begins to slowly unravel.